Carla Kelly started writing Regency romances because of her interest in the Napoleonic Wars, and she enjoys writing about warfare at sea and the ordinary people of the British Isles rather than lords and ladies. In her spare time, she reads British crime fiction and history—particularly books about the American Indian Wars. Carla lives in Utah and is a former park ranger and double RITA® Award and Spur Award winner. She has five children and four grandchildren.

Carol Arens delights in tossing fictional characters into hot water, watching them steam and then giving them a happily-ever-after. When she is not writing, she enjoys spending time with her family, beach camping or lounging about a mountain cabin. At home, she enjoys playing with her grandchildren and gardening. During rare spare moments, you will find her snuggled up with a good book. Carol enjoys hearing from readers at carolarens@yahoo.com or on Facebook.

After graduating with degrees in history and political science, **Eva Shepherd** worked in journalism and as an advertising copywriter. She began writing historical romances because it combined her love of a happy ending with her passion for history. She lives in Christchurch, New Zealand, but spends her days immersed in the world of late Victorian England. Eva loves hearing from readers and can be reached via her website, evashepherd.com, and her Facebook page, Facebook.com/evashepherdromancewriter.

A VICTORIAN FAMILY CHRISTMAS

Carla Kelly
Carol Arens
Eva Shepherd

HARLEQUIN
HISTORICAL

Recycling programs
for this product may
not exist in your area.

ISBN-13: 978-1-335-40737-5

A Victorian Family Christmas

Copyright © 2021 by Harlequin Books S.A.

A Father for Christmas
Copyright © 2021 by Carla Kelly

A Kiss Under the Mistletoe
Copyright © 2021 by Carol Arens

The Earl's Unexpected Gifts
Copyright © 2021 by Eva Shepherd

This edition published by arrangement with Harlequin Books S.A.

For questions and comments about the quality of this book,
please contact us at CustomerService@Harlequin.com.

Harlequin Enterprises ULC
22 Adelaide St. West, 40th Floor
Toronto, Ontario M5H 4E3, Canada
www.Harlequin.com

Printed in U.S.A.

CONTENTS

A FATHER
FOR CHRISTMAS

Carla Kelly

Merry Christmas to Jennifer Lunt Moore,
who also likes things maritime.

Dear Reader,

As both a historian and a writer of historical
fiction, I get my jollies out of pairing a real event
with a plot. I'm a lifelong student of the US Civil
War, and I enjoy things nautical. It's a pity the Civil
War at sea is often neglected, because Rebel
Captain Rafael Semmes is too good to languish in
a dusty textbook. *A Father for Christmas* turned
into a fun Yuletide brew: a widow and her son;
a reluctant Yankee hero; US diplomats; Captain
Semmes; ahem, British meddling in the Southern
cause—I was in writerly heaven. And a merry
Christmas to you!

Carla Kelly

Chapter One

December 1861

How shallow can a man be? Ezra Eldredge asked himself as he plonked his valise down on the bunk aboard the USS *Sullivan*, packet steamer bound for Portsmouth, Great Britain. *I know I can live for a few weeks without my valet. Can't I?*

Mackie usually travelled with him. He was a free Black, paid a fair wage—always had been—whose Yankee accent was more pronounced than Ezra's.

Mackie had objected to being left behind until Ezra had explained. 'I prefer having you with me, but I dare not,' he'd said that last night before taking the train to Boston from New Bedford. 'Here we are in December of 1861, Mackie, at war. Rebel commerce raiders are prowling the oceans. They would have no qualms about selling you into slavery, if they captured you.'

'I see, Mr Eldredge,' was Mackie's quiet reply as he packed that valise. 'Will you be taking along Mrs Eldredge?'

Ezra always took Priscilla with him. 'Not this time.'

Consequently, his valise did not contain the charming miniature of his late wife, dead these ten years. Priscilla had graced him with her presence on all business trips, but not this time, and by design.

She probably would have come along, if he hadn't just endured his thirty-fifth birthday, complete with cake from his employees at the ropewalk, that wonderful one-thousand-two-hundred-foot-long brick building he had taken a chance on after his father's death. 'A shed is good enough for your workers,' he had heard from other merchants. But it wasn't, not in coastal New England's frigid winter damp. He'd taken a chance and prospered as the best rope twiners and twisters competed to work for him. Soon Eldredge cables, miles of them, graced the most beautiful clipper ships ever to sail. A man could be proud of that and he was.

So many candles on his cake—lit, of course, outside, for safety. They had still been on his mind that evening as he'd readied for bed, then looked down at Priscilla's miniature on his night table. For some reason this time the sight of her twenty-five-year-old loveliness reminded him that she was always young and now he was not. Thirty-five. Good Lord.

This time, he gazed at her image and thought he detected a little reproach, a mild scolding, from as generous a lady who ever lived. This time, she seemed to silently remind him that lonely years had passed, and what was he doing about it?

The obvious answer was nothing; he had no second wife, no hopeful heirs. His heart had broken with those two deaths, hers and their son's born too soon. In grief, he'd thrown himself into turning New Bedford Ropewalk and Marine Supply from a small firm into New Bedford's largest such emporium. If he wanted to puff up the matter, he doubted there was a better marine business in all of New England.

He enjoyed success, but who cared? Could it be that Priscilla's sweet silence in the miniature was starting to nudge him into action beyond business?

'Why now, my dearest?' he asked the miniature. 'You know I'm busy. I haven't time for another wife. There's a war on.'

Why had he never noticed that thoughtful look the miniaturist had somehow captured even in so small a frame? He knew that look. The matter was something to consider when he returned from England, not now. Ezra knew this was no time to travel, but he was an ambitious man. The ropewalk and marine supplies were already increasing his fortune during a war where President Lincoln had declared a naval blockade of the southern coastline.

Everyone had said the war would be over by Christmas,

which, at this point, was less than a month away. No one had told the Rebels that, though.

The letter from Courtney and Howe, solicitors, located in Salisbury, had changed matters.

In efficient legalese, they had explained that his English mother's late father had left her several thousand pounds. All he needed to do was show up at Melton Manor, near Salisbury, Wiltshire, to collect. Andrew Melton, Mama's uncle, would do the honours. Courtney and Howe had confirmed that with the passing of his mother, Maude Melton, six months previously, the legacy was now his.

The amount made him smile. Now he could safely invest in railways. He knew that ropewalks would eventually become a relic as sails vanished. His business sense assured him that once this miserable war ended, Americans would be moving West, travelling by rail.

So to Wiltshire he would go. Travel by steamship meant a shorter voyage than under sail, where the winds ruled. Curious about being aboard a steamer for the first time, he wasted no time returning to the deck once his gear was safely stowed.

He moved to the railing on the port side and watched Boston recede. For the next two weeks he had nothing to do but eat and read. He had left both his business and his home in capable hands.

That reminded him of what his housekeeper had said to him before he'd left. 'Mr Eldredge, come home with a wife,' she had begged. 'Your father did, years ago.'

He had, but was Ezra's business his housekeeper's business, too? He had told her so, in no uncertain terms, surprising himself.

She had been undeterred, and had dropped unhappy news on him next. 'Cook wants to retire from service. You will need to replace her when you return.'

'*What?*'

She'd given Ezra a kindly smile. 'Don't fret, Mr Eldredge,'

she'd replied. 'I'll stay here, but do be thinking about a re-placement for Cook.'

'If I must,' he had grumbled.

That had earned him a finger-wag. 'Seriously, sir. You're so set in your ways you'll be turning into an old man too soon.'

As he leaned on the rail, he reflected on the conversation. *Am I turning into a geriatric before my time?* he asked himself. Surely not.

'Ezra Eldredge?'

Oh, God, I know that voice. Ezra blanched in horror and turned to face the barrage of sound that was Rectitude Blake. 'I had no idea you were travelling to England, Mr Blake. How, um, delightful.'

Rectitude Blake was a prosy, fat fellow who rejoiced in the friendship of the illustrious Adams family, from John through Quincy and now to Charles, serving as United States envoy to England's Court of St. James. The fact came up at every opportunity, appropriate or not.

As if on cue, the man said self-importantly, 'I am bearing a note from President Lincoln himself to Minister Adams. It's in regard to the Trent Affair.'

'Good for you, sir,' was the best Ezra could manage. With other Yankees, he had fumed over the recent news of the capture of two Confederate envoys heading to England and France on a packet boat much like this one but British. Over-taken by Captain Wilkes in the USS *Trent*, those Rebs now cooled their heels in a Washington, DC jail. What had hap-pened was a flagrant violation of all the rules of diplomacy, but there was a war on. Her Britannic Majesty was aghast, Prime Minister Palmerston appalled, and the French none too pleased either.

'P'raps you should keep the matter quiet,' Ezra said, even as he doubted the other man could. Seldom had a fellow been more ill named.

'Even the decks have ears?' Mr Blake bellowed out, laughing.

Ezra smiled weakly. 'Just think, laddie,' Mr Blake said. 'We have two weeks to renew our acquaintance!'

This voyage can't end soon enough, Ezra thought despairingly.

Chapter Two

After more than a week and a half, Ezra rued his thought that the voyage couldn't end soon enough. He had no idea that fickle fate would decree a quick end to the voyage in the way it did.

It happened on the morning Ezra hid below deck to avoid Rectitude Blake. He snapped his book shut at what sounded like cannon fire and stood up when the *Sullivan*'s engines stopped.

He came on deck and approached the railing, his eyes on the ship now alongside the USS *Sullivan*, which appeared to have no kind intentions.

He took heart at the flag on the other ship's mast—the Stars and Stripes—until seconds later, someone hauled it down and ran up the Stars and Bars of the Confederate States of America, signalling a Rebel commerce raider.

'Ahoy your captain,' he heard from the speaking trumpet, and saw a tall fellow in grey with blond hair and a soft Southern voice. 'Make yourself known.'

'You have some nerve,' Captain Trowbridge shouted. 'We're the *Sullivan* out of Boston, sailing to London with passengers.'

'You could be Noah's Ark, for all I care,' the man shouted back. 'I am Captain Semmes of the CSS *Sumter* and we are about to board you.'

Captain Trowbridge winced when the sharp hooks latched onto the *Sullivan*'s impeccable railing.

'Perhaps the Captain will be satisfied to relieve you of the cargo, then send us on our merry way,' Ezra suggested.

'That's a pleasant fiction. It's not what Captain Semmes will do.'

It wasn't. Two hours later, the *Sullivan's* cargo had been transferred to the *Sumter*, and the *Sullivan's* crew placed under close surveillance and threatened with incarceration in the brig. The few passengers stood and watched.

Captain Trowbridge couldn't bear it. He stared towards the Irish coast. 'Can you at least set us ashore in Ireland?' he asked his Rebel counterpart.

'Alas, I cannot.'

Captain Trowbridge muttered something under his breath that made Ezra wince. Then Captain Semmes asked the *Sullivan's* crew if anyone would like to join the glorious Southern cause. Two men stepped forward.

'Excellent!' Semmes said, rubbing his hands together.

'Now, hurry below, y'all, and get your luggage. I haven't time to waste.'

Ezra had no urge to remain on a vessel that was shortly to be fired and in mere minutes, like the others, he'd stuffed his valise. He wondered where in the world Captain Semmes planned to take them, knowing there was nothing he could do about it.

As it turned out, Ezra found himself on the rebel commerce raider, quartered with Rectitude Blake. *I must escape that man*, Ezra thought. *But how?* He went up on deck to watch what would happen next.

The crew of the *Sumter* knew what they were doing. 'I can't watch this,' Trowbridge groaned, and stormed below deck.

As the *Sullivan* burned to the waterline, Ezra found that he, too, couldn't bear it and returned to the cabin, hoping that the pompous diplomatist would leave him alone.

No luck. Rectitude grabbed Ezra by the lapels, panic all over his face.

'You have to help me,' Blake demanded. 'I am carrying significant secret documents intended for—'

'Yes, yes, I know,' Ezra said impatiently. 'You've told all of us!'

Blake's voice took on a wheedling tone. 'See here, I have this small package. Tie it to your thigh under your trousers, and no one will ever suspect.'

'No!'

'Where, sir, is your patriotism?' Rectitude demanded.

'Alive and well and too smart to involve myself in any scheme of yours,' Ezra snapped.

So how was it that he let Rectitude Blake talk him into strapping a letter addressed to Charles Adams, with *White House* stamped on the envelope, under his smallclothes and trousers? He decided it was self-interest. Before the water-proof pouch went around his thigh, he added his business card and two hundred dollars in greenbacks from his wallet. The Rebel bandits didn't need all his money. As an after-thought, he added his deck of cards.

He could only hope that Blake hadn't blabbed about the Lincoln letter to everyone on the *Sullivan*, now a smoking ruin.

On the morrow, Captain Semmes summoned the *Sulli-van*'s passengers, one by one, into his crowded wheelhouse and quizzed them on their reasons for travel. Ezra had no trouble accounting for his voyage.

Rectitude Blake's interview was another matter. Semmes came out frowning and the diplomatist was pale and sweaty.

Rectitude joined Ezra at the railing as the *Sumter* steamed along the coast of Ireland. 'He knows I have important papers because those two faithless seamen he took off the *Sullivan* told him,' Blake moaned. 'His first lieutenant is ransacking our cabin as we speak, looking for the package'

And I'm wearing it, Ezra thought with dismay. 'Maybe we'll get lucky and the *Sumter* will break down, giving him bigger problems than a letter that may or may not exist.'

To Ezra's surprise, the *Sumter* did break down that after-noon, as the commerce raider chased another packet ship flying US colours. The raider steamed along under full power until, suddenly, it didn't.

Ezra watched with satisfaction as the Yankee ship made its escape while Semmes went below. Ezra heard some banging, some cursing, but no response from the engines.

Captain Semmes came back on deck, wiping his greasy hands.

'Now what?' Ezra asked him.

'I have free run of the South Devonshire coast,' Semmes said. 'We'll sidle into Teignmouth by tomorrow evening. I know a mechanic there.'

'Could you let us harmless folk off and about our business?'

'Not a chance,' Semmes said as he walked away.

Upon later reflection, Ezra knew he should not have complained about the matter to Rectitude Blake. 'We're docking in Devon, but the Captain won't let us off. All I want to do is go about my business.'

Ezra gave it not another thought until the next evening when the *Sumter* sailed into Teignmouth under cover of darkness.

Rectitude Blake stood beside him at the railing. 'That letter on your person must get to our envoy,' he said, sounding more resolute than usual. 'Quite possibly it will make the difference between neutrality and the horror of England and France recognising the South's right of independence. Can you imagine the mess if the Union must declare war against England and France, too?'

'It won't come to that,' Ezra said. 'Would it?'

'You can see that it doesn't. Mr Eldredge, do you swim?'

'Certainly I do… Oh, no. Wait!'

'Think of your country, Mr Eldredge.'

With desperation giving the flabby man strength, Rectitude Blake heaved Ezra over the railing and into the water.

Chapter Three

'Jem, I promise you we will never move again,' Felicity Waring said as she wiped another glass her boy handed her and put it in the cupboard. She reconsidered. There was never any way to know what the future might hold, a lesson she had learned during the Crimean War. 'Let me amend that, son. Never during Christmastime.'

James Waring laughed, as she'd thought he might. After seven years, they knew each other pretty well. Seven years ago she had given birth to him, a child whose surgeon father of the same name had died of typhoid at the hospital in Scutari, tending others. She had followed her husband as far as Italy, and had remained there until their son was born six months later, no family present.

No family present, not then and not now. Her own genteel family in Derbyshire had been singularly unimpressed when she'd fallen in love with a surgeon in the British Army whose own father farmed on the family estate. No one had ever officially cut her off, but she had been told politely that her presence wasn't encouraged at family events.

The Warings had been kind but felt uncomfortable around her. James's mother could not read and his father had died shortly before his son, so there was no connection. *Too bad, too bad*, Felicity thought as she rubbed a non-existent spot off the last glass. *All of you have missed out on knowing a remarkable boy.*

There was nothing her own parents could do about the little legacy her Aunt Clara had left her. Unlike her mother and older sister, Felicity practised economy and managed well enough. At least it was the beginning of the independence she had ventured into now.

Jem stared at the packing crate. 'All of the plates, Mama?'

'Four of everything. I doubt Her Majesty Queen Victoria will visit, so we shan't require the full set.' It was their little joke.

And now, finally, The Move, the one that had taken her away from Derbyshire and her relatives with their condescension, and the oldish widower who had convinced her parents that she couldn't manage alone. Felicity absolutely could, but no one had listened. She hadn't actually sneaked away but she hadn't announced the matter with trumpets either.

Where to go? She'd remembered Torquay, near James's port of embarkation for the Crimea. It was a pretty place with pastel-coloured terraced houses and a spanking sea breeze, but it was out of her purse's range.

So she'd discovered Teignmouth, a modest seaside village a little further north. She found a house on quiet Brooke Street, and wasted not a minute in renting it. Within a week she and Jem were packed and gone from Derbyshire. Mama had complained, but only a little. So be it.

The house had come with modest furniture and curtains that looked better once washed. She had a little boy to help her put things away, the same boy who deserved an apology. This was a good time. She took his hand and sat him at the table.

'I know I promised you a father by Christmas, and I truly thought that Mr Pettyjohn was an unexceptional choice,' she said, holding his hands.

'I liked him, Mama,' Jem said. 'I thought you did, too.'

How to explain the unexplainable? At seven, Jem was old enough to understand some things, but this?

'He started telling me what to do, Jem, and I didn't like his ideas,' she said frankly.

'Mama, I know a small and diligent lad who doesn't like to be told what to do either.' Trust Jem to make her laugh.

She kissed his hands, even though they were grubby. 'I promise I will not tell you what to do when you are twenty-nine, as I am! We don't need Mr Pettyjohn,' she concluded, hoping that would suffice.

She looked around. The beds were made and the minuscule sitting room tidy enough. Another day's work would empty out the other crates. Perhaps then there would be time to meet her neighbour.

Neighbour in the singular, because her house was the last in the terrace. Her view across the street was of the river Teign, with little boats and buoys rocking side to side and now and then larger vessels. One neighbour would suffice. There would be church.

Church. Christmas.

'Jem, look in that smallish crate in the sitting room. You'll find the wreath that your father gave me for our door in Italy before he sailed to the Crimea. I believe our front door here already has a nail in the right place. I call that a good sign. Other people have kept Christmas here and we will, too.'

Jem had his doubts; she saw them on his face. 'Will Father Christmas have our change of address?'

'I believe he is good at that, son,' she assured him, thinking of the jumper she had knitted and the stockings, and a copy of *The Coral Island* written by R. M Ballantyne. Some of the words might be advanced for a seven-year-old, but it was a story of boys and shipwrecks and she wanted to read it to him anyway.

They looked through the crate together, which had other Italian souvenirs from Livorno, where she and her new husband had spent a blissful fortnight together before James's ship had steamed towards his death from typhoid after the battle at Balaclava.

Felicity had written to let him know that he was going to be a father. Whether he received it, she never knew. Every year about this time she told herself that he must have done and rejoiced. She had nothing else to hope for, so where was the harm?

Something about this move had made her surprisingly vulnerable to heartache, she discovered as she and her son rummaged through the crate. More than seven years had passed since her husband had sailed away to war in the Crimea. Wasn't it time for the mourning to end?

No tears, she scolded herself. *Cry later, if you must.*

Jem held out the wreath, with its delicate carving of ivy, her last gift from her husband. She didn't know yet what kind of a village Teignmouth was, but hopefully no one was inclined to steal. Here she was, seeing the wreath through a film of tears, probably because it was going on a door for the first time since her husband had given it to her. She dabbed at her face and muttered something about dust.

'This will do, Jem,' she managed. 'Do you need some help with it?'

He shook his head, took back the wreath and carried it to the front door, which she opened. 'See the nail?' she said, calm now, in control.

He set the wreath on the nail and they both stepped back in the modest entranceway. 'A little to the left,' she said and Jem obliged. 'There. Perfect.'

She started to close the door when she heard shrill whistles from the docks. 'What can that be?' she asked. She peered closer in the gathering dark to see what looked like lanterns bobbing along, carried by people in a hurry. 'Let's lock the door. I don't like this.'

'It could be something exciting,' Jem protested.

Felicity grabbed her son as a man in an overcoat ran towards their house, looking over his shoulder. She yanked Jem inside and tried to shut the door, but the man ran up the steps and pushed back when she tried to close the door on him.

'Go away!' she shouted. 'I'll… I'll call my husband downstairs. I'll…'

He forced his way in, shut the door, then sank to the floor, breathing hard, his eyes closed.

Terrified, she pushed Jem behind her and looked around for something to hit him with. Nothing. She knew there was a poker by the fireplace in the sitting room, but it was too far away. She backed up. 'You'll…you'll have to leave,' she said, aware that she had never been much good at sounding stern. 'I told you I will summon my husband.'

The man was sopping wet. He looked up at her from brilliant blue eyes. 'Please help me. I'm American. I was on board a steamer that was captured and burned by a Confederate commerce raider. I promise I won't stay long. Please.'

He did sound like an American. She frowned at him, less afraid for some reason unknown to her. She gave him a good look. He was wet, yes, but even water couldn't disguise the quality of his overcoat and the good leather of his shoes. Well, one shoe.

His sock was gone, too. She stared at his bare foot and, oddly, felt herself relax. 'You're missing a shoe,' she pointed out, then felt truly stupid. Clearly, he knew that.

'They were expensive shoes,' he said, in that funny accent, which suddenly struck her as hilarious. He couldn't have overlooked her smile. 'They were,' he said indignantly, sitting there in a puddle on the floor. He squeezed his beard and water ran out, which made Felicity turn away because she wanted to laugh so badly.

Jem laughed for her. 'Mama, should I get him a towel? Do you know which crate they are in?'

'I don't...think so,' she said, regretting her smile. Maybe Mr Pettyjohn was right. Maybe she did need someone to look after her. This sodden fellow with the expensive clothes could be a desperate killer.

Somehow she knew he wasn't.

Chapter Four

'Jem,' she said quietly. 'You'll find a towel in the crate beside my bed. Hurry. He's awfully wet. He could catch a cold.'

Jem ran up the stairs. She came no closer.

'Please, ma'am,' he said. 'All I ask is a little mercy. Not much. Just a little. I'm in a bona fide, certified pickle. I'm Ezra Eldredge, from New Bedford, Massachusetts.'

I wonder if I will regret this, she thought, amused at his comment. 'You won't hurt us?' she asked, even as something assured her he was harmless. She heard the whistles again, much closer.

'I could never do that,' he said firmly. He sat up, suddenly alert as someone banged on the door several houses away. 'I have to hide. Please help me.'

She reached for him and tugged him up. He staggered and righted himself. 'You really should get your husband to help you.' He gave her a little smile of his own. 'You said you had one on the premises.'

She knew she was a terrible liar. 'I'm a widow. You knew there was no man here, didn't you?'

He nodded. 'He would have been here lickety-split when you shrieked. *I* would have.'

She heard more banging, even closer. She looked down in dismay at the water on the floor. 'This won't work.'

They both stared down at the puddle, proof positive that someone wet had been there.

'No, it won't work,' he said. 'Is there a back door?'

She pointed. 'Open it,' he ordered.

She did, and watched, eyes wide, as he walked across the floor, dripping water everywhere, until he stood in the open back door. All was dark outside, to her relief. She jumped when a whistle shrilled from next door. She heard urgent voices.

'Mrs… Mrs…'

'W-W-Waring,' she stammered, terrified.

'Mrs Waring, who is England's most famous actress?' he asked.

'S-Sarah Siddons,' she said.

He pointed at her. 'No, it's you.' He looked over her shoulder. 'Ah, there is your boy. Hand me that towel, please. That should keep me decent.'

She smiled, because she knew precisely what he had in mind. 'Jem, that's a hand towel! Ah, well, sir. You won't surprise me.'

He rolled his eyes, then took a quick glance around. 'Are any of these crates empty?'

'That one,' she said, pointing. 'Hurry.'

She discovered in seconds how resourceful her unexpected guest was. 'Turn around if you wish, Mrs Waring, widow or not. I'm going to strip and dump my clothes in that crate, which you will close.' He tossed in his overcoat, ripped off his jacket, yanked his cravat loose and started on his shirt buttons as she stared at him. 'You've just moved in? No one knows you in this village?'

'We arrived yesterday,' she said, then couldn't resist. 'I thought I was moving to a quiet place where nothing ever happens.'

'How dull would that be? I'd squeeze myself into that crate, but I'm too big. Can you suddenly acquire a husband who is lying upstairs with a fever?'

She understood completely. 'I believe I can. I suppose I must.' She turned around. 'Jem, say nothing.'

Her son, the rascal, grinned at her. 'My lips are sealed,' he said, then giggled.

'No, this is serious,' she said quietly. 'When this man is as safe as we can make him, you and I are going to require a lengthy explanation before we send him on his way.'

Out of the corner of her eye she watched the rest of his

clothing drop into the crate, his smallclothes and one shoe last of all. She saw a nearly naked man with a practically useless hand towel around his waist dash upstairs leaving no sodden tracks now, followed by Jem. She bit her lip and looked at the soggy trail from the front door to the open back door, where it stopped. That would never do.

Wasting not a moment, even though men banged on her door, she grabbed the bucket of mop water she had meant to toss out earlier. She poured the water down the back stairs, into the darkness of the yard. 'Take a deep breath, Felicity Waring,' she murmured as she closed the crate. 'No. I am Sarah Siddons.'

'Open up!'

How to do this? Felicity knew it would not be hard to appear frightened: she was. She wrenched the door open and burst into tears. 'Thank God,' she cried. 'I thought you would never come!'

Two men, a third behind them, pushed her aside. She hurried after them, wringing her hands and sobbing that a crazy man had run into her house, then dashed out the back door. 'Here! I'll show you,' she said.

The older man in charge waved her away. 'Never you mind,' he called over his shoulder. 'We can see his trail, plain as day! Bolt your doors!' And they were gone. So much for her command performance in Drury Lane.

She did as they said, bolting the back door then hurrying to the front door. Before she closed the door, she saw the American's other shoe by the barren rose bush. Looking right and left, she picked it up and carried it upstairs to her bedchamber, where someone appeared to be sleeping.

'They've gone, I think,' she whispered, as though the constable lurked nearby, waiting to haul her to the magistrate for bad acting.

He turned over, bare chested, and smiled, which took the chill from her heart in remarkable fashion. To her surprise, and then her honest delight, he held out his hand and she shook it.

'Ezra Eldredge, proprietor of New Bedford Ropewalk and Marine Supply,' he said. When she said nothing but kept shaking his hand, he smiled. 'Your turn. I know you told me, but in the press of the moment I forgot.'

Embarrassed, she let go of his hand. 'Mrs Felicity Waring, widow of James Waring, surgeon with the Horse Guards in the Crimea.' She indicated her son, who left his perch on the window seat and came to her. 'This is James Waring as well. I call him Jem.' She knew it wasn't polite to stare at a half-naked man, even if he was in bed, or perhaps because he was in *her* bed, which had for some years been absent of a naked man. It was an unruly thought, and she blushed.

'Sir, considering things, let me see if I can find one of James's old nightshirts. I brought his trunk along when we moved here. I never could quite bring myself to…' She paused, wondering why her deep loss felt so immediate after almost eight years.

I am remembering other times, she thought, humbled by the power of memory.

'One moment.'

She went to fetch the battered trunk with the initials *JW* stencilled on top. She had earlier rejected the idea of discarding it, since it contained all that her son would ever know of his father. She hadn't opened it in years, but she did so now, fighting back tears as she searched and found the nightshirt. She sniffed it, then pressed it to her face. All the familiar fragrance that was James had long since vanished, to her sorrow.

One deep breath and another, she told herself.

She called for Jem, who came quickly, and handed him the garment. 'Give this to Mr Eldredge.'

'Is this my father's?'

She nodded. 'We'll get it back, no fears. Mr Eldredge needs it more than we do right now.'

She looked in the trunk as more memories washed over her. She knew her parents had thought her foolish to haul along such a useless item to Teignmouth. Mama had assured her it would be safe in Derbyshire. Some suspicion had told her this would not be the case. Her links to James Waring were slipping away, thanks to time and life; she wasn't certain how she felt about that.

Jem nodded and returned to her bedroom. She heard whispered words and the creak of the bed. 'All clear,' Jem sang out, which made Mr Eldredge laugh.

Feeling shy, Felicity entered. She no idea how old the man occupying her bed was, but he was at least clothed now. The most arresting thing about him were his distinctive blue eyes. She looked closer to see a much darker rim around the irises.

She saw his eyes grow smaller and wrinkles appear as he smiled. 'I know, I know. It's called a limbal ring.'

Felicity put her hands behind her back, as if she had been caught filching sweets. 'I didn't mean to stare, sir.'

'You're not the first.' He regarded her and then Jem. 'You two bear quite a resemblance to each other.'

'Jem has *his* father's eyes,' she said promptly. 'But you are right.' This was small talk getting neither of them absolutely anywhere, but she understood the matter. They needed to put one another at ease.

'Sir, I don't know what you did to be chased. Please don't give me cause to regret that I let you into my house. It was probably a naïve thing to do, considering that Jem and I have no male protection here.'

'No worries,' he replied with a wave of his hand. 'I'm relieved and grateful that you acted so promptly.'

'Then perhaps you had better explain yourself,' she suggested. 'Are you hungry?'

He nodded enthusiastically and she laughed, which made the man sigh. 'I haven't heard anyone laugh in nearly two weeks. Yes, I am hungry. I should come downstairs, but…'

'Oh, no,' she said hastily. 'You have no dry clothes. My first task will be to get your clothes out of the crate and hang them up in the laundry out of sight. Perhaps they can be salvaged. Then food. Come, Jem.'

'I do hope you can salvage them. Had I known someone was going to push me into the drink, I'd have brought along my valise.'

'Someone pushed you off the ship? What a scoundrel!' she said.

'Mrs Waring, he is a functionary of the US government so, yes, a scoundrel. I will tell you more after food.'

'I hope you will,' she said. 'This entire affair is peculiar.'

They started downstairs silently, but Jem started laughing by the time they reached the bottom. 'There's a stranger running from the law in my bed, and you're laughing?' she asked, half-exasperated but more amused. Jem's infectious laugh was so like his father's.

Jem took her hand. 'Mama, you promised me a new father by Christmas and…'

She stared at him. 'I don't think we expected *this* answer to a promise!'

'I like him,' her son told her.

It was time to bring out the heavy artillery. 'James Whittier Waring, you don't even know him! He's wanted by… by…who knows?'

Jem squeezed her hand and whispered, 'I still like him. May I at least pretend just for Christmas?'

I wish I were not an amateur at this business of child-rearing, Felicity thought.

She kissed her son's head. 'I did make you a ridiculous promise, didn't I?'

'You did, Mama,' he agreed, but he didn't sound crushed or even defeated.

'You have my complete permission to like him until then,' she said generously. 'I expect Mr Eldredge's story is interesting, and that he wants to be gone as soon as possible.'

'Maybe, but not too soon,' Jem said, illogically wise in that way of seven-year-olds. 'Everyone likes Christmas.'

'Forgive me and my silly promises?' she asked, after another kiss.

'P'raps,' he said. 'You may like him a little, too. What's the harm in that?'

Chapter Five

To his surprise, Ezra Eldredge had no trouble lying back in Mrs Waring's comfortable bed and relaxing for the first time in nearly a fortnight. Recent events reminded him that the last thing he should do was let go of his cares. He was obviously being hunted.

As both Warings had gone downstairs, Ezra removed the waterproof pouch tied to his thigh.

'Now I am to take this to Charles Adams,' he muttered under his breath. 'Was ever a man so put upon?'

He was hardly unpatriotic, but this additional task stuck in his craw. Wasn't he doing enough for the Union by increasing the workload at New Bedford Ropewalk and Marine Supply?

Even that notion was too much for a man with scruples. At least there wasn't a mirror he was forced to look into to see all the hypocrisy.

Ezra Eldredge, this civil war is going to make you even richer than you are already, he thought. *It won't kill you to get these documents into the proper hands.*

He heard footsteps on the stairs and Jem popped into the room with what Ezra already recognised as the relentless good cheer of a well-raised little fellow. His own son would have been slightly older had he survived the complications that had killed his mother and forced his early birth. What a horrible night that had been, with all anticipation dashed by disaster no physician had foreseen. 'How old are you, lad?' he asked, wanting to erase that earlier image, that terrifying night.

'Seven, sir,' the boy replied. 'Do you have a little boy of your own?'

'Alas, no,' Ezra said.

'Mam says I am a trial at times,' Jem offered. 'Then she kisses me and we forget it.'

It was an artless statement and Ezra couldn't help smiling. 'Until the next time?'

Jem nodded. 'You understand, don't you, sir?'

'I was a lad once,' Ezra said, even though he had trouble believing it. Where had the time gone?

'All I have is soup, bread and butter.'

He looked up to see Mrs Waring standing in the doorway. He disliked being a burden, but he knew he owed this woman a great deal. 'It will be better than anything I have eaten recently, I have no doubt,' he told her. 'I thank you.'

She set the tray on his lap and stepped back. He looked down, breathing in the fragrance of stew with more potatoes than meat. Mrs Waring gave him another hand towel. 'I don't know where the napkins are right now, but this will do. Excuse us, please. Come, Jem.'

He ate quickly, wanting more, but was even hungrier for uncomplaining company that didn't smell of brine and tar. He wished she and her son had stayed.

Ezra set the tray aside on the floor then reluctantly picked up the packet, wanting nothing to do with it but knowing he had a duty, much as he balked about the matter. He looked up, hopeful, when someone tapped on the door. 'Please come in.'

The Warings returned with tea and cups. Mrs Waring set the pot on the table, moving aside the miniature he had already noticed. 'Is that your husband?' he asked.

'Yes,' she said. 'Tea?'

He nodded and she poured him a cup. 'I should have everything put to rights tomorrow, Mr Eldredge. I can promise a better meal once I make a visit to the local market.' She gave him almost a boyish grin then. 'I'm not really much of a cook, though.'

He could enjoy this. 'Well, madam, that's what I deserve for blundering about from house to house in the dark with a magistrate breathing down my neck, and not enquiring about culinary skills.'

She laughed and he sipped the tea. Jem watched him, leaning on the bed. 'Go ahead and sit down,' Ezra said, gesturing to the foot of the bed. 'I need to tell both of you as much as I know about my current misfortune, since you have been so kind as to take me in.'

Mrs Waring moved the tray to a packing crate and sat down on the room's only chair. She looked at the packet in his lap. 'What is that?'

'Something that Rebel captain wants. The hand towel, please.'

She spread it on his lap as he opened the pouch. He sighed in relief to find the Lincoln letter dry. So were the two hundred dollars in greenbacks he had thrust into it.

Jem couldn't help himself. 'You're rich, Mr Eldredge.'

Ezra smiled as Mrs Waring glowered at her son. 'Jem, *really*,' she said.

'I own a ropewalk in a seagoing town in Massachusetts,' Ezra said, wanting to explain himself. 'You…uh…know what a ropewalk is, don't you?'

'Oh, yes. I've seen pictures of the one at Chatham Dockyard in Kent.'

'I also sell marine supplies. Our war between the states is keeping my company fully occupied, beyond the usual merchant marine trade.'

'A rich man,' Jem said under his breath, but not quietly enough to avoid another glare from his mother.

'It's nearly Christmas, and I do have a lapful of money,' Ezra said, laughing inside over the expressions mother and son traded. 'Let us charitably give your son the benefit of the doubt.'

'Perhaps this once. He does tend to speak his mind. I can remind him later that Father Christmas expects more from boys at such a time.'

Mrs Waring looked particularly handsome when she blushed. He liked the way her dark hair was so neatly parted in the middle and pulled back into a sleek chignon low on the nape of her neck. She looked as tidy as a mother could, considering that it was late and she must be tired. He knew *he* was. 'What a day this has been,' he murmured. 'I fear I am going to be a lot of trouble to you, Mrs Waring. Hopefully I will be on my way tomorrow.'

'If you have something dry enough to wear by then,' she replied. He noticed her frown. 'Surely the Rebels aren't after your money?'

'It's this they want.' He held out the envelope.

Mrs Waring stared at the envelope with a discreet *White House, Washington, District of Columbia* printed in the left corner, *Charles Adams* handwritten underneath. 'My goodness.'

'According to the envoy who foisted these on me, President Lincoln is trying to mend a few fences for the unfortunate way that two scoundrels calling themselves Confederate ambassadors were snatched from a British packet ship,' he said, not mincing his words.

'I don't understand government and war,' she said. Her face clouded over. 'I still don't understand the Crimean War.'

'I am sorry for your loss,' he said.

'Thank you. It's been nearly eight years,' she said softly. 'Some days it seems like only eight minutes. Odd, isn't it?'

'Eight or eighty, it stings,' he remarked, thinking of his own sadness, remembering other lonely Christmases when loss seemed so much sharper.

'You know loss, too?'

'I do. A wife and child.'

She glanced at her son, whose eyelids had started to droop. 'I'm grateful for what I have.' She looked at the watch pinned to her apron bib. 'It's late. Let me see Jem to bed. When I return, you can explain what's going on.'

When she came back, he told her everything. 'Is this Teignmouth?'

'Yes. It's a seaside village close to Torquay, without the

high prices,' she said, which suggested some facts about her own circumstances.

'Captain Semmes thinks to repair his raider, then steam to Spain. Here I am, a wanted man.' He looked at the pretty lady sitting so composed beside the bed. 'I have tumbled you and your son into this bumblebroth, but I vow I will extricate myself as soon as I can.'

'How?'

It was a good question. He had only one answer. 'With your help?'

'All I can,' she said firmly.

'Could you go to the harbour tomorrow morning and see what you can learn about this situation? I hate to impose, but there you have it.'

She smiled at that. 'Mr Eldredge, I have lived a boring life for the past…oh…years and years. What do you know? I get up the nerve to move away from my trying family, and things start to happen. This might be an eventful Christmas. Goodnight, sir.'

'Where will you sleep? I could move somewhere else.'

She regarded him with the same good humour that her son possessed in equal abundance. 'There is a small room off the kitchen with a little bed. Your feet would hang off the end of it, so I'll sleep there.'

'Moving away from trying relatives,' he mused.

'Perhaps your life has been boring, too?' she teased.

'I believe it has, Mrs Waring,' he replied. 'Let us see what new trauma tomorrow brings, shall we?'

Chapter Six

After a night of fitful sleep, Felicity brought her unexpected guest toast and porridge a little on the overcooked side, with milk and sugar. When she produced tea after a return to the kitchen, she saw the disappointment in his eyes.

'I have no coffee,' she said.

He waved away any apology. 'I don't suppose you expected to serve an American breakfast in your bed, did you? Hopefully I will not trouble you beyond another day or two.'

It was his turn to apologise when she felt her face grow warm at his casual words about being in her bed. Her embarrassment vanished when he declared, 'I am an uncouth American, Mrs Waring. Forgive my indelicacy. I am damned lucky you opened the door to my sorry carcass in the first place.'

'Yes, you are,' she said, relieved when he laughed, because it lightened her heart. 'I am going to skulk about the dock and find out what the *Sumter* is up to. Hopefully it will be gone. I've never skulked before, so it will be a new experience.'

'I should escort you,' Mr Eldredge said. 'Ladies shouldn't go unaccompanied any place where there are sailors. And skulk? Never! See there. I am well aware of the niceties.'

Laughing, she closed the door on him. Jem was already sitting up and rubbing his eyes in his room across the hall, so he was downstairs in mere minutes for his porridge, still buttoning his shirt. Felicity took out their two shopping baskets and handed him one, after he'd finished his breakfast.

'In addition to trying to sort things out at the dock regarding a certain missing person, we have the more legitimate task of buying food for the larder,' she told him, mindful of how well they worked together, mother and son, since they had no choice in the matter. 'And there is the matter of a Christmas goose.'

At least the rain had stopped. When she knelt down to wrap Jem's muffler firmly about his neck and tuck the ends in his coat, he did the same for her, much as he always did. 'We are a team, aren't we?' she whispered as she touched her forehead to his. 'Let's go.'

She looked about as they walked towards the river's mouth, noting where the greengrocer's was located, spotting a man selling eggs and cheese and milk. She smelled plum pudding when they passed a bake house. She regretted, for the tiniest moment only, her retreat from her parents' house in Derbyshire, where there was a cook. Maybe next year she could attempt plum pudding.

She did stop at a poulterer's and threw herself on his mercy when he rolled his eyes at another goose for him to cook, and at such short notice. She explained her recent arrival in Teignmouth, and made no objection to a larger sum than she wanted to pay.

Another row of businesses on a busy street took them to the harbour. Felicity stared at the steamer in the dock, flying that odd flag.

'The *Sumter*,' Jem read as he pointed to the name in gilt.

The sails were furled, which made the ugly smokestack stand out. As she watched the ship, Felicity noticed a handful of people milling close together on its deck. She wondered which man had pushed Mr Eldredge overboard last night. His story suggested deep and nefarious doings.

Onward, Felicity. It's time to skulk.

She looked around the dock, wondering how one went about asking questions without arousing suspicion.

Some townsfolk stared at the steamer, while others glanced and walked on. Felicity noticed the one constant on the dock closest to the *Sumter*, a fishmonger. She edged closer.

The big woman's arms were flecked with scales of the

fish she was gutting and cleaning with a wicked-looking knife. Jem stood back, his eyes on the fast-moving blade.

'Herring, mum,' the woman said, not missing a stroke of the knife. 'How many?'

'Six, if you please,' Felicity said.

The woman pulled out six fish of equal length from a barrel. Felicity looked over her shoulder at the *Sumter*, not sure what to ask.

She shouldn't have worried. The fishmonger was the garrulous type. 'Engine trouble, that's wot,' she said. 'Remember when it was just sailing ships with them pretty lines and no chimney stack belching smoke? What is the world coming to, I ask ye?'

'We live in a modern age,' Felicity said. 'I suppose it's called progress.'

'A damned shame, if you ask me,' the woman grumbled.

'Do you have any idea how long it will be here?' Felicity asked.

The fishmonger shrugged. 'Four or five days, if you ask me,' she said as she wiped her nose with her slimy hand and continued working. Felicity reminded herself to give the fish a thorough wash, before she figured out how to cook them.

Slap. Down went fish number five of the six she wanted.

I should have asked for more fish, Felicity thought, *except that we don't need even this many.*

She must get more information quickly.

'After dark, I heard a terrible racket. People shouting and running, and whistles. Whatever did that mean?'

'Someone escaped,' the woman said.

Felicity stepped back and opened her eyes wide, hoping she wasn't overdoing it. 'My goodness! Is he dangerous? Should we keep our doors locked?'

The woman leaned closer so Felicity did, too. 'What I heard was that he run orf with something the bloke what steers that ship claims he nicked.' She pointed past Felicity with her dripping knife to a skinny little man trying to keep up with a tall blond fellow in a grey uniform. 'And there's our mostly useless magistrate.' She lowered her voice. 'I heard something about a house to house search today.'

'Though why our good Queen Victoria would have anything to do with slave holders and rebels I couldn't tell ye. Merry Christmas,' she added incongruously, and slapped down a seventh herring. 'For t'little 'un.'

Felicity paid her and forced herself to stroll slowly away from the dock, buying eggs and bread on the way, when all she wanted to do was run home.

'Mama, what'll we do if they search our house?'

'Shh.'

She didn't want to think about consequences but couldn't help wondering if she would be nabbed as an accessory and transported to New South Wales. Come to think of it, did the government still transport felons? She had no idea. 'I'll think of something, Jem. Don't you worry.'

Better paste a cheerful smile on her face. Her neighbour was peering at her through lace curtains. Should she wave or not? Felicity didn't know her yet, and she hadn't time to make an acquaintance now.

To her dismay, the curtains closed and the front door opened. A tidy lady somewhere on the sunny side of ancient waved to her. Felicity stopped, trapped by good manners.

'My dear, I have been wanting to meet you! I am Mrs Honeycutt. It's good to see someone living next door.'

Felicity forced another smile on her face and gave a proper nod. 'I am Mrs Waring, and this is James, my son. My husband was—'

'Was looking out that window earlier,' Mrs Honeycutt finished for her. 'He's a fine figure of a man!' She tittered into her hand. 'Ye might want to remind him that lace curtains don't hide much!' She gave Felicity a roguish look. 'You're a lucky lady!'

God in heaven, Felicity thought in a panic. *Now what?*

She had no choice. Not one tiny iota of a choice, not if she was going to remain even another fifteen minutes in this neighbourhood, no, in this town. Maybe in all of Devonshire.

Sarah Siddons, where are you when I need you?

She took a deep breath and perjured herself beyond redemption, she who never told a lie.

'I will definitely tell my husband to behave himself behind the lace curtains in future,' she managed to say with what she hoped was wifely concern.

'Do that, Mrs Waring.' Again that laugh, which suggested to Felicity that it had been a long time since Mrs Honeycutt had enjoyed any such view. 'He'd put a spring in any woman's step! Congratulations, dearie!'

'Oh, my, well…yes,' she said, then continued the perjury, even as Jem stared at her with his mouth open. 'Hurry on ahead, darling. Papa is waiting for us.'

To her relief, Jem ran ahead. Felicity took another deep breath. 'He arrived yesterday from Massachusetts, America,' she began. That was true. 'He has a maritime business there.' Still true. 'He's here for Christmas and we couldn't be more delighted.'

Chapter Seven

'Your mother said *what*?'

'She had to, sir! That old lady next door saw you standing at the window... Sir, were you wearing your nightshirt?'

'Good God.'

Jem had flung the door open and rushed into the sitting room, where Ezra waited and shivered, dressed in his slightly damp clothes retrieved from the laundry. Coming right behind him was Mrs Waring, looking...complicated. He braced himself for the worst, wishing his throat wasn't so scratchy. His head ached.

'Mr Eldredge!'

She closed the door and shook her finger at him, which struck him as hilarious. He had been married and knew better than to laugh. And he *was* guilty as charged.

'Mrs Waring, I didn't realise anyone was looking in your upstairs window,' he said.

She plumped herself down in one of the chairs and stared at him. 'There she was, complimenting *me* on such a fine-looking husband!'

'Well, thank you to Mrs... Mrs...'

'Honeycutt,' she snapped. 'Don't you even try to make me laugh because I won't!'

She stared at him a little longer. 'Your trousers have shrunk, Mr Eldredge.' She peered closer then looked away, her face red.

'Wool trousers shrink when one is pushed into the water, but they're all I have. I feel achy, too.' He glanced at Jem. 'According to your son, I am now Mr Waring.'

She threw up her hands in dismay. 'What was I to do?'

'It was a monstrous stretcher, Mama,' Jem said. 'You never lie.'

'No, I don't, but we can't have Mrs Honeycutt thinking I entertain unclad gentlemen in my house,' Mrs Waring said with some dignity. 'I couldn't think of anything else to say.' She handed her son the basket of fish. 'Dearest, put this in the kitchen, please.'

Jem did as she asked while Ezra came and sat beside her. 'I owe you such an apology,' he said. 'May I ask—what did you tell her?'

'That you own a maritime business in Massachusetts and weren't we lucky that you could be here for Christmas,' she said.

'I had better remain here through Christmas then,' Ezra said, even as he wondered why the inconvenience didn't bother him. He hadn't enjoyed Christmas in years. Maybe it was time to change that.

Mrs Waring's expression turned from piqued to concerned. 'You must remain if I am to maintain any credit at all in Teignmouth as a virtuous woman.' She touched his arm. 'It's worse, much worse. A fishmonger at the dock told me that the ship's captain has convinced the local magistrate to conduct a house-to-house search today for someone who escaped with valuable papers belonging to him.'

'That puts a different spin on things,' Ezra said grimly. 'Captain Semmes knows what I look like. I can't cut and run because Mrs Honeycutt has, ahem, ample proof that you are a married woman. What if she should talk?'

She looked away, but not before he saw the dismay and embarrassment on her face.

'Mr Eldredge, I have led a quiet, respectable life since the death of my husband. I have a son to rear by myself.'

'You're doing that well,' he said, then couldn't help himself. 'He's astounded that you told lies, which speaks to your excellent character.'

She skewered him with a look that made the hairs rise

on his neck. 'What would you have done?' she demanded. 'Why did you have to stand at the window in the altogether?'

'I'm a moron?' he suggested, which made her lips twitch. He thought that a good sign.

'Do be serious! You are a wanted man, even though I don't want you. Mrs Honeycutt now knows I have a husband here for Christmas. That scoundrel captain can identify you on sight.' She sighed the great sigh of the supremely put-upon. 'What are we to do?'

It was a pickle; no denying it. Ezra took the smallest comfort in that she had said 'we' and not 'you'. He stared at her. She stared back. Silence.

Her brown eyes looked into his blue ones. He watched her chin go up as she appraised him and, for all he knew, found him wanting in the extreme. He sneezed. 'Beg pardon.'

'Don't you dare become ill.' She grabbed his beard suddenly and gave it a good yank.

'Ow!'

'You deserve that and more.' Not letting go of his beard, she turned his face towards the light then called, 'Jem, could you bring my scissors from the sewing basket?'

'The little scissors that look like a bird?' Jem asked, as he started up the stairs.

'The big ones, the shears.' She let go of his beard, to Ezra's relief. 'They need to be sharpened, so you might feel some pain, sir.'

'Why do I have the feeling that you hope I do?' he asked wryly.

'Because you are an impediment to my life, Mr Eldredge, and I'm not going to be transported to Australia as an accessory!'

She was right. He couldn't leave her house in his too-tight, too-short trousers; he had no other clothes, except an overcoat. No hat. The beard was a fearsome giveaway to his identity. He was proud of it, but she was right.

'Very well, do your worst,' he said with calm resignation. Jem returned with the shears. There was no mistaking the interest in his eyes. Ezra doubted Jem had ever seen his mother in high dudgeon. Mrs Waring's brown eyes might have been deep pools of umbrage and irritation at the moment, but he had seen compassion in them last night. Her nose was just this side of masterful, but only contributed to the elegance close to his face now as she surveyed the work ahead. When she pursed her lips in concentration, he had a roguish thought that he slapped down, after allowing it to frolic about for a second. She wasn't more than a kiss away.

She led him into the kitchen and then to the laundry. Jem trotted along beside him, carrying the shears.

'Mr Eldredge, sit you down,' she ordered, pointing to a stool.

'That's Mr Waring,' he reminded her, then wished he had not.

She flinched and her face crumpled. He watched tears gather in her eyes. She blinked and turned away, then squared her shoulders in a motion he could only call gallant in the extreme.

Mr Waring, you were a lucky, lucky man, he thought as she turned around to face him.

'My husband was the best of men,' she said, her voice soft. 'Remember that while you borrow his name.'

'I will, Mrs Waring.'

She pulled on her bibbed apron and tied it. He had no trouble admiring her figure, but it was a mother's figure. The days of any man spanning her waist with his hands were gone, but it only added to the air of comfort she gave off, now that she wasn't quite so angry with him. He wondered how hard it had been for her to give birth alone, with her husband dead and buried.

'Thank you, Jem.' She took the shears and clacked them close to Ezra's ear.

He closed his eyes when she began to cut, which made her chuckle. 'It's not a death sentence,' she reminded him. 'If you grew it once it will grow again.'

He enjoyed the feel of her fingers on his face. Gently

now—her anger seemed to have expired—she ran her hand against his cheek and pulled out the beard far enough to cut close to his skin. She was careful, humming as she worked.

'There. I will get my husband's shaving kit and you can do the rest. My goodness, Jem, that is a lot of beard on the floor. What a pretty colour. Gather it up, Jem. Put it in the stove.'

She returned with the late Surgeon Waring's shaving gear, her eyes suspiciously red, which touched his heart. 'Take good care of this. You'll need it with you when you leave.'

'When I get to London, I'll buy my own set and return this to you,' he assured her.

'Thank you. Jem would like it someday.'

She handed him another towel, then a bowl of hot water. 'I found some of James's clothes in the trunk, a pair of trousers and a jumper I knitted him,' she said, the wistfulness in her voice obvious to anyone with ears and a heart. 'He was a little taller than you, and a bit wider around, so I know I'll have to take in the trousers and hem them. That can wait, because you're going back in that infamous nightshirt after you've eaten.'

'Why, may I ask?' He took off his shirt and shook out the hairs, then put the towel around his neck. He lathered up, then began to scrape away.

'Without the beard, at least you don't look fifty,' she said.

'I am not even close to fifty!' he protested. 'I just turned thirty-five.'

'You could have fooled me,' she said, very calm. 'The fact remains that your blue eyes are somewhat distinctive as well. You're going back into my bed and there you will remain when the search reaches this house.'

'I'm sick?' He didn't feel too good. That harbour water had been cold last night, and he had floundered around in it too long. The ache between his shoulders wasn't going away.

'Yes. I'll lower the shades. You will keep the blankets high around your shoulders and your eyes closed. I will invent some illness and cry a few tears.'

Ezra had to admit that there was no grass growing under

Mrs Waring's feet. She really didn't want to go to Australia. 'Mrs Waring, I'm impressed. For someone who never lies, you have a breath-taking ability.'

She narrowed her eyes and shook her finger at him again, which was starting to make him think she was hilarious.

While he shaved, he heard her in the kitchen, then smelled something wonderful. He had his own moment then, remembering Priscilla supervising the cook in their tidy house on Mott Street while he shaved and prepared for a day at his office next to the ropewalk. The memory flooded his heart and he couldn't help swallowing a few of his own tears.

He forgot Jem was still in the laundry. 'I'm sorry, lad,' he managed. 'I was just remembering my own departed spouse.'

Jem nodded. 'Mama cries now and then.' He spoke in a matter-of-fact way, his voice lower. 'She doesn't mean to scold you. When she does that to me, I usually get a kiss and then a smack to my seat. I think that really means she loves me.'

Ezra chuckled and continued shaving, imagining a smack to *his* seat. When he finished, he looked in Surgeon Waring's shaving mirror, startled to see someone that looked closer to forty. He turned his head. Maybe thirty-five, if he squinted. Why had he buried his face in all those whiskers?

'Luncheon is ready,' he heard from the doorway, and turned to her.

'Will I do?' he asked.

Mrs Waring put her hands together at her waist and appraised him. 'I believe you will,' she said. She smiled at him, and his heart did a funny little flip. Well, hell's bells, that was medically impossible, but he definitely felt something, what, he wasn't sure.

'Sit down and eat, Mr... What is your Christian name again?'

'Ezra.'

'I shall call you Ezra. We do have a charade to maintain.'

'I don't mind,' he said, then said something else that took away some of the hollow feeling in his heart. 'Back in Massachusetts, no one calls me anything but Mr Eldredge. I like to hear my name.'

'And I have been Mrs Waring since…well, for ever so long. Call me Felicity, please.'

Chapter Eight

Luncheon was a simple affair of bread, cheese and boiled eggs eaten in the kitchen. Felicity apologised for the meal. 'My parents had a cook in Derbyshire, of course, but moving so far away meant some necessary retrenchment. I will learn to cook.'

'You brought home several herring,' he pointed out, then quickly realised what he'd just said.

This wasn't his home. But even with all the crates, and his perilous situation, Felicity's house on Brooke Street felt like home. He asked himself why, knowing it boiled down to simple things, as so much in life did. He shaved himself in Felicity's laundry. He smelled kitchen fragrances. He heard a boy talking and a mother answering. Had matters gone according to plan, this would have been his own home in New Bedford, his own life.

Recalled to the moment, he tried to lighten the mood. 'Yes, you did bring herring…here.'

From the uncertainty on her face Ezra could tell she floundered, too. He had to give a palm to the lady; she recovered better than he did. 'I bought them in an attempt to skulk,' she said seriously.

'I can cook them for you.'

'I accept,' she said, more at ease. 'They won't grow a minute younger in the pantry.'

'We can spare the little fellows until dinner,' he assured her. 'You're right, the three of us need to agree on a plausible fiction, in case that dratted Rebel does insist upon a house-to-house search.'

'After Jem and I have cleared the table.'

'I can help.'

She went into the laundry and returned with a broom and dustpan. 'Make certain there are no auburn hairs uncollected. If I must skulk for you, you must sweep for me.'

He laughed at that, which cut through whatever tension, real or imagined, was left in the room. He swept.

'Right, then, we three,' Felicity said after the chores were done, 'need to figure out a good story to satisfy any house-to-house search.' She looked at him. 'Mr War… Ezra…you will concede the necessity of pretending to be unwell, which will keep you under bedcovers and your eyes closed.' She peered at his face. 'Come to think of it, you don't look precisely at your best.'

'I have the headache.' She didn't need to know that everything else ached, too.

'What is the matter with Mr… Ezra…'

'Better call me Papa,' Ezra said, not looking at Felicity when he said that, not wanting to see the longing on her face after too many years. He understood such longing, but he didn't want to see it.

The boy grinned, then ducked his head when Ezra glanced his way. 'I won't mind that, sir. Papa.' He giggled. 'Mama, why must he keep his eyes closed?'

'Because his eyes are deep blue and quite memorable,' Felicity explained. For some reason, she blushed.

'Why, thank you,' Ezra teased. 'Jem, the captain of that wretched commerce raider knows what I look like. That's why the beard had to go. Your mother has declared my eyes memorable. Ergo, I must keep them closed.'

Jem nodded. 'Mama made you cut your beard. You are disguised!'

'Isn't she amazing?' Ezra said.

'Stop it, you two!' Felicity said, then laughed.

Why in the world did this nonsense suddenly feel so good? Ezra looked at mother and son with perfect clarity and something more. He knew that however this experience turned out, he would remember it for a lifetime.

'Do be serious,' Felicity begged both of them. 'In the interest of telling the truth…' she emphasised those words, staring him down '… I told Mrs Honeycutt that you are my husband, arrived here in time from Massachusetts to celebrate Christmas.'

'That won't do, you know,' he said. 'They're looking for precisely who you described.'

'I know. It was all I could think of,' she admitted. 'I'm not good at inventing fanciful commentary.' She regarded him a moment. He saw her hesitation, and knew she was a lady with good manners. He could help.

'Why am I in England in the first place? Is that what you'd like to know?'

'I am curious,' she said. 'I suppose it's not my business.'

'There's no mystery to the matter,' Ezra explained, feeling on solid ground again. 'My mother was from Wiltshire, about a hundred miles from here, I gather.'

'Yes about that.'

'She was a Melton from Melton Manor, a landed family near Salisbury. I have inherited a tidy sum from her father, so here I am, ready to collect.'

'You're not a diplomatist or ambassador?'

'No.' He shuddered elaborately. 'Spare me such a fate! A wretched fellow by name of Rectitude Blake was carrying important documents to our American ambassador to the Court of St. James, Mr Charles Francis Adams. Blake was so terrified that Captain Semmes would find them that he made me attach them to my leg. Then damned if he didn't throw me overboard! Beg pardon.'

'Overcoat and all,' she said, then looked towards the laundry. 'Your overcoat had better disappear. Jem, would you put it in my…in your bedroom?'

'Yours would be better,' Ezra said. 'And if you have any of your late husband's clothes, they should go on pegs in there, too.'

She nodded, her eyes troubled. 'This is becoming a deep game.'

'I hope you will continue to play along.'

'I will. I must.'

They had a good plan in an hour, after Ezra assured Felicity that he could easily mimic his mother's Wiltshire way of speaking, if he had to say anything. 'The bigger burden falls on you, if I am to be ill and quiet. Why have we moved here? There must be a reason.'

Some thought required pacing back and forth, so Ezra paced. 'I have it. You moved here from Derbyshire, you say?'

'I did.'

'Let us say I was a merchant in...in where?'

'Manchester,' she said decisively. 'It's been in all the papers that the mills are beginning to suffer because they cannot get cotton easily from the Southern states. You are ill and have lost your employment and we must retrench. That's why we moved!' she concluded triumphantly.

'You're rather good at prevarication,' Ezra joked.

'Should I say anything?' Jem asked.

'The less any of us say, the better,' Felicity replied. 'I had a younger brother, a positive scamp, who drove my parents to Bedlam, upon occasion. When called on the carpet, he concocted the most amazing tales. He always said too much.' She knelt beside her son. 'If we truly are interrogated, Jem, we must not *offer* any information. We merely respond to questions.'

'You continue to impress me, Felicity,' Ezra said, and he meant it. 'If you ever choose to follow a life of crime or serve in the government, you will succeed beyond your wildest imaginings.'

'Ezra, you're no help,' she replied. This time, that pretty smile did reach her eyes.

'I must assume that your brother is either in Newgate or Parliament,' he said.

The pretty smile left her face. 'Luke was with the Seventeenth Lancers at Crimea. He died at Balaclava in the charge.'

'You lost too much in the Crimea.'

'I did,' she said simply. 'We'll not lose anyone else to stupid governments, shall we?'

'No, madam.'

What else could he say? He knew there were times when words failed. She was standing next to him so he put his arm around her shoulders. When her hand slipped around his waist and she leaned against him, he pressed her head to his chest.

To his further gratification, Jem came close too. There was room for him.

'I shan't be melancholy,' Felicity said as she stepped back and the lovely moment ended. 'If we pull off this charade, I will ask something of you.'

'Anything you like,' he said, and he meant it. He also wanted to hold her close again, because she fit so well beside him.

'It's simple. Before you go to London or to Wiltshire, spend Christmas with us. It's only two days away, and after all, I did tell Mrs Honeycutt that you were here specifically for Christmas.'

'This is hardly onerous,' he assured her. He leaned closer to breathe in the scent of her rose talcum powder. 'Your son has already asked me to remain for Christmas. He said you owed him Christmas with a gentleman.'

How she blushed! There wasn't a soul in the Waring family who would have been any good at poker. Ezra wondered if the late Surgeon Waring was any better at hiding his true feelings. At least he, Ezra Eldredge, was quite a dab hand at poker; he could bluff with the best of them. He looked down at the pretty lady beside him, the one who fit so well there. At least no one here would imagine that he was feeling emotions that hadn't cluttered his life for years. He had things to do.

Didn't he?

Chapter Nine

The search reached the Waring household in late afternoon, while Felicity was hemming James's old trousers, sitting close to the bed where Ezra lay in her husband's nightshirt, eyes closed because the light hurt them. Jem read to him.

She knew Ezra was curious about her promise to Jem to have Christmas with a gentleman, but she waited until her son concluded the chapter, then sent him to his room to finish unpacking.

Jem had protested, of course, which touched her heart. To her delight, if not her surprise, her son and their guest had already developed a rapport that she found endearing. She also knew that although Jem was long past the age for naps, they had been up late last night after the excitement of Ezra's precipitate arrival. She gave Jem a few minutes to either unpack or pout, his choice, then peeked in his room. Arms thrown out, confident in slumber as in other aspects of his life, he slept.

She gave Ezra his orders next, which included trying on her husband's trousers. They fitted well enough around the waist after all—braces would help, but she didn't have any— and two inches off the legs would suffice, if they didn't require close inspection. 'I wish I had more of his clothes, but this will have to do,' she told him.

'I can wear my own trousers,' he said.

'No. They're too tight.' *Too tight for me to look at*, she thought, then felt her face grow warm. She nearly laughed out loud, wondering what Mrs Honeycutt would say about them. After all, her elderly neighbour had seen Ezra in far less.

'You're finding this altogether too amusing,' was his comment. 'Do ye think Teignmouth has anywhere I could buy gentlemen's apparel?'

'You'll be in London soon enough. Ask your ambassador about a tailor. He'll take your measurements and you can have a suit and more waiting for you when you return from Wiltshire, if you pay him enough.'

'Felicity Waring, you are brilliant,' he declared. 'I never would have thought of that.'

'You're a man,' she said, and knew that needed no amplifying, especially since he had been married before and must have heard similar from his wife. When all he did was smile, she knew she was right. He had a wonderful smile.

He was frowning when she returned to the room, the trousers over her arm and sewing basket in hand. He held out the sealskin pouch that had been wrapped around his leg. Felicity knew it must be hidden somewhere else, but his expression suggested it might involve her.

Oh, no, was her first thought. The second was more charitable. *Well, perhaps.*

He cleared his throat and winced. 'I've left my two hundred dollars in there. I daren't spend American money here. Felicity, would you do the honours this time and tie this around *your* leg? I shouldn't put it on, in case our scheme fails and they nab me.'

Felicity took the pouch from him without a word and he turned his back so she could so as he asked, wondering how her life had gone from completely ordinary to far too exciting in a mere twenty-four hours.

'There,' he said when she told him he could turn around. 'You can tell your grandchildren someday that you had a personal connection with an American president whom I think will go down in history as a great man. The war has only begun, but time will tell.'

'Is this one of those wars that everyone predicts will end by Christmas?' she asked.

He grimaced. 'It will be a long war. President Lincoln's

letter might smooth things over with your government.' He sighed. 'I never thought to be in the middle of this.'

'I didn't plan to open my door to a desperate man.'

'Yet here we are.' He gave her a sideways glance. 'You may tell me this is none of my business, but something Jem said intrigued me. He said you had promised him a father by Christmas.'

'I did. Mr Waring, I owe you an explanation.'

'Mr War… Oh. Yes.' He rubbed his forehead. Felicity wondered if it hurt. He didn't look too sanguine, and she knew it wasn't just his current predicament.

She turned up one trouser leg and pinned a hem. 'I moved here for two reasons.'

'Which are…?'

As she pinned the other leg, Felicity realised she had never explained why to anyone, principally because no one would have understood. 'You won't laugh if I tell you?'

'I might,' he said. 'I won't know until you speak.'

'That's honest, at least. After Jem was born in Italy, I re-turned to my parents' home in Derbyshire,' she began, as she hemmed. 'I hadn't much choice.'

'How old were you?'

'Twenty-two.'

He winced. 'Twenty-two and a widow.'

He leaned back and put his hands behind his head.

She watched him with a pang. James used to relax like that, except that she was generally curled up next to him. So nice. So many years ago. She looked at her unexpected house guest, really looked at him. Too many years ago.

Head down again. Back to hemming those trousers. 'It has been going on nearly eight years now. Jem told me last year that he wanted a father. I made him a foolish promise that he would have one by this Christmas. I had a year to fulfil that promise, after all.'

'No contenders?'

'Some. My parents are well respected and, like your Wilt-shire great-uncle, landed gentry.' She tried, maybe not too

hard, to subdue her scorn. 'One or two respectable men said
they would overlook the fact that my late husband was merely
a surgeon and not a physician, and the son of a farmer.'

'Dogs,' Ezra said, his voice flat.

'Enter Mr Pettyjohn, a friend of my parents and an older
gentleman.'

'I sense trouble.'

'Not at first. He was everything my parents wanted for
me. After a few visits and his confidence grew, he assured
me I was too young to manage alone and needed a firm
hand.'

'The nerve of him.'

'If you make one more comment, Ezra, I am going to
march down to the CSS *Sumter* and turn you over to that
Rebel captain myself!'

She thought that he might laugh, but he didn't. He stared
at the ceiling instead. 'I was told by one and all to buck up
and look for another wife. I didn't want to then, and I said so.'

'Did they leave you alone? No one leaves women alone,'
she told him tartly. 'We're at the mercy of every well-wisher.'

'They had to. I became too busy at the ropewalk, too busy
selling marine supplies, too busy making money.' He rubbed
his hands together. 'In New England, no one bothers a man
making money. You weren't that fortunate.'

'No,' she said, at peace with him. 'Mr Pettyjohn took me
in hand as much as I allowed, but the last straw certainly
surprised him. If I'm honest, it surprised me, too. I don't
suppose he knows what to make of it, even now. Maybe I
was foolish.'

Ezra sat up then and turned towards her, careful to keep
the coverlet around him. 'I doubt you have done a truly foolish thing in your life, madam.'

'Thank you,' she replied quietly. 'That means more to me
than you will ever know.'

'What did Mr Pettyjohn do?'

'This: one day he said, "Since your handwriting is so
excellent, my dear, I will let you address these greetings to

my clients." He handed me a stack of three hundred blank envelopes.'

'Good God, is he the Prime Minister?' Ezra exclaimed, but his eyes were kind. 'Archbishop of Canterbury?'

'A successful barrister.'

She folded her hands in her lap. The hemming could wait. It suddenly mattered to her that this man she had only met yesterday understood her. Maybe she *was* foolish. After Christmas, and if things went well, she would never see Ezra again. She hoped she could trust him, because this mattered to her.

'I looked at him, smiled sweetly, as I have been taught, and said, 'Mr Pettyjohn, I prefer that you *ask* me if I will address these envelopes.' He laughed at me.'

Ezra was silent so long that Felicity felt that same dread she had felt last autumn when Mr Pettyjohn had declared, 'How can it possibly matter how I word something so un-important?'

She picked up the hemming again and continued, her heart heavy. Ezra leaned closer and put his hand over hers. All he said was, 'I'm the other kind. I ask. Priscilla taught me that.'

She was about to put her hand over his in gratitude when someone pounded on the front door. Felicity leaped to her feet and ran to the window. She lowered the shade and blew out the lamp by the bed.

'Turn over and face the wall,' she ordered.

He didn't. As she bent over him to draw the coverlets higher, he took her face in his hands, kissed her cheek, and said again, 'I ask.' He smiled at her. 'That was strictly for courage, Sarah Siddons. It's time for your best performance. I need to get that letter you're wearing to London. Apparently I must become a hero.'

Chapter Ten

Felicity didn't dare look down at her bodice because she knew she would see her heart leaping about in her breast. She smoothed down her hair and took her time on the stairs. Jem popped out of his room, alarm on his face. She put her finger to her lips. 'You might want to go and sit beside Papa,' she said. He nodded in understanding.

She took her time opening the door. 'Yes, gentlemen? To what do we owe this visit?'

She recognised the constable as the man who, with two others, had rampaged through her house yesterday. She favoured him with a smile, even as she quaked inside. 'Did you find the awful man who dripped water from my front door to my back door?'

'No, we didn't, ma'am,' he said. He looked at the magistrate standing beside him.

The magistrate wore that self-important look of a man with power. So did the man in uniform next to him, the dratted ship's captain who was probably at this moment keeping the man in her bed on edge.

Man in her bed.

Don't you dare blush, Felicity, she ordered herself.

'Yes?' she prompted again.

'Are you new in Teignmouth?' the magistrate demanded.

'I am, sir. We moved here mere days ago.'

'We, madam?'

'Myself, my son and my husband.'

'We would like to speak to your husband,' the magistrate said, feeling himself on firmer ground now from his expression of relief. Perhaps he felt no more confident that women should have an opinion than Mr Pettyjohn did. Her chin went up at that thought.

'Yes, you may. He is upstairs and ill.' She slapped down her first card. 'I don't think he is contagious.'

Captain Semmes stepped back, and she silently applauded.

'We're new here, sir,' she confirmed. 'In fact, if you can recommend a physician...' She let her voice trail off. She slid the second card onto the table. A lip quiver wouldn't hurt. 'I'm worried.'

A glance at the Rebel captain suggested that he did not like the direction of the conversation. 'I cannot imagine life without him,' Felicity pleaded. That was simple enough; tears helped. She had no trouble thinking of her dear husband dying alone among his patients in Scutari to be harrowed by her emotions.

The magistrate appeared less bothered by the thought of catching a potentially fatal disease.

'We *will* speak with your husband,' he insisted.

'Certainly, gentlemen. Please, follow me,' she said, her heart pounding.

Oh, please, Ezra, be really sick, she thought.

With the shades down, the room looked nearly funereal. She sniffed the air and wondered how Ezra had made himself vomit. She decided he was an even better actor than she was. This was turning into a Christmas to remember.

Ezra gave a grunt and then coughed until Felicity's own throat hurt. He was facing the wall, the blanket high on his shoulders. Jem sat in the chair by the bed. 'Mama, I was reading to Papa, but I'm afraid he—'

'Never mind,' she said hastily. She sat on the bed and patted Ezra's shoulder. 'My love, may I get you some water?'

'Later,' he croaked in an English accent, then added, 'Dearest. Sorry about the mess.'

'Never mind that. These men are conducting a search for a scoundrel from the...the...'

'CSS *Sumter,*' Captain Semmes said, sounding proud but too loud for a sickroom, even this imaginary one. 'He stole valuable documents from me and I am determined to get my hands on them…and him.'

Felicity blushed to think of that arrogant man's hands anywhere near the sealskin pouch tied to her thigh. 'Then perhaps you had better keep looking for him. My husband wasn't…'

Again that loud voice. 'Sir? What do you remember of last night?'

More coughing from the sick man.

My word, he is convincing, Felicity thought.

He tried to sit up, but she patted his shoulder. 'Don't tire yourself,' she whispered.

'My wife told you I was sick,' Ezra managed to rasp out, still not facing them. 'I know nothing.'

The magistrate tried next. 'Yes, she did, but you're the man of the house and….'

'And what?' Ezra croaked, then coughed again. 'Don't be a blockhead, sir. She was downstairs. I was not. Do you not believe my lady wife capable of informing you of what happened?'

'Now, now, my love, don't exert yourself,' she urged. She put her hand on his forehead to further the charade, but suddenly it was no charade. Ezra was burning up. 'Jem, get me a cold, wet cloth from the kitchen,' she ordered, then turned around to face the interrogators. 'Gentlemen, please leave now. He is ill! If I remember anything else beyond what I already told the constable last night, I will inform you.'

Felicity leaned over and laid her cheek against Ezra's, fearful for him, wanting the men to leave. When she straightened up, she motioned the men towards the door. 'You know everything I know, sirs. Mr Waring knows nothing.'

'I suppose you are right,' the magistrate said, even as he looked back at Ezra as if expecting him to give precise coordinates of where the thief could be found, since obviously a woman had no such skills.

'Please, sirs,' she said again, and ushered them out of the door, down the stairs then into the street.

One deep breath followed another as she sighed with relief. Jem came out of the kitchen with the requested cloth. 'We don't need this now, do we?' he asked, hopeful. 'They're gone.'

'Ezra really is warm,' she whispered, as if the searchers crouched by the keyhole.

'I wondered,' Jem said. 'When I sat beside the bed to read to him, he looked... I don't know. He didn't look good. Then he vomited.'

'Stay here, son. I'll take that compress upstairs.' She climbed the stairs slowly, wondering what had happened to a perfectly ordinary move from one shire to another. She quickly discarded that shallow thought, which only smacked of self-pity, an unwelcome emotion that had clouded earlier years without her dear surgeon.

I can and will get this man healthy and on his journey, she thought as she opened the bedroom door.

She drew the curtains enough to let in a little welcome sunlight, then went to the bed, contemplating the man looking up at her. He blinked a few times then closed his eyes.

'I feel wretched,' he croaked. 'I felt a little ragged this morning, but this came on so fast. No need to act. Hell's bells, what a useless guest I am.'

Felicity smiled at that and placed the cool compress on his forehead, surprised that it didn't sizzle and pop. He *was* hot. 'You're not a guest, strictly speaking,' she said, before she winced at how rude that sounded. 'I mean...'

'No need to apologise,' he said quickly. 'I barged in here, upended things, and have caused you unnecessary alarm.'

'You have.' Ezra had done something else that she had to acknowledge: he had altered her placid, boring life, which had been turning her into a bland sort of female no man could find interesting. She sat down on the bed, surprised at this self-revelation. 'Then tell me why I am less upset about this than I should be?'

'Because you find me charming and utterly irresistible,'

he teased, obviously striving for a light tone, even as his nose ran.

She handed him her handkerchief and he gave his nose a good blow. 'By the time I return to America, I will have no manners left at all,' he muttered. 'I promise you I will feel better tomorrow, so I can be on my way and you can resume your Christmas.'

She could have agreed; perhaps she should have agreed, but hadn't he promised her something more? 'One moment, sir. Didn't you agree to remain here for Christmas for Jem's sake, after I made such a botch of assuring him there would be a man in my life again?'

'I'm a pathetic specimen,' he tried to argue. He turned his head away to cough.

'We will manage, sir,' she told him. 'At the moment, you're better than nothing. I must go out.'

'I wish you wouldn't leave me.'

Touched, she wiped around his lips with the compress. 'There now. I am going to speak to Mrs Honeycutt and find a physician.' She looked around. 'And the mop.'

He was coughing too hard to answer, so she left him there, told Jem not to let anyone in, and hurried next door. Mrs Honeycutt sat her down, interest written all over her face.

'Would you like some tea, my dear?'

'Thank you, no. My…my husband is quite ill. He was soaked in a rainstorm a few days ago, and it seems to have caught up with him.'

'I thought he looked quite fit, standing there in the window,' Mrs Honeycutt said. There was no overlooking the gleam in her eyes.

They laughed together, Mrs Honeycutt obviously pleased, and Felicity even more curious what the man in her bed actually looked like. She doused that unruly thought with the reason for her visit. 'Mrs Honeycutt, could you give me directions to a physician? I do believe Ezra will be more comfortable if he can cough less and perhaps sleep tonight.'

Mrs Honeycutt obliged and Felicity hurried to the High Street, a short stroll that reminded her all over again how pleasant this village was. After Ezra was on his way, her life would return to normal.

The physician was out, but she gave her request to the man's wife, who said she would pass it on.

She was passing an inn, the Coach and Four, when the shrill sound of a driver's yard of tin startled her and she moved closer to the wall of the building. She watched as the Exeter Coastal Carriage disgorged dishevelled, grumpy-looking people.

On a whim, she went inside to enquire of the publican when the coaches generally left for London. Ezra would need that information after Christmas. What she learned made her frown.

'Ordinarily, mum, the coach leaves around eight every morning, with another leaving at noon,' he told her.

'Ordinarily?' she asked. 'Is there a different Christmas schedule?'

He leaned forward and looked around, then whispered, 'Our almighty magistrate, upon whom the sun never sets, has ordered us to let him scrutinise every man that gets on board for the next week.' He leaned closer. 'The captain of that damned Confederate steamer is certain the thief what took all his money and robbed the passengers before murdering a coal stoker is still in town.'

Felicity gasped. 'Murder?'

The publican shrugged. 'That's what he said. Nasty customer.'

Whether he meant the captain or the felon, whose crimes seem to have grown exponentially with each retelling, Felicity had no idea. She thanked him and hurried home.

She quieted her nerves and went inside, taking a mop and bucket upstairs to clean the floor by the bed. At least he hadn't got anything on the sheets.

'I'm sorry,' he whispered. 'I should leave but I can't.'

She sat down beside him, threw caution out the window

and put her hand on his neck. 'You realise that's the only nightshirt I have from my husband, and it's going to Jem someday,' she said gently. 'I will launder it. The physician will be here soon enough, after he has attended the difficult delivery of a baby.'

'Sorry to be a bother.'

The bad news about the mail coach could wait; this wasn't the time. She had a really poorly man on her hands. She helped him out of James's nightshirt, which made her smile. Mrs Honeycutt had been right about Ezra Eldredge's physical attributes.

Chapter Eleven

For a moment, Ezra couldn't remember where he was, or why he was naked in bed, or who this man was who pummelled him then listened to his chest. He looked up and saw Felicity and remembered, grateful for her calm presence.

'I'm such a bother,' he managed to say, which meant she sat beside him, glared at the physician, shouldered the man aside and took him in her arms.

'You're no bother, my love,' she whispered in his ear. 'Let Mr Canning do what he must, and I will help.'

'I am a most fortunate man,' Ezra whispered back, then relaxed and let Mr Canning pummel some more. He heard the physician and Felicity discussing him in low tones that bounced into his ears but never quite penetrated his brain. Someone held him up and poured something noxious down his throat, and that was that.

He woke hours later, dressed now in a nightshirt that belonged to an earlier era. Felicity sat beside the bed, her late husband's mostly hemmed trousers in her lap, her head bowed over them as she slept.

The room was getting light. When he reached out to touch her, she opened her eyes in surprise. 'My gracious, you frightened me with such a fever. You said you'd been feeling low but, heavens, *this* low?'

'Remind me not to let anyone throw me into the sea ever again. What day is it?'

'Christmas Eve. Do you wish to sit up?'

He did, so she plumped another pillow behind his head, gently scolding him because he should have said something. 'I don't read minds, Ezra,' formed the gist of the scold, which reminded him forcefully of his own Priscilla, who could nag and admonish then give him a whopping kiss. He didn't expect that from Felicity Waring, a woman he had known not even three days, but he knew he wanted it. He lay there and realised he had been alone too long.

I am delirious and delusional, he thought. *This will pass, and I have to get to London. Maybe not today, however. And didn't I promise someone something?*

Ezra fingered the lace on his cuffs. 'This is a little grander than I am used to.'

'It is on loan from Mrs Honeycutt,' Felicity told him. 'After Mr Canning left, I went next door and asked to borrow a clean nightshirt. Since I had already gone there to enquire about a physician, she was not suspicious. Are you hungry?'

'Something light. I would hate to repeat that unpleasant performance.'

'Of course,' she replied, and went to the door. 'It's from the same source as the nightshirt. I told Mrs Honeycutt that I am no cook, and she produced a magnificent consommé, perfect for the sickroom. There is also a dried apple compote.'

He felt much better when she returned with a tray. She set it on his lap and efficiently tucked a napkin into the top of his nightshirt. She stepped back. 'Can you manage? Do you feel better?'

'I think so. I feel as if my head doesn't quite belong to the rest of me, though.'

'You had a lot to say last night after the physician left,' she said as she sat down. 'He warned that the draught might make you a little talkative.' She looked away, as if considering what she should say.

'It couldn't have been that awful, Felicity,' he chided, after a few spoonfuls of the consommé.

'You kept asking for Priscilla and became a little tearful when she did not answer.' He saw all the sympathy in her eyes.

'She was an excellent wife,' he said simply, and turned his attention to the broth before him until it was gone.

In silence she took away the bowl and spoon and set the apple compote before him. It went down more smoothly than he'd thought it might, considering the state of his throat.

Afterwards she removed the tray and, returning from the kitchen, she sat beside him. He watched her quiet demeanour, finding her serenity entirely to his liking. He liked his life to be orderly. Since the crew of the CSS *Sumter* had boarded the *Sullivan*, nothing had been orderly. Despite his low state, he felt energised for the first time in years.

That wasn't anything to tell this pleasant lady sitting there so peacefully; she would consider him a stodgy fellow. No wonder she'd thought he was fifty years old. Maybe he had felt that way for too long. And here he was, suffering through a nasty cold, his schedule in shambles, and minding it less than he'd thought he would. How odd.

'You have something on your mind,' Felicity said. 'You'll feel better soon and be on your way.' She frowned. 'Except, sir, there is an impediment.'

'I am a man of business,' he said. 'There is always an impediment.'

'The magistrate is going to closely watch the Coastal Carriage for the next week at least, hoping to nab the scoundrel who robbed Captain Semmes of valuable documents and money and murdered someone. I can't recall who.' She spoke very calmly, but he saw the twinkle in her eyes and knew she didn't believe a word of it.

'The extent of my villainy is that I was thrown in the water. Believe me?' he asked.

'I do. Apparently, the captain has concocted a marvellous taradiddle to bait a magistrate who, in my opinion, is a little dense.'

He laughed at that, which made him clutch his throat and wince. 'A moron or not, the magistrate is making my departure problematic.'

'More than problematic,' she contradicted. 'It has become dangerous.'

'I suppose it has.'

'The *Sumter* will give up and sail eventually,' she said.

She was right, but he felt the need to get the Lincoln letter to the ambassador. 'Felicity, as much as I loathe Rectitude Blake, I understand his urgency. Your country and France could decide to recognise the Confederate states. Right now they recognise the South's belligerent status, which is why that damned captain can steam into Teignmouth, ask for help and get it with no risk.'

'What would be the difference if England recognises the...the Confederacy?'

'England could throw all her maritime might south and we would have to declare war against your country. France, too, perhaps.'

Felicity sat back in her chair. He saw the fine lines of exhaustion around her eyes. She was tired and she didn't need this sort of trouble, not someone trying to settle into a new village with no fanfare.

'You do need to get to London,' she said.

'Maybe I could leave tomorrow.' Ezra tried to sit up.

She easily pushed him back against the pillows. 'Tomorrow is Christmas Day. Maybe the day after.' She shook her finger at him. '*When* I am convinced you can sit up.'

'It's a mere cold, madam,' he told her. 'Tomorrow.'

'Mr Canning said it has settled in your lungs. Don't argue.' She patted the trousers in her lap. 'I'll take these away and you won't be able to go anywhere.'

Thank God he was smart enough to know adamance when he heard it. They traded gaze for gaze. 'You, madam, are a martinet.'

'I am,' she agreed sweetly. 'If you stood up now, you would fall down. Maybe in a day or two.'

She was right and he knew it. 'If you insist.'

'I do.'

Something happened then. He couldn't have explained it to a board of directors or his banker, but he knew he had a friend and ally in this quiet lady who had already saved his bacon more than once. He ached all over. He knew he needed another draught of whatever Mr Canning had given him, but he needed to thank her. Maybe it was a leap of faith that she understood him. It probably didn't amount to a hill of beans, because he would soon be gone and mercifully out of her life.

Onward, Ezra, he thought.

'You have been to considerable trouble for me, and I thank you,' he said. That was too proper, too stiff. After all, this woman had probably helped him into the nightshirt he was wearing. He thought she had even taken him in her arms when the physician had been wrestling with him. He could do better.

'Felicity, you're a wonder.' He meant it sincerely.

'You needed my help.'

'It's more than that. I realise now that I have been getting stodgy and dull.'

'I suffer from the same complaint,' she said. 'After a while, once the sharp pain is gone, it's easier to retreat into a sort of complacency, isn't it?'

'I believe it is.' He had to laugh. 'I suppose I owe Mr Blake an apology for objecting so strenuously when he first wanted me to hide that Lincoln letter. I was getting set in my ways.'

'I know the feeling,' she told him.

He took another chance. 'Is that why you moved here?'

She touched his hand lightly. 'I already told you about Mr Pettyjohn.'

'Ah, so you did. Poor Mr Pettyjohn. Were there any more?' Where was his nosiness coming from?

He put his hand over hers for a brief moment. 'I want to know more about you because I know you are my friend.' Well, that was blatant; it was also the truth. He moved his hand away.

She didn't take it poorly. She turned rosy, and something besides exhaustion came into her eyes. 'Your friend? Well, then I can tell you this.'

He watched her face, seeing what he knew was stamped on his face from time to time: a certain infinite sadness to be parted too soon from a loved one, and the wish to bend time, and the knowledge that such things were impossible but the wish existed anyway, because they were only human.

'I wanted a fresh place to begin again,' she said finally. 'I cannot have what I most want, so I need to move on. It took me almost eight years to admit that to myself, but here I am.'

'Will you remarry eventually?' he asked, curious because now he understood his own restlessness in New Bedford, all his quarrels with himself. 'I have lately wavered between staying for ever as I am or looking around.' He leaned back because his head was starting to ache again. 'Felicity, I could have arranged for the barrister in Wiltshire to handle all the paperwork with my attorney in New Bedford. After a few months I would have received a bank draft from his counting house to mine. I didn't need to make this trip.'

'Yes, you did,' she said quietly, 'and for the same reason I needed to move. We're both trying to live again, aren't we?'

She was right. All he could do was nod, speech impossible.

'Good for us, Mr War... Ezra,' Felicity said. 'I shall look around Teignmouth for a seafaring man who isn't too rough about the edges, and you will find a nice lady once you are safely back in New Bedford. Think of the stories you will have to tell your children someday.'

'I will, indeed,' he said simply. 'Thank you for listening to me.'

'We both needed this bit of truth-telling, didn't we? I feel better already.' She laughed. 'And will feel even better when you are on your way and safe!'

'When this whole business is done and I return to Massachusetts, I'll see things differently,' he told her. 'Why Devon? Do you like rough seafaring men?'

'Not particularly,' she said with a smile. 'They smell briny. Oh, stop laughing! I know that a change of scenery wasn't necessary, not really, but I wanted it anyway.' She stood up and folded the trousers, putting them at the end of the bed. 'You'll laugh, but I blindfolded Jem and he stuck a pin in a map of England. Presto! Devon.'

'That is both utterly ridiculous and absolutely right,' he said.

'It is, isn't it? I didn't have a business to tie me down, as you do.'

He turned his head to cough. 'You're right. I will be gone soon enough, and you can go about the task—hopefully pleasant—of making a new life for yourself and Jem here in Devon.'

'I suppose,' she replied. 'I'll have to count my shillings and pence with more vigilance, but I am good at that.' She must have given herself a little mental shake because he heard the wistfulness leave her voice and the resolve return. 'It is Christmas Eve, which for you will be broth and bed and perhaps, if you are willing, a reading from Luke Two.'

'I'm all a-twitter with excitement, Felicity,' he teased.

She attempted sternness and failed marvellously. 'Ezra, you are not, and never will be, an "a-twitter" sort of man.' His heart nearly stopped when she took his hand, held it to her cheek briefly, then left the room.

Friend, I am going to miss you when I leave, he thought.

Chapter Twelve

'We don't have a Christmas present for Mr Eldredge,' Jem reminded Felicity as she stirred the chicken broth brought over by Mrs Honeycutt. Their neighbour had come to enquire after Ezra's health, since she had recommended Mr Canning.

And that ended that. Jem was only seven, after all, and not skilled in prevarication, or even the need for it. Felicity felt more relief than dismay for she was not a liar either.

'Mr Eldredge? Mr Eldredge?' Mrs Honeycutt sputtered, her eyes wide. 'But you are Mrs Waring! *Who* is upstairs in your bed?'

Felicity put her hand on Mrs Honeycutt's arm. 'Thank you for bringing over this food,' she said quietly, then took a deep breath. 'Thank you for your concern for Mr Eldredge.'

'Mama!' Jem said. 'We weren't….' He stopped when he realised he had spilled the beans first. Tears welled in his eyes.

Felicity held out her arms to him, and he went into them and sobbed. She kissed the top of his head. 'Never mind, my love. Let me move the pot from the hob and we will explain ourselves to our neighbour.'

Through all this Mrs Honeycutt stared with a dazed expression, until her own mothering instincts took over. 'Jem, I brought some ginger biscuits, too,' she said, and her eyes were kind. 'Dry your tears and sit over there. It cannot be that bad. We will ask your mama to pour you some milk while she and I have a chinwag.'

He did as directed, after Felicity encouraged him with another kiss, followed by a little tap to the seat of his trousers to move him in the direction requested. When he was eating, Felicity turned her attention to her neighbour and poured them both tea, amazed that her hand didn't shake.

Quietly, with glances at her son to make certain he was not overcome by guilt, she explained the situation to Mrs Honeycutt. 'What could we do?' she finished, after another pouring of tea. 'Mr Eldredge needed our help. He is trying to get that Lincoln letter to his country's ambassador in London. It's a letter no confederate pirate—for that's what Semmes is—has a right to possess.'

Mrs Honeycutt leaned forward. 'Is the letter safe now?'

'As houses,' Felicity assured her. She patted her thigh. She prayed silently, then asked the question that would determine everything from Ezra's freedom to her own reputation in Teignmouth. 'What will you do with this information, Mrs Honeycutt? Jem and I are throwing ourselves on your mercy.'

Her elderly neighbour hesitated not a moment. 'We must find a way to spirit Mr Eldredge out of Teignmouth, mustn't we?'

Felicity sighed in relief. 'All Jem and I want to do is live here quietly, with no tumult.'

'I think you should,' Mrs Honeycutt said.

'Jem and I went to the market square yesterday and saw the constable and his associates watching the Exeter Coastal Carrier. Mr Eldredge will never get past them.'

'I suppose he will not,' Mrs Honeycutt agreed. 'Is he well enough to travel?'

'Not yet. Mr Canning thinks several days of bed rest will help. Mr Eldredge wants to leave right now, so I took away those trousers of my late husband's that I shortened for him.'

Mrs Honeycutt laughed. 'Dearie, you are amazingly resourceful. Why are men so stubborn when we have their best interests at heart? Never mind. I trust he will go nowhere on Christmas Day.'

'Not as long as I hide those trousers,' Felicity assured her. 'His own trousers shrank after he was thrown in the water. He can't wear those.' She blushed. 'I didn't know where to look.'

'*I* did,' Mrs Honeycutt said wickedly, and Felicity giggled.

'Thank you for the loan of the nightshirt, by the way,' she said.

'Even after all these years, I can't bring myself to discard everything.'

'I know what you mean,' Felicity said, because she did. 'What else do we have that is tangible?' *I have a son*, she thought, and *memories*. Suddenly, she wanted more, but that didn't bear comment.

Felicity walked her neighbour to the front door in quiet contemplation, relieved to have an ally but uncertain with this new thought, one more complication in a Christmas that had got out of hand. 'I will think of something,' Mrs Honeycutt assured her. 'You keep pouring chicken broth down Mr Eldredge's throat.'

'We will. Oh, dear. Christmas.'

Mrs Honeycutt put her arm around Felicity. 'Didn't anyone ever tell you that the worst time to move was during the season of Yuletide?'

'You're right,' Felicity admitted. 'I need to find a good man who knows better than to move in December, and who will overrule me if I suggest it.'

Mrs Honeycutt gave her a measuring look, not the kind that meant betrayal of Ezra but camaraderie.

'I gather you're not a cook,' Mrs Honeycutt began cautiously.

'Not yet, but I am hopeful of improving,' Felicity replied, equally cautious.

'Let me help you this year,' her neighbour said. 'If you can arrange for a cooked goose—? Oh, you have? I will bring over the rest.'

'That's too much,' Felicity protested.

'Not at all. For the last few years I have been nibbling a bit here and there until Christmas has turned into just another day. I will do my best at short notice.' She clapped her hands. 'You can tell me what you and Jem like, and I can provide cooking lessons through the coming year. My gift to you.'

Felicity knew better than to object, not with that determined glint in Mrs Honeycutt's eyes. 'I could use the help,' she said quietly. She put her hand out. 'Maybe even more than that, the friendship.'

Felicity sat by Ezra's bed, she and Jem, for most of the day. When Mr Canning returned that afternoon to check on his patient, he found a quiet man gazing back at him, someone with his face washed and hair combed.

'You are a natural nurse, Mrs Waring,' he said, after a quick listen to Ezra's chest. 'And you, sir, are a lucky man.'

'I know,' Ezra said. 'Sir, you have no idea.'

That's enough from you, Felicity thought as she ushered Mr Canning towards the door.

'I promise to keep him in bed. Jem and I will make certain Mr Waring does not "spring from the bed to see what was the matter".'

'Ah, a quote from that delightful American poem written by Clement Clarke Moore,' Mr Canning said.

'Among my many talents, Felicity, is reciting that bit of Yankee doggerel entirely by heart,' Ezra said, when she returned from ushering out the physician.

'Entertain us, then. I can begin, '"Twas the night before Christmas…"'

He continued, to Jem's amusement, then he dozed, aided by a smaller draught of medicine. She and Jem tiptoed downstairs, where her son repeated his initial worry. 'What can we give him for Christmas, Mama?'

'Let us go to the stationer's and get him a dip pen and pad,' she decided. 'He probably lost his, and it won't cost too much.' She didn't add that Mr Canning had handed her a bill for his services. She could pay it, with some monetary stringencies in January.

Jem nodded. They bundled up and found what they needed. The proprietor also threw in a small bottle of ink and wished them Happy Christmas. Felicity agreed to Jem's request for roasted chestnuts, particularly since the temporary stand was located by the posting house for Exeter Coastal Carriage.

The constable and his partner stood at the entrance, looking intimidating enough to make potential riders and Christmas shoppers make a wide arc around them. They had a perfect view of the High Street in all directions.

'Mrs Waring.' Felicity froze. Jem gripped her hand convulsively.

'Yes, constable?' she replied coolly.

'Is Mr Waring feeling better?'

'Yes, he is, thanks to a visit from Mr Canning,' she said. She shook her head sorrowfully. 'I doubt it will be a good Christmas for him, however. And you? Will you be here tomorrow?' She hoped it sounded like polite conversation.

She must have succeeded, because the constable sighed. 'T'magistrate says we will be here until that Rebel commerce raider steams away.' Another sigh. ''One more week,' says he. Blast and damn, says I.'

They strolled away slowly as she wondered how to manage the impossible and get their house guest away safely. Nothing came to mind. She looked at Mrs Honeycutt's house.

If you do have an idea, please share it, she thought.

Ezra was awake and tugging at the lace around his neck. She sent Jem downstairs with the pen and tablet, and instructions about finding a twist of paper and twine to wrap it.

'What may I do for you?'

'It's these blasted buttons,' he said. 'Too small. Would you undo two or three?'

She sat beside him on the bed. He leaned forward obediently, then startled her with a kiss on the cheek. 'I owe you more than you will ever know,' he said, before he lay down.

'I… I'll bring up more broth later,' she said. 'And…and we'll read in the book of….' She trailed off. Heavens. It was just a harmless peck on the cheek. The second one, as she recalled. She would excuse the first one last night as delirium.

'Luke?' he offered. She heard the amusement in the single word.

'You're teasing me,' she declared, on more sure ground, although heaven knew why.

'I would never.' He closed his eyes. 'Hush now and let me sleep. I have to get well as fast as I can and out of your hair. I'm in a hurry to do my business and get home to my rope-walk, where no one will throw me in the water.'

'I suppose you are in a hurry,' she told him, then surprised herself. 'I believe I will miss you, Mr Eldredge.'

'Whatever happened to Ezra?' he joked.

She returned some inane comment, then closed the door on her way out and leaned against it. She tried to tell herself that it was a harmless gesture, a mere peck on the cheek. She almost succeeded in believing it, but not quite.

Whatever happened to Ezra? She frowned and wondered instead, *Whatever is happening to Felicity?*

Chapter Thirteen

Christmas Eve passed easily, until it didn't. Ezra grumbled, but Felicity and Jem insisted he stay in bed. They pulled up two chairs and everyone took a turn reading from the Gospel of St. Luke. Jem ended up sitting on the bed, showing their unexpected guest how to do cat's cradle if he ever got bored. And then he leaned against Ezra, who smiled for the first time. Felicity watched their heads together over the twisted string, heard them laugh, and thought how much her own dear surgeon would have relished being part of his son's life.

'What do you do for Christmas at home?' Jem asked their guest.

Felicity knew this was a harmless question, not a probing one requiring the wisdom of the ages. But, look, were those tears in Ezra's eyes? She wanted to leap in and change the subject, but to what? She had planned nothing special this Christmas, what with moving, and second-guessing herself about the wisdom of what her mother had called an impulsive act unworthy of a widow. She hadn't considered that her son wanted more, needed more.

'Jem, let's not prod,' she began.

Ezra stopped her with his hand on her arm. 'No, it's a good question,' he said. 'Sit down again, Jem. That's better.' He took a deep breath. 'Lately, I have done nothing.'

'No goose? No kissing ball? No carol-singing?' Jem asked, wide-eyed. 'Not even any marzipan? We did that and more in Derbyshire.'

So we did, Felicity thought, startled. *I depended on my mother to make up for my shortcomings and she did. I was determined to mourn. Shame on me.*

'Nothing at all, even on this best of days,' he said, almost as if his spoken revelation equalled her silent one. 'I give my housekeeper and cook the day off and eat leftovers. I might even go into the office.' Ezra looked at her. 'That's wrong, isn't it?

She nodded, yanked out of her own self-pity. 'You should be making merry with your friends.'

'What do you do?' he asked, his expression bleak. She had no answer.

Quiet, she ushered her son to bed, curling up with him for a few minutes and promising him they would have a good Christmas tomorrow.

I hope that is enough, she thought as he nodded, cuddled closer, then slept. *I can do better, son, starting now perhaps.*

Almost against her will, Felicity returned to her own room to ask Ezra if he needed anything before she said goodnight. It took all her courage because between Jem's room and this room, where she usually slept, she knew she didn't want the merchant from America to leave so soon. The thought had been growing by the hour, even if she had tried to stuff it away in some unused corner. Ezra's honest description of his usual Christmas Day had dragged itself into the open to blink, stretch and look around. Something had happened, but what could she do?

'I... I wish my late husband could have been part of his son's life, as you have so kindly been this evening.' There. That statement took all the courage Felicity possessed. She knew better than to say more, but perhaps, just perhaps...

It went no further, to her real chagrin, but at least she knew.

'What I have learned in these few days, is that I need to get home to New Bedford,' he said. 'Being around you and Jem makes me realise that I am wasting valuable time. I believe Priscilla would be vexed if she knew I was still single. I gather that you feel that way about your surgeon.'

She took a chance. 'We had so little time. I do want more.' Mama, a stickler for niceties, would have been horrified at such frankness.

'You'll meet someone here in Teignmouth.' He chuckled. 'Someone who will *ask* you instead of *let* you.' He lay back on the single pillow, after she moved the other one. 'I am determined to feel much, much better tomorrow and perhaps devise a way to get from here to London without the scrutiny of the magistrate. I have troubled you and Jem enough.'

'Perhaps you should warn the single females in New Bedford of your intentions,' she teased, even as her heart broke.

'Take out an advertisement in the newspaper?' he joked back.

'Something more subtle,' she suggested. 'Engage a fife and drum band.'

'I'll do it at the first opportunity! But now, goodnight, kind lady. Thank you again for everything.'

The end. She said goodnight and closed the door.

This was the conversation she had needed. Ezra couldn't wait to leave. She thought about that as she lay in her narrow bed off the kitchen, reminding herself that he was far from home, and missed his fellow Americans. Through no fault of his own, he had been put in an untenable position.

I hope you do find someone in New Bedford, she thought, even though deep in her heart she knew she didn't mean it. She wanted him to find someone right here. Her.

Early, but not too early, on Christmas morning, the poulterer delivered the roast goose, already cooked and stuffed with sage and onion dressing. Felicity paid close attention to his instructions on how to keep it hot for the noon meal.

She was spared from too much introspection on the state of both the bird and her heart by Mrs Honeycutt's arrival with spiced apples, turnips and plum pudding. They made several trips for the food, giggling like schoolgirls and trying to be quiet. Felicity stood a moment to frown down at the harbour, trying to will the CSS *Sumter* away and out of her life.

'Don't worry about that today,' Mrs Honeycutt said. 'I have a plan.'

To Felicity's relief, soon the cooking range was warm

enough, thanks to her neighbour's expert management. Porridge held off both males, who agreed to be served breakfast upstairs while Mrs Honeycutt worked her magic, soothing Felicity's heart in the process.

Mrs Honeycutt shook her head over Felicity's tablecloth and napkins and returned to her own house, coming back with the needed items, as well as more pickles and mincemeat she claimed to have forgotten.

Jem made trips downstairs, at first to sniff the air in the kitchen, then to filch a bread roll, all flaky and well buttered, also from Mrs Honeycutt's endless kitchen. When he came back and asked for another for Mr Eldredge, Mrs Honeycutt herself went upstairs and told them they had ten minutes to appear, dressed and ready to eat.

To Felicity's relief, Ezra appeared less shaky and decidedly on the mend. The trousers she had shortened and hemmed fitted well enough, at least for the distance between Teignmouth and London, provided he wore his overcoat and that they could work out how to get him there. The dark blue jumper she had knitted for James gave her a pang. Perhaps Ezra wouldn't mind returning it.

The question, 'How are we going to get you out of here?' ran around in her head, but that could wait, especially since it kept bumping into, 'How can I ever induce you to return?'

They exchanged Christmas presents, modest affairs, while the goose rested in the dining room. Jem approved of his own jumper and gave a whoop at his copy of *The Coral Island*. Felicity displayed the proper amount of delight at Jem's present of a blue hair ribbon, even though she knew he had appropriated it from a tangle of ribbons in her stocking drawer and smoothed it out somehow.

Thank goodness she had found something earlier for Mrs Honeycutt. Between mashing turnips and spooning out stuffing, Felicity had managed an earlier dash upstairs of her own, startling Jem and Ezra, who had been playing cards. 'I'm teaching him poker,' the American said.

She rummaged in her dresser for a lace collar that would

suit Mrs Honeycutt's black dress. The collar was nearly new, or as good as. 'I trust poker is a harmless, educational game.'

'Well, no,' he said with a smile. 'He'll probably gamble away your house and send you to the poorhouse.'

'Ezra!' she exclaimed. 'You are a bad influence.'

She smiled to herself as they laughed and Jem tried to shuffle the deck, spilling cards everywhere.

Perfect. The gift was wrapped and ready for Mrs Honeycutt's turn to open a present, when the men of the house were finally allowed downstairs. 'It suits me fine,' she said, admiring the lace collar.

Ezra touched her heart with his delight in the new dip pen and pad. 'Jem, this is just the souvenir I need of my odd stay in England.'

We're just an odd stay, Felicity thought, welcoming the offhand remark, which would help her forget him soon enough.

'Mama thought you needed a pen,' Jem said. With the optimism she knew and loved about her son, he bowed. 'Maybe you can write to us now and then.'

'Maybe I can,' Ezra said, with a sidelong look at Felicity that made her hope for the smallest second, until she reminded herself how much he wanted to leave. 'Yes, I will,' he amended, which warmed her heart.

Even one letter from you will be such a kindness to Jem, she thought. *And to me.*

'I wish I had gifts for you all,' he said. 'I will send you something from New England. What would you like?'

'Maple syrup,' Felicity said promptly. 'I hear it is excellent.'

'It is. And you, Mrs Honeycutt?'

'The same,' she said.

'You won't be disappointed,' he told her.

'So far you have not disappointed me,' she said with a twinkle. Trust Mrs Honeycutt. Who knew a dignified-looking widow could be such a rascal?

'Ah, well. Good thing,' he said hastily, his face red. 'What about you, Jem?'

'I'll think about it, Mr Eldredge,' her son said.

Mrs Honeycutt put her hand to her mouth. 'I forgot *your* present, Mr Eldredge,' she said, getting to her feet and heading to the door. 'Felicity, you seat the gentlemen in the dining room because the food won't wait. I'll be right back.'

What could you possibly have forgotten? Felicity asked herself as her neighbour darted next door and she allowed Jem and Ezra to escort her into the dining room.

Jem had said grace and Ezra was carving the goose when she returned. Felicity heard her leave something with a rustle to it in the sitting room before she joined them. 'It will keep until we've eaten,' Mrs Honeycutt said.

What a meal. Jem said it best, after he polished off a substantial portion of plum pudding, which finally finished their Christmas feast. 'Mama, we were ever so fortunate to move next door to Mrs Honeycutt,' he said.

'Weren't we just?' Felicity replied. 'She has promised to teach me everything she knows.'

Jem nodded gravely. 'God bless us, every one,' he said, which made them laugh.

'I can't move,' Ezra said. 'Dear ladies, this far exceeds my usual Christmas dinner.'

Your dinner of scraps and sorrow? Felicity thought with a pang. *Mine, too.*

'Jem, this is our cue to rise, clear the table and begin the dishes,' Ezra said.

'One moment.' Mrs Honeycutt held up her hand. 'I have a plan. Stay where you are. Come with me, Felicity.'

A black dress, and an equally drab crinoline lay draped over the sofa. 'Bring my hat, dearie,' Mrs Honeycutt said, pointing.

'These are yours,' Felicity said in a low voice.

'Aye, they are.' To Felicity's relief, her widowed neighbour smiled. 'Mr Honeycutt used to tease me unmercifully that I could not ever throw anything away.' She turned serious, but her eyes were no less kind. 'I told him I only kept the things I treasured.'

Felicity leaned closer. 'Will I know when it's time to… to…?'

'Let go of some things? My dear, you already know. Trust yourself.'

Mrs Honeycutt shook out the dress in the dining room, as Ezra and Jem watched, then looked at each other. 'Stand up, Mr Eldredge,' she said, then handed the dress to Felicity. 'Hold it up to him, dearie.'

Felicity did as directed, close enough to Mr Eldredge to admire his remarkable blue eyes. She could try to memorise them, but what was the point?

She thought of Mrs Honeycutt's comment. *Enjoy the moment,* she thought. *Sometimes it is all we have.*

Mrs Honeycutt walked around the two of them, muttering to herself. 'Yes,' she said decisively. 'I can add a flounce. Nothing to it.'

She took the dress back and stood right in front of Ezra when Felicity stepped back. 'Tomorrow, sir, I am taking my sister—you—to Exeter to catch the train to London. She is a recently bereaved widow in deep mourning. Such a sad state of affairs at Christmas, wouldn't you agree?'

Felicity laughed at her neighbour's audacity. 'Will it work?'

Ezra clearly wasn't sure. 'Uh…' was all he said.

Mrs Honeycutt poked his chest. 'You will get safely to Exeter, and with any luck there will be no one there on the prowl for you.'

He took the dress from her, held it up again, then kissed Mrs Honeycutt's cheek. 'I believe you are a thoroughgoing rascal, and quite the heroine. Will you come all the way with me to London?'

'That depends. If our dim-witted magistrate is thinking further ahead than I expect and has nasty fellows on the lurk when we arrive in Exeter, I might have to. Nothing indicates he is that clever. You will bring along your own clothes and change in a convenient nook.'

'Then I give you back your widow's weeds and go on my way rejoicing?'

'Precisely. We'll get you out of Teignmouth, Mr Eldredge.'

We'll get you out of Teignmouth.

After a brief visit to the US Embassy in London, then a bolt to Wiltshire for his mother's inheritance, he was going to vanish from England for ever. It wasn't fair and she hated it. She turned away, unwilling to display sudden tears she couldn't explain.

'Felicity, I don't think you like to see widow's weeds,' Ezra said.

'It's not that,' she admitted before she thought. 'I just…'

'She told *me* she's going to miss you,' Jem said suddenly. His face clouded over. 'I will, too. That's why I feel like this, isn't it, Mama?' He put his face into her apron, and muttered. 'Who's going to remind him about cat's cradle?'

'We'll have to trust him to muddle along by himself,' Felicity said. She bent down to kiss him, and took a swipe at her eyes at the same time. When she looked again, Ezra's attention rested on the plum pudding and Mrs Honeycutt watched her with sympathy.

I don't need your sympathy, Felicity wanted to tell her.

'Here, sir. Let me take the dress. I will add a flounce, and we two sisters will walk to the posting inn tomorrow morning at seven of the clock.'

Christmas was over just like that. Mrs Honeycutt took the dress and hurried away. Felicity cleared the table with Jem's help, something he had become accustomed to doing, because it was just the two of them and no one else. She washed and Jem dried in silence.

'You are an efficient pair,' she heard from the doorway, where Ezra leaned, watching them, his hands in his pockets.

Lending him James's dark blue jumper hadn't been a good idea. James and Ezra were not alike in looks or build, but that jumper… She had knitted it in Italy while she'd waited for James's letters from Scutari. She had finished it after his death, weeping over it as she waited in Livorno for their baby to be born. James had never even seen it.

'That's another Christmas present for you,' she said.

'What?'

'The jumper you are wearing. James never even laid eyes on it, so I cannot be sentimental about it,' she said, hoping her voice expressed only disinterest. 'I don't need it back.'

He said nothing. He left the kitchen as quietly as he had entered it, another man gone from her life.

'Mama, we should read the first chapter of *The Coral Island* tonight,' Jem said, draping the damp drying cloth over a chair.

'What?' she asked, impatiently, then regretted the dismay on his face. She usually never raised her voice. 'Yes, let's do that, son.' She pasted on a smile, wished the oblivious American heartily to the devil, and said goodnight to this miserable, marvellous Christmas.

Chapter Fourteen

He nearly went to Felicity that night. After all, she knew the proper dose for the potion Dr Canning had authorised and he didn't. Ezra lay on her bed in her room, feeling monumentally sorry for himself.

No one cared much for introspection, but lying there alone he forced himself to think about someone besides himself. Since the double sorrow of losing a wife and a son, he had gone about his business as best he could. He lived in a fine house, his housekeeper kept him organised, his cook well fed, and Mackie kept him tidy. Nothing disturbed his life, his plans or his ledger's bottom line. The trip to England had also been well planned and destined to earn him even more money.

Everything had gone wrong from start to finish. He stewed and fretted, wishing Felicity would at least come in and pour him the right dose.

Ezra Eldredge, you are behaving like a spoiled child, he thought, even though it pained him to take an honest inventory of his actions in recent years.

Perhaps on the trip to London he would have time to examine his faulty character.

A soft knock on the door roused him. He strode across the room in his ridiculous nightshirt and yanked the door open. Felicity stepped back in surprise, then narrowed her eyes. Somehow he knew she was counting to ten to keep from exploding at him, and felt suddenly diminished. His wealth and prestige meant nothing here.

He waited for her to speak because he was suddenly ashamed of himself. She had done so much for him already.

He could mull it about and attempt more self-examination later, but the fact remained: What a small man he was.

'I came to give you that last dose,' she said. 'Get into bed, Ezra.'

Meekly, he did as she said, feeling very embarrassed. She measured the draught and handed it to him, following it with a sip of water from the carafe. 'There now. I will make certain you are up by six so you can dress.'

He looked for a smile—hoped for one maybe—and saw one lurking, which perversely irritated him. 'You're going to enjoy that, aren't you?'

'I believe I am,' she said. 'It won't be as bad as all that. You'll get to London and everything will be nice for you again.'

That stung. At least he was aware enough to realise that perhaps, just perhaps, she had him figured out, weighed him in the balance and found him sadly wanting. 'It hasn't been my usual Christmas,' he said, hoping that was enough explanation.

'Or mine,' she said. She reached into her apron pocket and handed him several coins and pound notes. 'You have no money. This is all I have at short notice. It should get you to London, at least, where hopefully your own countrymen in the embassy will help you from there.'

'This is all you have?' he asked, then could have slapped himself because it sounded like he was complaining that it wasn't enough. 'I mean, I shouldn't take all your money.'

Ouch, such a level stare from this lady. It certainly put a sparkle in her eyes. Damn, but she was a pretty woman. 'I… I will promptly repay you, as soon as I get to London,' he stammered. 'Never fear.'

'Excellent. I'll be getting my quarterly funds immediately after the new year, in case it slips your mind.'

Ouch, again. When Priscilla got a mood on her like that, the only thing he could do was take her in his arms and give her a fat smooch on the cheek. It had never failed to make her laugh. Without a word he pulled Felicity close and gave her a fat smooch, hoping it worked. Good God, she felt wonderful.

To his everlasting relief, she gave him a brief smile instead of a well-deserved clout. She wasn't done with him, though. 'You are a big baby.' She reached into her apron pocket again. 'Here are more handkerchiefs. Your nose is running. Goodnight.'

A big baby, am I? he thought as he tucked himself into bed and gave his nose a hearty blow.

He didn't argue; he needed to remind himself that he wasn't the only person who had been discommoded by the doings of Captain Semmes and his Southern cause. His last thought was how to part in friendship from this magnificent woman who had done so much with so little.

He awoke, if not refreshed at least feeling less achy and more human. This day would either see him in London or twiddling his thumbs aboard the CSS *Sumter*, President Lincoln's letter never to reach Great Britain's prime minister.

Breakfast was porridge with Jem, who gave him a length of twine for cat's cradle. That little gift made Felicity smile. 'You're raising your lad beautifully,' Ezra told her when Jem went into the laundry room to wash. 'He is as kind and thoughtful as you are.'

It gave him a bit of unholy glee to see her startled and then fuddled by a compliment. 'He's my son. I'm doing my best,' was all she said, and it humbled him, he who had become a distant cousin to humility.

Dressed in suitable grey, Mrs Honeycutt came in through the back door and handed Ezra the black dress, as well as a petticoat to go under the crinoline.

Resigned to the inevitable, Ezra let himself be led into the laundry room. 'I'll keep my trousers on,' he said as he pulled off his jumper. He looked around for Felicity, but saw only Jem and Mrs Honeycutt. He held up his arms as the old lady dropped the dress over him.

When he pulled it down, Felicity stood there, holding out

the sealskin pouch. He took it from her; it was still warm, which made him blush like a fool and remember that she had worn it against her thigh. He imagined her thighs were worth a second glance.

You're already an ass, he thought, disgusted with himself. *This is business and you need to get on with it.*

He hoisted his dress and strapped the pouch to his trousered thigh. Felicity helped him step into the petticoat and crinoline then tied them expertly at his middle. She smoothed the dress down, appraised the effect, then nodded, apparently satisfied.

'It's too tight across your shoulders,' Mrs Honeycutt announced unnecessarily when he squirmed at the constriction. 'This cloak will cover a multitude of sins.'

Will it cover the sins of pride and complacency? he asked himself as he slung it about his shoulders.

'As long as it gets me to London,' he muttered.

Felicity left and returned with a travelling case and a black reticule. 'For your own clothing. I put in James's nightshirt,' she said as she handed it to him.

The elderly widow sat him down at the kitchen table and settled a black hat with a heavy veil on his head. 'There you are, young man,' she said, sounding gruff and emotional at the same time. 'Don't cross your legs, sit with your knees together. I am amazed how much room a man can waste on the train with his legs spread.'

'I suppose we do that now and again,' he admitted.

'Now and then?' Mrs Honeycutt slapped his back with surprising strength. 'You're not really God's gift to women, you know.' Whether she meant men in general or him in particular, he hadn't the courage to ask.

He glanced at Felicity to see her lips twitch. 'Mrs Waring, I will do as your neighbour insists, but I promise you that when I return to New Bedford and find a lady to court, I will remember to *ask* her for favours, and not *let* her help me.'

He meant it as a joke, but it wasn't a joke. He sat there in a black dress, his face covered in mourning veils, his legs together, and wondered why women even tolerated men. He pulled the veil back over his hat. 'I mean that.'

'Then you have learned something useful,' Felicity said.

Mrs Honeycutt put on her own sober hat, headed towards the front door and gestured to him. He stood up, but stayed where he was until she was out of sight. He took Felicity's hand. 'What have you learned through all of this?'

'That Jem still needs a father. I promise to start looking. Teignmouth is as good a place as any.'

'You're equal to it,' he said, smarting from her honest answer and spotting her son watching this exchange. 'Jem, will you get my overcoat and put it in the valise?'

Jem took the valise and went upstairs. Ezra turned back to Felicity, took her in his arms and kissed her.

He meant it to be an *I'll show you* sort of kiss, just to prove that men did have their uses, even spoiled ones. He discovered that Felicity knew how to furnish a scorcher of a kiss. James Waring had been a damned lucky husband.

He broke away first because she was too close, pressing against him. Or perhaps he was pressing against her. He liked the feeling, however it came. 'My goodness,' he whispered. 'I don't think you'll have to look too hard, Lissy.'

'I like that name,' she said, and kissed him gently this time, which was even harder to pull away from. He was so aware of her and how capable she was. She brought him back to earth quickly. 'However, I would *never* kiss a man like that as a way to introduce myself.'

'Then why did you kiss me like that?'

He couldn't help a little more unholy glee to see her stare and stammer. 'Well I… It's just that…' She collected herself. 'I wanted to. That is all.' Her cheerful nature righted itself. 'If I were you, I wouldn't try that with a New Bedford lass until you are dressed like a man.'

He laughed, and dropped the veil over his face again. 'The neighbours would really wonder.'

He had to leave. Jem returned with the valise and Mrs

Honeycutt called to him from the front door. He touched Lissy's cheek. 'You've taught me a few things. Thank you.'

'Don't forget them, Ezra.'

'I shan't. Goodbye.'

Chapter Fifteen

Leaving Teignmouth proved to be simple. The magistrate and Raphael Semmes himself watched the ticket window of the Exeter Coastal Carriage. Captain Semmes even helped Ezra with his valise, stowing it on the carriage, then taking the 'widow's' hand, fortunately gloved in Mrs Honeycutt's spare pair.

'You made a conquest,' Mrs Honeycutt joked. It was easy to give her a withering stare under the safety of the veil.

At the train station in Exeter, Mrs Honeycutt saw no one that she knew. Once he had bought his ticket with Lissy's money, he found a door labelled 'Broom Closet', slipped inside and removed the dress and petticoat. On went the jumper. His overcoat was a little tighter from its trip into the harbour, but at least it hadn't shrunk as much as his trousers had, which Lissy had already burned. He had no hat, so he was no gentleman. At least Mrs Honeycutt let him keep the gloves, ill fitting as they were. He handed over her widow's weeds with a bow.

He kissed her forehead, took her hand in his and whispered, 'Dear lady, I owe you a great debt.'

'Oh, go on,' she said, even as her face turned rosy. 'Get that letter to your ambassador, go to Wiltshire, make more money, and go home.'

'Yes, ma'am,' he said, and gave her another kiss. When she was close to him she asked, 'Perhaps one last visit to Jem and Felicity?'

'If I have time,' he temporised, suddenly shy, and wondering at himself. 'Goodbye.'

Mrs Honeycutt waved him off to his railway compartment, and watched until the train pulled out, which gratified him. His late mother used to see him off when he went beyond New Bedford. He enjoyed the memory.

He sat back and felt as though he was relaxing for the first time since the CSS *Sumter* stopped the unfortunate USS *Sullivan* and scuttled her. 'I'm getting out of Devonshire,' he murmured, speaking softly because he shared the compartment with others. 'At last and thank God.'

Easy to say. Why he felt something lacking he couldn't have said. Well, yes, he could if he were being honest. He was missing two people.

Don't be ridiculous, Ezra, he thought. *You have much to do, and your business at home needs you.*

In mere hours he was in London, and shortly after that at the United States Legation in Great Cumberland Place, City of Westminster. He had trouble convincing them that, yes, he was a gentleman, in spite of his ill-fitting garb and no hat. He also had quite a story for Ambassador Adams.

Despite the doorman's obvious scepticism—perhaps Ezra's Yankee accent helped—he eventually found himself seated in the well-appointed office of Charles Francis Adams himself, and his son Henry, one of his secretaries.

He told his tale of adventure to the men. When he mentioned Rectitude Blake, both Adams rolled their eyes. 'I had been informed he was headed our way,' the ambassador said. 'You will make me a happy man if you assure me that he is still on board the *Sumter.*'

'To my knowledge, he is,' Ezra assured the man. 'The *Sumter* is undergoing repairs in Teignmouth, but rumour says they are bound for Spain.'

Charles Adams laughed. 'That is if Captain Semmes doesn't murder the prosing old busybody first.' He leaned forward. 'As you have just said, Blake was carrying something with him that we sorely need if we are to stay out of war with Great Britain.'

'He gave it to me and pushed me overboard,' Ezra said, then patted his thigh, where he'd relocated the pouch next to his skin after he'd changed in the broom closet. 'Sir, if you will direct me to a more private spot, I will drop my trousers and produce a document kept safe in a sealskin pouch.'

Father and son laughed and pointed him into the next room, where Ezra dropped James Waring's trousers. He also took out his business card and the two hundred dollars.

There was something else in the pouch, a name and address on a square of card. Lissy had drawn two flowers on it as well, one pink and the other blue, with five petals. Pretty thing. It would be a good memory.

When he returned to Adams's office, tea and biscuits waited. Ezra handed the ambassador his business card— 'Just so you know, sir'—then handed over the Lincoln letter.

With a nod of apology, Charles Adams read the letter, sighed with relief and handed it to Henry to read. 'Will it help our Union cause?' Ezra asked.

'Didn't you read it?'

'No, sir. It wasn't addressed to me.'

'I'd have been tempted, were I you,' Charles Adams said. 'But, yes, I know this will help. You have done a signal service for your country.'

There wasn't anything else to say. Henry Adams poured tea and the biscuits went around. Charles Adams set down his cup and nodded to Ezra. 'What are your plans now?'

'I'm past due in Salisbury to collect a bank draft from a relative of my late mother.'

'We'll see that you get there.' Charles Adams looked him over. 'Henry, take this casual-looking fellow to Markham and Sons in Regent Street. He needs some clothing that won't embarrass the United States.'

They all laughed. 'I have two hundred American dollars. Will that buy me suitable garb, two pairs of extra trousers, shirts and smalls and maybe an overcoat? Oh, and a hat.'

'I'll have your money changed here, but you will accept a gift from the US Legation for your clothing and expenses, since you have done us a huge favour,' the ambassador said.

'Oh, but—'

'Don't argue, Mr Eldredge, or I will turn into my father and grandfather—President John Adams himself—and give you a Yankee scold!'

They shook hands, and the ambassador turned Ezra over to his son. Henry saw him to Regent Street, and stayed there until the proprietor had a tailor measure him and agree to produce the clothing requested in a week.

'Now I will take you to Maurigy's Hotel a few doors down, register you, and see to your needs until you get on the train to Salisbury,' he told Ezra. He smiled sympathetically. 'This has been quite an ordeal, hasn't it?'

Less than you would imagine, Ezra thought, thinking of only kindness in Teignmouth.

He shrugged as they walked along Regent Street. 'Maybe I needed a jolt from my complacency,' he admitted. 'I met brave people who hid me, then healed me, and helped me to escape so I could do something useful for my country. I really cannot complain.'

He couldn't. After a good night's sleep and a close shave with James Waring's razor, loaned by a lady he had to admit he missed more than a little, he ate a good breakfast. Henry Adams arrived to shepherd him to the railway and send him on his way.

Before he boarded, he took Felicity's card from his pocket and held it out to Henry. 'Do you know anything about flowers?'

'It's a forget-me-not, Mr Eldredge,' Henry said with a smile. 'I'd say you have a friend in Teignmouth.'

He carried that thought to Melton Manor, where he explained his whole story again. Great-Uncle Anthony Melton turned him over to his solicitor to sign documents. He was assured there would be a bank draft ready for him in a few days.

'I remember your mother well, Ezra,' his great-uncle told him that night over sherry in the sitting room. 'She was such a sweet lady.' He laughed. 'My God, can you grasp the consternation we all felt when she met and married an American?'

Ezra smiled. 'I hear my parents fell rapidly in love.'

'That's what Maude always claimed,' Anthony took a sip. 'She said the Eldredge men were well nigh irresistible, with an eye for English ladies.' Another chuckle. 'Have you succumbed as well?'

'Oh, no,' Ezra said, 'although I was well tended in Teignmouth by a widow and her son.'

'Merely well tended?'

Much more, he thought suddenly. 'It was more,' he admitted. 'She risked her reputation to keep me hidden.' He smiled. 'And her son taught me cat's cradle. His father died in the Crimea.'

'Are you going to pay her another visit?'

'No. I'll write to her, though. Yes, I will do that.'

Ezra could tell his answer did not impress his uncle. It didn't impress him either.

Why am I being so stubborn? he asked himself as he undressed for bed that night.

Why, indeed? Lissy had thoughtfully sent along the last of Mr Channing's medicinal draught, so he downed the final dose, then lay back to stare at the ceiling until the draught hurried slumber along.

He felt himself relax, which permitted his mind to wander, but not so much that he couldn't process rational thought. He could plead with himself that a man could only stay away so long from even a successful, well-run business. Common sense dictated such.

What was *in* that draught? Common sense deserted him; it vanished.

He lay there alone in a bed for two, and found that he desperately wanted Lissy Waring. He forced himself to consider the merits of the single ladies he knew in New Bedford or Boston. Some were charming. He asked himself honestly, 'Ezra, do you want to bed any of them?'

No, he didn't. When he thought, 'What about Lissy Waring?' he felt himself growing warm again. She might be a twenty-nine-year-old widow but, Jerusalem Crickets, she could kiss. His last coherent thought before the draught finished him off was the notion that maybe she could teach *him* a thing or two.

He slept soundly.

no man, money to be made, plans to put into action. He sat still, stared at the wall and allowed the other side of his brain to speak to him, this time without the benefit of a medicinal dose. It was never a loud voice—certainly in recent years he had barely heard it. It was the side of his brain trying to tell him love wasn't something that happened only once.

He heard it now. He looked at the note again. 'I am an idiot,' he said out loud, then said it louder, telling himself that plans can change.

Do I or don't I? he asked himself.

It was the question he continued to ask himself as the train took him back to London. His rational brain still took pleasure in scolding him that he was too old to be so foolish. It reminded him of money to make, which meant more time in the office and no time to marry again. The other side gently reminded him that he had plenty of money already, and where was the harm in marrying again and having plenty of love, too?

He knew he was being inevitably drawn back to Teignmouth, but for now he had to focus. Waving away the racket in his head, he took a hansom cab from the station to Great Cumberland Place, where Henry Adams met him once more. They shook hands, Henry telling him that his father had gone immediately to the Court of St James after Ezra had left for Salisbury.

'Any success?' Ezra asked, as they started towards Regent Street and dinner.

'Diplomacy is not something to rush, he tells me. He did mention a slight thaw, so we will leave it at that. Are you in the mood for steak and kidney pie? Tomorrow morning we'll pick up your new clothes from Markham and Sons.'

He was in the mood for Anadama bread and clam chowder from his own kitchen in New Bedford...clam chowder with blobs of butter and clams raked that morning from the beach. He thought of Felicity's admission that she was no

Chapter Sixteen

Ezra left Salisbury after several pleasant days at Melton Manor. The solicitor handed him a bank draft for a sizeable amount, which he knew would further his aim to invest in railroads. This legacy would make him more than well off; it would make him rich.

Great-Uncle Anthony furnished him with more funds to see him comfortably home and then surprised him with an overcoat that almost fitted. 'Just leave that shrunken coat in your room. The housekeeper will see it to the midden.'

'With pleasure!'

The new overcoat was of handsome black wool, understated and elegant. His old overcoat, looking more than forlorn, he left hanging in the dressing room. He reached into the pocket to retrieve his Christmas pen, ink, and tablet from Jem.

Better check the other pockets, he told himself. And changed his life.

The other large pocket yielded lint and wadding that might have been a railway ticket from years ago. The inside pocket yielded a folded note.

Curious, he opened it, and felt his eyes mist over. It had to be Jem's handwriting. He stared at it, reminded again that if life had been kinder, it could have been his son's note. He read it.

I didn't want you to leave. Mama didn't either. She told me. Please come back. That is what I want from you for Christmas. You asked. Remember?

Stunned, he sat down on the bed. The more hardened part of his brain tried to remind him of time and tide waiting for cook. He doubted she had ever seen a clam and wondered what she'd think of them.

'Yes, steak and kidney pie.'

The train from London to Exeter moved at a slug's pace, stopping at every tiny village and hamlet, when Ezra wanted it to race along. No! Too fast! He needed more time to think, more time to say exactly the right thing to the woman he loved. He was thirty-five years old, feeling again those joys, doubts, fears and exaltations that men much younger than he felt.

He had been through this anxiety before, the will she, the won't she? At least he wasn't worried this time how he would support a wife. He had a fine home, a carriage and horses, a summer cottage on Nantucket Island and a cook. He chuckled. Especially the cook. The smile left his face. His housekeeper had informed him that his cook was retiring. Maybe he could cajole her into staying a few more years.

Lissy could always say no. He was going to ask a lot of her. All Priscilla had had to do was move three blocks to his house, not three thousand miles to a new country at war. Priscilla had known Ezra since they'd sat next to each other in the children's Sunday school at New Bedford's Congregational Church. Felicity had never seen him at his best. What was he *thinking*?

Cold reality nearly made him leap off at Lyme Regis. She had seen him sick, nearly naked, complaining, frightened. She had emptied his chamber pot and wiped his face and chest of smelly fever sweat. She was probably relieved to have him gone. In despair, he took out Jem's note. It calmed his heart and kept him on the train to Exeter.

As they bowled into Teignmouth on the Coastal Carriage, Ezra looked towards the harbour first, relieved past all measure to see that the CSS *Sumter* had steamed away.

Good riddance, he thought.

He knew an ocean crossing now would be rough and

the seas stormy. He walked slower and slower, stopping, nearly turning back, then moving on and feeling every year of his age.

He didn't make it past Mrs Honeycutt's house. Did the woman spend all her time watching out that dratted window? Then he remembered what he owed her and returned her hug when she came out and embraced him.

'Mrs Honeycutt, you were right,' he said, holding her off. 'I couldn't stay away. I love Felicity. Do I even have a chance?'

The old lady had such a twinkle in her eyes. 'I can't say, sir, but she's been moping about for a week.'

Ezra Eldredge, man of business, man in love, took a long look at Lissy's neighbour. 'Mrs Honeycutt,' he asked, 'have you ever wanted to travel to America?'

'I'm too old.'

'No, you're not,' he responded promptly. 'I like your cooking. I have a good kitchen in New Bedford that needs a cook. Interested?'

He kissed her cheek and left her staring after him, her mouth open.

He squared his shoulders and walked up the steps to Number Eleven Brooke Street. He had come here before, soaking wet and running for his life. This was different.

He knocked on the door, reminding himself to breathe. The years fell away and he was a young man again, wanting a woman, wanting this woman, and no other, not ever.

Jem opened the door and gasped. Ezra put his hand over the boy's mouth. 'Let's see what she does,' he whispered. 'Shall we?'

Jem nodded and Ezra took his hand away. He straightened his cravat and handed his new top hat to the boy, to his future son.

'Jem, who is it?' he heard from the kitchen.

'Someone with a question,' Ezra called out.

She was at the door in a moment, staring, her hand to

her heart. She was so beautiful to him, even though her hair looked wild from the kitchen's heat.

James, I will treat her well, he thought. *Don't ever worry about her.*

'I'm a fright,' she managed to say.

'Hardly.' It was his turn. 'I came here to *ask* you to marry me,' he said. His throat felt as dry as the Sahara. A person would think he had never proposed before. 'I came here to ask you if you love me as much as I love you. I came here to ask you to be my wife, the mother of my children, and an American eventually. I came here to ask if I could raise Jem as my own son. I already love him like my own. I'm asking, sweet lady.'

She was in his arms in seconds. He held her close until he felt Jem pressing against his side. They opened their embrace to include the boy. 'I asked,' he whispered into her hair. 'Please, Lissy, please.'

She nodded. 'All you had to do was ask. Americans are so brash and pushy. I will marry you. I love you.' She kissed him, another scorcher.

'It's winter. I might be seasick,' he warned her as she nestled close. 'You'll see me at my worst.'

'I already have,' his love told him.

'Dear lady, you are too easy,' he scolded playfully, now that he knew she was his. 'You don't even know if I have a house, a good reputation, or a cook.' He smiled at that. He knew he had a cook right next door. Mrs Honeycutt could mull it over and come in the spring.

Felicity made a face, then touched her son's head. 'Jem, do those things matter?'

Jem shrugged. 'Not to me.'

Ezra leaned down and kissed the top of Jem's head. 'Thanks for the note.'

'Note?' his Lissy asked.

'It'll keep, won't it, Jem?'

The boy grinned at him.

Lissy looked from one to the other as her face rosied up. 'I sense a conspiracy.'

They nodded in unison.

'You're not telling me?' she asked, then kissed them both, a gentle kiss for her son, and a more energetic one for Ezra, suggesting that his voyage home would be a lot more enjoyable than the voyage out. 'Let's start packing.'

She came to him that night, stepping around packed crates. To be scrupulous, they actually met at the bottom of the stairs. In her embrace, Ezra duly noted that her nightgown was thin. Perhaps she had come to him for warmth. When he suggested such reasoning, she kissed him again. 'Ezra, I know you are joking.'

He pressed against her.

'I do believe this is no joke,' she murmured, and pressed back.

'I do not tease about business or love,' he managed to say before both nightgown and nightshirt came off right there at the foot of the stairs. Luckily, Jem was fast asleep.

He carried her upstairs to her bed and put her in it. 'I know *I* am putting the cart before the horse,' she said as he lay down beside her. 'But, sir, why were *you* headed downstairs?'

'To see if two would fit in that little bed off the kitchen. We'll never know now.'

He discovered to his pleasure that she was more than just a beguiling kisser. 'I don't think I've forgotten a thing,' he whispered later into her neck. He cuddled her close in total euphoria. 'Neither have you, apparently.'

'It's not something one forgets,' she replied, and snuggled back.

He was still a gentleman; better put her at ease. 'My love, when I was in London, the ambassador acquainted me with registry offices. He assured me I can find one in Plymouth. I suppose it is not a romantic venue for a wedding, but it is a legal one. What say you?'

'Aye, my dear Ezra. First thing tomorrow morning. We can take the train from there to Bristol for the packet boat.'

He drifted off, but not before breathing deeply of rose talc, making plans, wondering what his neighbours on Mott Street would think when he carried Felicity Waring Eldredge across the threshold, her son beside them. He knew they would fall under her spell, too.

He felt charitable enough to admit that he owed posturing, cowardly, prissy, prosy, smug Rectitude Blake a debt he could never repay. His gratitude would not extend to naming a baby after Rectitude, however. Some things were never meant to be. He laughed softly at the thought, and closed his eyes.

* * * * *

Author Note

As mentioned in this story, US Minister Charles Francis Adams spent the Civil War years attempting to call Great Britain to account for allowing the building of five warships, purchased by the South to use against the North. To the United States, this constituted a violation of neutrality.

Captain Rafael Semmes, who indeed skippered the CSS *Sumter*, both in this story and in real life, became more famous later as the Captain of the CSS *Alabama*, a commerce raider built in England and responsible for the taking of sixty Union vessels. The *Alabama* was finally trapped in a French port in 1864 by a Union warship and sunk.

Following the war, and with Minister Adams's able assistance, the United States formally demanded reparations for the damage to US shipping from neutral Great Britain for allowing the building of warships intended solely for use against the United States.

In 1872, international arbitrators—a tribunal of Great Britain, the United States, Italy, Switzerland and Brazil—ruled in favour of the claim of the United States. Britain was required to settle the matter by a payment of fifteen and a half million dollars. This sum was balanced by damages of nearly two million dollars owed to Great Britain by the United States for illegal Union blockading, and also for fishing rights in an unrelated matter. The claims were paid in 1872.

The Alabama Claims established a precedent for settling disagreements using international arbitration that continues to this day.

As for a Lincoln letter… President Lincoln and Secretary of State William Seward did correspond with Prime Minister Palmerston and others to apologise for the Trent Affair and smooth over matters.

As for a personal letter from Lincoln... Who knows? Lincoln was famous for his human touch in matters of both war and state. That he should have written such a letter as my character Ezra Eldredge was grudgingly forced to deliver to Charles F. Adams, is not out of the realm of possibility, making this fictional account probable, if not factual.

And that is the fun of historical fiction.

A KISS UNDER
THE MISTLETOE

Carol Arens

This story is dedicated to the memory of
Cheryl Arens Powell. You gave the world
a sparkle, which we feel even now.
Love cannot be separated.

Dear Reader,

I hope this Christmas finds you celebrating with
family and friends. Over the past year or more, I
think we have all come to appreciate that there
is nothing more important. May this anthology of
Victorian family Christmas stories bring you all the
joy of the holidays.

If you have read *Wed to a Wallflower*, you will have
met Lady Kirkwynd. Perhaps you suspected she
was not the vixen she appeared to be, or if she was,
she had a very good reason for it. In *A Kiss Under
the Mistletoe*, you will discover who the lady is and
meet the family she is devoted to. You will discover
why the baron renting her estate cannot resist her,
even knowing of her reputation as a fortune hunter.

I wish you the very best of health and joy this
Christmas.

Carol Arens

Chapter One

Kirkwynd Manor, Coniston, England
15 December 1891

Baroness Kirkwynd knelt beside an empty trunk. Her bedroom felt too chilly because the fire had not been laid in the hearth and a gusty evening wind huffed against the window.

She pleated and folded her navy-hued satin evening gown then, with a flick of her fingers, dropped it inside. She was grateful to finally lay the scandalously low-cut garment to rest.

It had done her reputation a great deal of damage, labelled her a coquette…a hussy, and had not helped her attain her goal.

Sadly, coquette and hussy were among the kinder words she had overheard regarding her. The other, harsher judgements? She did what she could to forget them, reminding herself that she was not, in truth, that person.

That forward woman had been born of a desperate attempt to secure a wealthy husband. Yet she was no different in what she sought than any other lady of society. It was only that, by necessity, she had gone after it more aggressively than most.

On no less than four awfully expensive occasions, she had competed for the attention of eligible gentlemen and done so against beautiful debutantes in the first flush of youth who had family fortunes to offer a suitor.

While Louisa was known for having a comely face and figure, she was well past the flush of youth and as far as her fortune went, it was but a wish upon a star.

After failing so miserably in her last attempt to capture

an earl, she had quite given up. What reasonable lady would
not do so after being intentionally bumped into Ullswater by
a rival in pursuit of Lord Hawkwood's attention?

She had not wanted to attend his house party in the first
place but duty was what duty was. She had given the attempt
her best effort and failed. Now everything was changing.

'Auntie Louisa?' Five-year-old Emily stood behind her,
rested her heart-shaped chin on Louisa's shoulder and peered
into the trunk. 'Will Father Christmas find us when we move
to the cottage?'

Louisa turned, gathered her niece onto her lap and hugged
her close.

'Of course he will, little goose!'

'But the cottage is deep in the woods and he is used to
coming here. What if he leaves our gifts for the tenant?'

'Father Christmas knows precisely where you and your
brother are. You have nothing to fear.'

How wonderful it would be to have someone reassure
Louisa that all would be well. To be able to lean into reassuring arms, if only for a moment, would be such a relief.

She shook her head to scatter the wistful longing. There
was no one; there had not been since her husband had died.
For the past two years it had been she alone holding the
household together. The responsibly had lain squarely on
her shoulders…and they were pitifully slender shoulders.

Strong, though. Challenge by challenge she had made
them so.

'Mother wishes you to come downstairs. Brother is be-
devilling Mrs Hooper.'

She set her niece off her lap and rose quickly. Poor Mrs
Hooper was already confused by the changes of late without
eight-year-old Bram pestering her with questions.

When Louisa had come to Kirkwynd Manor as a bride,
Mrs Hooper had been serving as cook. Even though she was
no longer the cook, she still fancied herself as having the
position and puttered happily about the kitchen. That was
lovely, helpful even, except that despite still having a talent

for preparing delicious food, the sweet, elderly lady was as likely to serve cake for dinner as stew.

When Louisa had been forced to let the rest of the household staff go, Mildred Hooper had remained. It would have been heartless to set her adrift in the world.

If she could give the woman nothing else, she could provide her with a roof over her head. A modest one but, still, it was a roof and Louisa was determined to make the cottage a cosy haven for her family.

Oh, but she would dearly miss living in Kirkwynd Manor. It had been a place of security in a life that, before she had wed Chester, had not been secure.

Living with her father for the first eighteen years of her life, she had been vulnerable to every unsound choice the man had made. The only responsible decision he ever made concerning her had been to marry her to a man much older than she was.

Naturally, she had been hesitant at first. Like all girls, she had dreams of a grand passion to sweep her away. In the end, her marriage had been the best thing to ever have happened to her. In the ten years she had shared with Chester, she had not been hungry, cold or afraid.

From her first day at Kirkwynd she had felt at home. A home that since Chester's death she had been forced to fight for. Her husband had been a good man, even a wealthy one. Sadly, poor financial investments had drained the estate. When he'd died and the debts been settled, little had remained. What was left, she had spent making herself appear to be a lady of means, a desirable society catch.

In the end it had gained her nothing, except that society viewed her as a woman who spent lavishly, flirted even more lavishly, and in the end…

In the end she had spent all she'd had and hadn't found husband who might save the estate for the heir, eight-year-old Bram, who was no doubt merrily beguiling Mildred Hooper in order to get his way in something.

While Louisa had not succeeded in wedding a wealthy

husband, she had managed to secure a tenant. The income the rent provided would keep the estate secure for a time.

Rushing into the parlour, she smiled at her sister-in-law, Lena, who sat straight backed, impatiently tapping the arms of her wheeled chair.

'He's followed her into the kitchen and the last I heard he was trying to persuade her to prepare dessert rather than a healthy meal.'

Beyond a doubt Lena would like to be the one dealing with her charming and lively spirited son. Tragically, the carriage accident that had left her a widow had also left her disabled. Not hopelessly disabled... Louisa would not accept that. Every day she worked with her sister-in-law, exercising her weak legs in the expectation—or hope—that Lena would walk again.

Perhaps she would not, but one must have hope. Louisa would never by word or deed let Lena think she did not have faith.

Walking along silent hallways on her way to the kitchen, passing by rooms without servants going about their business, Louisa's heart dragged. She was going to have a difficult time holding tears at bay when they moved out tomorrow. But she would, of course. No one would be better off for her giving in to them.

Ah, but ahead of her light spilled out of the kitchen doorway...light and laughter.

Whatever Bram was telling Mildred made the older woman happy.

Happiness was what mattered in the end. The size of one's dwelling had little to do with it.

Perhaps dessert instead of dinner would be just the thing.

16 December 1891

Arriving at Kirkwynd Manor well after dark in a hired coach, Hugh Clarke helped the driver unload the luggage trunks then dismissed the fellow with a large gratuity. Being as late as it was, the driver had earned it. Besides, being this close to Christmas, it was right and proper to spread goodwill.

Waving the man farewell, Hugh carried his three-year-old ward into the manor house. Arabella was asleep and the weight of her small body sagged trustingly against him. Her head lay on his shoulder. He felt the tug of her curled fingers while she sucked her thumb.

It had been a long day of travel from Liverpool, where his manor house was undergoing construction. The child was exhausted.

Once inside, he exhaled a great sigh of relief. He had been assured that the manor would be clean and ready to move into but one could never be sure of a promise being kept until one saw for himself.

Going up a wide flight of stairs, he strode along a hallway, opening doors, until he found a room with a bed.

Moonlight streaming in the window shed enough light for him to manoeuvre safely without tripping over something.

He peeled the blankets back on the bed. Sniffing, he determined that, indeed, the linens were fresh. Reassured, he removed Belle's shoes, laid her down, then snuggled the cover under her round little chin.

He spread the swath of her curly dark hair over the pillow. The bed was large, making her look even smaller than she was.

The chamber was chilly. Since he had not been expected to arrive until morning, he could hardly have expected Lady Kirkwynd to have arranged for someone to kindle the fire.

He might be a baron but he was not a helpless one. In fact, he had been rather handy before he'd inherited the title from a distant uncle.

Kneeling before the hearth, he was grateful to find kindling and logs.

The Baroness must have a reliable staff...or the remnants of one since she had fallen on dire financial circumstances. His presence here attested to that.

He was fortunate to have discovered the estate was for rent. It was not something one was lucky enough to find all that often.

More fortunate still to discover the place to be in good repair.

With the frivolous reputation Lady Kirkwynd had, he'd half feared he would bring his young ward to a dishevelled place.

Gossip had it that the woman was vain, extravagant, and had spared no expense in her pursuit of a wealthy husband. It was rumoured that in doing so she had reduced the estate to poverty.

Perhaps he should not judge the Baroness, having never met her. But, truly, he did know her type…painfully and intimately knew it. He had been engaged to a woman of like morals who had returned his ring, a ring that meant a great deal to him, by messenger when a fellow of higher rank and wealth had come along.

Even now, six months after Victoria's betrayal, the sting and shame of heartbreak lingered like the sharp end of a pin poking at the pleasure he typically felt at this time of year.

Despite the occasional heavy heart, he was grateful for the near escape. But even feeling grateful, it was unnerving to think he had found 'the one' and then discovered she would not have been a good match. Not for him and not for Belle.

Vanity like Victoria's, and he supposed, Lady Kirkwynd's, was a vice hard paid for. Indeed, had the Baroness not procured him as her tenant, her estate would have fallen to creditors.

Hugh's expectation was to reside here for a year. What, he wondered, would the intemperate lady do after that?

It was unlikely he would see much of her since Kirkwynd Cottage, where she was to have relocated, was a distance away in the woods. Coming in earlier, he had spotted chimney smoke being whisked away by the wind and had assumed that was where the cottage was…right at the point where wooded land rose towards rugged-looking fells.

One thing was certain, he would do his best to avoid Lady Kirkwynd. His dearest wish was to never cross paths with another false-hearted fortune hunter.

Having been played for a fool once, he would not do so again.

A broken engagement and a crushed spirit had been enough to keep him from revealing his position in society to Lady Kirkwynd. As far as she knew, he was a merchant dealing in textiles.

Which he was. It had never seemed prudent to give up the profitable venture when he'd inherited his rank and estate.

In some ways, becoming Mooreland had been a burden. In truth, he had been content as Mr Hugh Edison Clarke. Were he still, he might have sought an uncomplicated, loving marriage like his parents had had.

And marry he must. It was expected of a gentleman of society…a duty. Sadly, as said gentleman, he would always wonder what a lady really wanted of him…his title or his love.

But duty was what duty was. But perhaps duty could wait a short time.

Ah, but he did have a lady's love. A small sweet lady whose moist thumb had just fallen out of her mouth and lay slack on the pillow.

One day, he would need to teach her not to suck it, but she was still young enough for it to appear charming and babyish.

Now that the room was growing warmer, he ought to see to the task of unpacking their trunks. But first he would put the wedding ring both his mother and grandmother had worn, the very same that Victoria had scorned, in a safe place. He had not trusted the heirloom to be packed randomly in one of the trunks and had carried the precious ring in his pocket.

He placed it in a desk drawer then stood over Belle's large bed, gazing down at her.

She had not been happy about leaving home at this time of

year, fearing that Christmas would not happen anywhere but at home. But the renovation of his estate house was extensive and had reached the point where everyone must move out.

The timing was good for the staff, though. With no Christmas events to be hosted, he had given them leave to spend Christmas with their families. It was the right thing to do, allowing them time off. It was not as though he had not grown up without the help of servants. Surely he could manage until the New Year without their services.

He had hoped to have Belle's nurse accompany him but her elderly mother had fallen ill and it would have been unconscionable of him to ask her to work over Christmas.

Now here he was, just him and Belle.

Tomorrow he would go into Coniston Water and see if there was a lady looking for a bit of income, just until after the first of the year when his own staff would join him here.

And 'here', he suspected, was going to turn out to be an exceptionally beautiful place, once he got a look at it in daylight.

He went to the window, gazed out. A large and ancient-looking tree grew beside the house, its width spreading nearly corner to corner.

The view through bare branches was stunning. He would have enjoyed arriving last month when the bright colours of autumn had been upon them. But still, even without leaves, the limbs shifting in wind and moonlight were a magical sight.

Living here was going to be quite satisfying. Belle had been asking for a dog and he'd had to refuse because of the construction. Perhaps now would be the time to fulfil her wish. A puppy for Christmas would be just the thing, as long as his landlady approved.

A movement from below caught his eye. He peered hard, trying to make out what he was seeing.

There was a woman…and a mule. A mule?

Unless he was mistaken, the animal had a wardrobe trunk tied on a rope behind it. The woman appeared to be trying to persuade the creature to drag it along a narrow path leading towards the woods.

As far as he could determine in the darkness, the beast was refusing, stubbornly resisting her tugs on the bridle.

The petite lady was not going to win in a contest of strength. She must have come to the same conclusion because she went up on her toes to speak into the beast's ear. The stubborn animal backed up a step.

Apparently at the end of her patience, she shook her head, causing moonlight to ripple in the strands of her loose, dark hair. She stamped her foot, pointed towards the smoke column rising into the cold night.

The mule nudged her arm, brayed.

Seeming to accept defeat, she spun about then strode to the trunk, sat down with a thump. She gazed up at the sky, looking, in his opinion, run into the ground. He felt her weariness all the way up here to the second-storey chamber.

Even with that he was struck by how uncommonly lovely she was.

What was going on here? Why was she trying to transport a trunk late at night when she ought to be abed?

Given the plainness of her gown, she could only be a servant. A servant who was no doubt being taken advantage of by the flighty Lady Kirkwynd!

This would not do!

Rushing to the bed, he bent over it to be sure Belle was still sleeping deeply, then dashed out of the room, down the stairs and into the night.

He would hire the woman right out from under the Baroness's nose if he could.

Chapter Two

'Sometimes I wonder if you are worth the cost of feeding,' Louisa mumbled to the mule. 'I did not mean that…truly, I could not have managed moving everything to the cottage without you. Take your rest, my friend, you have earned it.'

She had as well, so she sat upon the trunk and let her weary muscles relax. At least this trunk was the last of what needed to be removed from the house.

From the exceptionally clean house. She had made certain that her tenant would find it tidy when he arrived tomorrow. Oh, yes, her hands were blistered and her back ached but there had been no money to pay anyone else to move the family to the cottage.

Thankfully, the moving was nearly finished. If Willard demanded a moment of rest before completing this last task, he would have it.

Being obliged to sit on the lid and gaze at the sky, so crisp and clear on this late autumn night, was as far from a hardship as one could get.

She shrugged her shawl tighter about her shoulders. How wonderful it was, she thought, that the treasure of stars winking overhead was offered equally to both wealthy and poor. She had been poor, wealthy and then poor again so she understood what a great gift this was.

A yip, a pattering of paws through dry leaves, drew her attention to the path.

'Well, hello, Bernard.' She clapped her hands on her lap. Her nine-month-old puppy bounded towards her, made a leap for her lap. Tail wagging, he tried to lick her chin. 'What are you doing outside so late, you little scamp?'

Suddenly, his throat rumbled in a growl.

'If you wish to appear a proper hunter you must not wag your tail.'

But what had him alarmed?

Footsteps crunched on the path! They could not possibly belong to anyone who lived here.

If only Bernard would bark and raise a fuss while he dashed for the unseen intruder, she would feel somewhat safer.

Leaping up, she bolted behind Willard, using his solid stubborn body as a barrier between herself and whoever her dog was greeting.

The intruder became visible when he strode into a shaft of moonlight. Tall and leanly built, he squatted down to pet Bernard. The man did not draw away when the pup madly licked his face.

How nefarious could the fellow be?

He could certainly not be any more handsome.

Her heart was galloping, which was to be expected under the circumstances, but what she could not determine was the reason it was acting so.

Was it because the man was a stranger…or was it because he was a handsome stranger? There was a difference, after all.

'I am sorry if I startled you, miss,' he said, rising to his full stature. 'But I saw you from the window and wondered if you could use a hand with the trunk.'

'From the window?' She glanced up, saw the panes of her chamber softly illuminated. 'May I assume, then, that you are Mr Clarke?'

He nodded. 'Half a day early. I hope it does not inconvenience you.'

'It is quite all right.'

Her tenant had a friendly look about him. Even in the dark she thought his eyes bore a kindly expression. His hair spoke of a man who had an easy nature, too. A stern fellow would wear it contained, every strand obedient. But Mr Clarke's hair waved in loose curls about his face. One short hank even dipped across his forehead, teasing the arch of his brow.

'Welcome to Kirkwynd, Mr Clarke. I hope you find everything to your liking.'

'As much as I have seen seems quite satisfactory.' Bernard jumped about, pawing at the knees of the fellow's trousers. The fact that her tenant did not seem to take umbrage spoke well of him. 'I trust I have you to thank for it?'

She noticed he was staring at her hands, which were clutched on Willard's harness. A shaft of bright moonlight shone on her ragged nails as if pointing them out.

'You were promised a residence in good condition and so it is.' As if she would present her beloved home as anything less than cherished.

With a nod and an arched brow, he stared at her fingernails. 'If I may say so, it is unconscionable of Lady Kirkwynd to require you work so late…and, I imagine, far too hard. Is there no man to help you?'

What? Heat flashed in her chest, flared from her cheeks. Anger? Embarrassment? Some odd twist of the two more than likely.

The man had mistaken her for a servant, which, when she thought about it, was understandable. She looked nothing like the lady she had presented to society. Not that he would recognise her as that person since she was certain she had never met him.

Oh, but she had no reason whatsoever to be ashamed. It was not a disgrace to be a hard-working servant, neither was it a disgrace to do what one must to protect her family.

She stepped out from behind Willard, keeping her hands hidden within the folds of her skirt.

'Bernard, come here at once,' she said, while gathering an appropriate response to his misguided assumption of who she was. But what was an appropriate response? She had every right to be offended…and yet she was not, not really.

Rather she was intrigued at the way his smile lifted the corner of his mouth more on one side than the other.

'Does the dog belong to you?'

'He does. As you can see, he is something of a rascal.'

Mr Clarke's expression indicated he appreciated that trait in a pup. For all that she still felt the nip of what he'd said about her—but of course not her but 'Lady Kirkwynd' making her work so hard—she did find his smile appealing.

Once she told him who she was, he would probably feel badly for what he said.

If she managed to keep a sense of humour about it, they would no doubt share a good laugh, and she did want to begin her relationship with him on a good footing.

'Does your employer approve of you keeping a dog? I would not think she would.'

'Truly, Mr Clarke, why would you assume so?'

'It is only that her reputation as a social climber would not indicate a care for animals. You must know she is perceived as a—'

'Why would it not? One is not exclusive of the other. Lady Kirkwynd approves of dogs…and mules.' Honestly, no one knew what she was known for better than she, herself, did.

Willard chose that instant to continue along the path. The weight of the trunk slowly moving across the ground crunched what leaves had not been scattered by the breeze.

'I would not have thought—'

'One should not presume to know what Lady Kirkwynd is thinking.'

'Of course not. I only wondered because my daughter has been asking for a puppy for some time now. What do you think, miss, will your mistress allow it?'

Now would be the time to set him straight on who she was but, oddly, she did not. Or not so oddly, really, because he was smiling at her, and it was such a handsome smile, the explanation stuck on her tongue.

Setting him straight would have to wait for a time when he was not looking at her the way he was, warmly, in the way that a man did when he felt a certain draw towards a woman.

It would be nice to bask in it for a moment before she shattered his image of her, admitted to being a woman he clearly disrespected. What could it hurt to feel appreciated by him for just a bit longer? To share that particular sort of yearning with a man? Just for another instant, only?

Perhaps she would tell him in the morning when moonlight was not casting him in such a pleasing light.

'She will give it some thought, I'm certain. But now I must be going. If Willard arrives at the cottage before I do, he will wake the house with his braying. He'll rile the household as sure as anything.'

There was something about coming in range of the cottage that always made him quite vocal, no matter what the time of day or night.

'I imagine your employer does not appreciate being awoken at odd hours.'

'Yes, she does enjoy a good sleep.' Greatly enjoyed it, but with two young children requiring care at all hours, she was awoken more often than not. 'If there is anything you require you will find me at the cottage. You cannot miss it since it is at the end of the path. Good night, Mr Clarke.'

'Wait… I would like to offer you a position, an easier one than you have now, I would wager.'

A position? For a wage?

If he knew who she was he would not offer it. But he had made an incorrect assumption and she was not disposed to correct him on it, especially now with a proposal of employment having been made.

'What sort of position do you have in mind?'

If it was not indecent or immoral, she would give it a great deal of thought.

Father Christmas could use a bit of help if the children were not to be disappointed on Christmas morning.

'My foster daughter, Belle, is only three years old. She needs a nurse and her own nurse will not arrive until after the new year. I promise to pay you a better wage than you would make with the Baroness.'

Better than her wage of no wage at all? How remarkably interesting. It would be foolish of her to turn down his proposition.

'I will give your offer serious thought, Mr Clarke.' It was what she said but, truly, she had already made up her mind. Caring for a third child ought to be a simple enough thing. Bram and Emily would be over the moon to have a playmate. 'I will come by tomorrow and give you my decision.'

'Do not let fear of what Lady Kirkwynd has to say about it sway your decision. I will find you a permanent position on my staff if need be.'

'Goodnight, Mr Clarke. We will speak of it tomorrow.'

Goodness, but the man did have a tainted opinion of her. Somehow, she was going to have to keep her identity secret. The last woman he would think fit to influence his daughter was the avaricious Baroness Kirkwynd.

She followed Willard down the path and then…she could not help it…she cast a glance back over her shoulder at her tenant.

He was walking towards the house, but then he stopped, cast a glance back over his shoulder at her.

Waving his hand, he smiled.

Returning his smile made her feel warm and happy… womanly. As if she were…well, never mind. Dwelling on certain things was simply pointless.

Walking again after the mule, she sighed. Pointless or not, she listened for the sound of his footsteps walking away in the dark.

'I'm sorry to be late coming in, Lena.' Louisa hurried into the front parlour a step behind Bernard. Knowing her sister-in-law would be worried, she had rushed from the stable to the cottage, become winded and got a stitch in her side.

What a great relief to stand in front of the cosy hearth, to feel warmth seep into her shawl. To lift her skirt and luxuriate in a pleasurable twirl of heat whispering up her stockings… It made her sigh aloud.

'Willard became stubborn and stopped to rest, and then I met our tenant, Mr Clarke,' she explained.

'Did you? What is he like, besides early?' Her sister-in-law leaned forward on her elbows, clearly eager to hear all about the man who would be living in their house.

Warmed, Louisa took off her shawl and draped it over the back of a chair, then she sat down, her muscles melting into the soft cushions.

'He is hard man to interpret. On the one hand he seems kind...he took to Bernard right off. I imagine he is a good father to his little daughter. But at the same time I wonder if he is judgemental.'

'Why would you think so?'

Lena had round eyes, the shade of Coniston Water when the sun was shining on it. They blinked at Louisa in anticipation.

She smiled inside, thinking of how they reminded her of Chester's eyes. Lena was only a few years older than Louisa's thirty but, still, the resemblance to her older brother was unmistakable.

'Well, he thought I was a servant and that Lady Kirkwynd was working me far too hard.'

'Oh, but you do work too hard, sister. I feel so horrible for it. I ought to be able to help.'

'You do help. And you are making good progress at standing. Before you know it, you will be chasing after the children again.'

'I will, of course...but in the meantime I will set Mr Clarke straight about who you are.'

'But you cannot.' Doing her best to disguise her weariness, Louisa pushed up from the chair. 'Here, let's see if you can stand for a few seconds.'

'Whether I can stand or not does not influence what I will say to Mr Clarke. My tongue is in perfect working order.'

With an arm about Lena's waist, Louisa lifted her, keeping hold of the waistband of her skirt.

'Well, you must contain it because he offered me a position. His daughter needs a nurse until his staff arrives in January.'

'The last thing you should have is more responsibility.'

'Not the last thing. Just think of it. Having another little girl at the cottage would be a delight, especially at this time of year. Bram and Emily will be thrilled to have a friend. And we need not lose sleep any longer about Father Christmas's visit. We will have the money we need for plenty of gifts.'

'I think it is you who would love to have another child in the house, wage or no wage. I'm sorry you and my brother were not blessed.'

Lena's weight began to sag against her arm so she set her back down on her chair.

It was true that she and Chester had wanted a child, had been saddened each month it did not happen, but some things were simply not been meant to be.

And other things were. She had learned to embrace her life as it was and found joy in it.

Returning to her chair, she sat down, shrugged her shawl around her shoulders. Cold was beginning to penetrate the cottage walls.

'But I have been greatly blessed with your children. You know I adore them.'

'And they adore their auntie. Now...tell me, what does our Mr Clarke look like? Is he handsome? You know it is not too late for you. Women have children at your age every day.'

They did, of course. What they also had were husbands. In Louisa's experience, those were not easily come by. Blushing young brides of good family were greatly preferred over widows desperate to save the family home.

'It was dark so it is hard to know for sure.' She did not reveal that there had been moonlight, which had revealed quite a lot about their tenant's good looks. 'I think perhaps his eyes are brown, soft brown and friendly. His hair is short-ish, but with wavy curls that tickle his neck. He is tall, lean. Bernard took to him right off.'

'He would, of course…but how did you take to him? Rather well, I would guess given the way you noticed the curls… Tickling his neck, didn't you say?'

'It hardly matters. The man does not even know who I am and he has heard unkind things about Lady Kirkwynd.'

'I think it is for the best then that he doesn't know. We would not want to lose care of the child.'

'Yes, for the time being it will be best if I am once again Louisa Copeland. I should not feel horrid for keeping this to myself since he has yet to mention he has a title. He referred to himself as Mr'

'I suppose he must have a reason for it but, still, this is a bit of luck fallen into our laps…or yours, but I will do what I can to help. The children only know you as Auntie Louisa so they will not give you away.'

'In the morning I will tell him I accept. But only on the condition that I care for his daughter at the cottage.'

It was not as if she could abandon her responsibilities here.

For as wonderful as it would be to live at the manor house, the cottage was now her home.

She intended to make it a comfortable one, a joyous one rich with the sounds and scents of Christmas.

Merry and bright despite their altered circumstances.

Chapter Three

'Take me outside, Papa. I want to play down there.' Belle stood on the tips of her toes, peering over the windowsill.

Dawn had risen bright and beautiful this morning, if nippy. What a sight it had been earlier, gazing out of his chamber window and seeing the sun peek over the fells... watching while golden rays reflected off the lake in glimmering streaks.

He had not missed the spectacle, having risen before dawn in anticipation of performing tasks he had never given a great deal of thought to. Tasks that had been second nature to Belle's nurse.

One of those tasks was taming Belle's hair. Oh, he had tried, done what he thought was right and run a brush through it. Sadly, all he had managed was to turn her pretty curls into fuzz. Even tying it back with a green ribbon had done little to contain it.

At least he'd had better success at preparing breakfast. Belle claimed he made the best toast she had ever tasted.

He must remember to thank whoever had been thoughtful enough to lay in food in the pantry. He had brought a few things along, but nothing as delicious as the strawberry jam that he slathered on Belle's toast.

No doubt the woman he met last night was the one he owed a debt of gratitude to...indeed, the very lady whose pretty face had appeared unexpectedly in his dreams, several times. Dreams he had woken from each time when he'd been about to claim her lips in a kiss.

Funny, he could not recall ever having dreamed of Victoria. And kisses? She had been miserly with them. That alone should have warned him something had been wrong.

The lady from his dreams, a stranger whose name he did not even know, had seemed eager to share a sweet moment in his embrace.

But what was her name? He ought to have asked since he had offered her a job, one that would require her to live under his roof.

Of course, she would have lived under this roof already, in the servants' quarters. The room he would offer would be far nicer.

At least, he would offer it if she came by to give him an answer as she'd said she would.

He truly hoped she accepted because he was not completely certain Belle's shoes were laced properly...or even if they were on the correct feet.

'Would you like to take a walk and visit a puppy, Belle?'

Spinning about, a great grin on her face that flashed the dimples accenting the corners of her mouth, she dashed towards the chamber door. She snatched his trouser leg while charging into the hallway.

'Come on, Papa! Hurry! I loves puppies!'

And he loved her. What an unexpected blessing she had been in his life. She might not be a child of his blood but she was of his heart and had been since the day her mother had died and left the infant girl in his care.

If the unnamed lady of last night accepted his offer, would she be good with Belle?

It would have been wise to discover such an important thing before he offered her employment. For all he knew, she did not like children.

She did like dogs, though, so that did speak well of her character.

Still, had she not looked so tired, so small and taken advantage of, he would have thought a bit more before making the offer.

Seeing where she lived, how she lived, would be helpful in judging her fitness to care for Belle.

Perhaps he would even meet his landlady. The opportunity might arise for him to point out that she overworked the woman he hoped to snatch from her employ.

Overworked on his behalf, he suddenly realised. Now, that was an unsettling thought.

Belle skipped happily ahead of him along the path through the woods, singing something he could not quite hear.

'What are you singing, Belle?'

'About Christmas trees and presents! And snow!' Suddenly, she stopped, spun about. 'I can hears the puppy!'

Yes, he heard it too. They must be nearly there. He had to increase his pace to keep up with her.

The cottage was where the woman had said it would be, at the end of the path. What she had not mentioned was how quaintly pretty it was.

He would not have guessed the style was one that would suit a woman of Lady Kirkwynd's reputation.

Modest and charming were two traits the woman was not known for.

Perhaps society judged her too harshly. A person who lived in a home with flower boxes under the windows, filled with green boughs bedecked with pinecones tied in tartan ribbons, did not fit with the one he had heard of.

Even the white fence circling the cottage presented a welcome, with bare-branched roses twining among the pickets. He was anxious to see what the roses looked like next spring.

The dog from last night ran out of the porch, raced for the gate, yipping and leaping, his tail wagging madly.

A boy, about eight years old, rushed out of the cottage, followed by a girl of about five.

The woman he met last night appeared in the doorway after them, pausing for a moment to look back at someone inside. 'Will you be all right? We won't be more than a couple of hours.'

There was much more about this lady than her name, which he did not know. It had not occurred to him that she might be a mother...or a wife...but there were children.

His gut took the oddest turn, thinking she was married.

She had not seemed married in his dreams! No...indeed. She had seemed...his.

Dreams! Who could explain or understand them? He had been taken with her when they'd met last night. Her delicate beauty combined with her obvious inner strength had left him undone. Those were not the qualities that haunted his dreams, though. Rather it was her smile...the seductive shape of her lips.

'Auntie Louisa!' the boy called. 'I think the tenants are here!'

Auntie! The fist tightening his chest loosened. The question in his mind was why had it tightened in the first place.

He had only just learned the woman's name, after all.

Louisa. A pretty name...delicate sounding and at the same time strong. It suited her.

She turned. Spotting him, she smiled and waved.

In his dreams she had been alluring but wispy. Here in the—well, in the flesh to be honest about it, she was even more appealing.

'Good morning, Mr Clarke,' she greeted him. She walked briskly towards the gate where the children and the dog waited. Her smile shifted from him to Belle. 'We were just on our way meet your lovely little girl.'

Belle popped her thumb out of her mouth long enough to say, 'I is Belle.'

Louisa opened the gate. Everyone pressed through at once.

If Belle was overwhelmed by the attention being lavished upon her, she did not show it, even though it was not something she was used to. Back at home in Liverpool there had been no children for her to play with...no dog to leap up and lick her cheek.

Belle laughed in a way Hugh had not heard her do before. Until this moment he had not thought her to be lacking in any area of her life. He had given her everything he'd known how to.

'What a pleasure it is to meet you, Miss Belle.' Louisa bent slightly to offer his child a warm greeting.

While Louisa introduced her niece and nephew, Hugh studied her, the curve of her cheek when she smiled and the soft, sultry sound of her voice. He could not recall when he had been interested, preoccupied really, in a woman so soon. From his first glimpse of her out of the window last night, he had wished to know more of her.

It was not only her evident beauty that drew him. Indeed no. He had met many beautiful women. His attention had never lingered on any of them the way it did on Louisa.

For all that this was only the second time he had encountered her, she completely intrigued him.

She moved with the grace of a lady but her hands were worn with work. Her figure was neat and trim, her movements efficient and at the same time unhurried.

One compelling thing about her was that for all her apparent self-assurance, beneath it she was vulnerable.

It was hard to say how he knew such a thing, just a sense...of her. He did not recall having 'senses' about people before. In this case it must have been to do with the fact that he was having a difficult time not thinking about her.

He was doing far too much of it when there was only one thing he ought to be wondering about.

Was she going to accept the position as Belle's nurse?

'We are going to gather twigs, greenery and such to make wreaths for the cottage. We were hoping that you and Belle would join us. We can discuss the business matter you mentioned last night.'

'Please, please, please, Papa!' In her excitement, Belle hopped on one foot, up and down, then switched to the other foot.

'As you can see, nothing would give Belle greater pleasure. I will also enjoy it, Miss...?'

'Louisa Copeland, but since we are neighbours, please call me Louisa.'

Neighbours? Yes. He supposed that was true…but employer and employee was what he hoped for.

Which meant he should not call her Louisa. Miss Copeland would be more appropriate.

He rubbed the back of his neck, wondering what to do, how to answer without offending her.

The children dashed off the path, the dog romping beside them. 'Is it safe for them to go into the woods on their own?'

'Bram and Emily know the area well. You need not worry.'

'I can't recall seeing my foster daughter happier. She does not have other children to play with at our home in Liverpool.' He was silent for a moment, watching Belle's red wool coat vanish then reappear among the tree trunks. 'Have you made a decision on my offer, Miss Copeland?'

Black hair tied back in a green bow caught morning sunshine, warmly winked red-brown shimmers at him as they followed the children into the woods. Apparently, she was not enslaved to what society considered a proper hairstyle. He liked that for a couple of reasons. One was that she had beautiful hair and, in his opinion, it would be a crime to keep it wound tight in a bun. The other reason was that she was not likely to judge him for the mess he had made of Belle's hair this morning.

Surely it must mean something that both she and Belle wore green ribbons. Although Louisa's results looked far better than his did.

'I am considering it.'

But not agreeing to it…and she was frowning while she said so.

It unsettled him to think he might have to petition a lady from town for the job.

While any one of several women might do an adequate job of caring for Belle, Hugh had not missed the expression in his child's eyes when Louisa had smiled at her.

There had been something special in that smile…something of longing…yes, a need of a child for a mother and a mother for a child.

It was not the sort of expression he had ever seen pass between Belle and Miss Preston, her current nurse.

Here was one more thing he sensed about Louisa. She had no child of her own but was a mother at heart.

Wasn't it interesting how one could read so much in a glance, in a smile?

Louisa laughed under her breath and pointed at the children, who had stopped to toss leaves in the air. The sultry sound kicked the breath right out of him. How did someone so tiny, so angelic looking have a laugh like…well, he did not know what for certain but angelic was not quite it.

'Isn't it sweet how they get along like they have known each other for ever?' she asked.

He nodded, again struck by the realisation of what Belle had been lacking in her life. How could he never have been aware of it?

'What can I do to convince you to take the position of Belle's nurse? You would be able to move out of the cottage. There is a large room beside hers, which I imagine you would be comfortable in.'

'I would like to accept, of course. Anyone would adore caring for such a dear little girl. But I do have two conditions.'

He cocked his head at her. Quite honestly, he was ready to consent to whatever she wanted because he very much wanted her to stay in the room next to Belle's…the one two over from his.

Not that he had anything untoward in mind…not on purpose at any rate. If she moved in, he would need to remind himself hourly that she was his employee and it would be wrong to pursue his attraction towards her.

Of course, she would only be in his employ until Miss Preston's mother recovered. Until that time he could pursue her friendship. The house was far too large for only him and Belle. Adult company would be welcome.

'Firstly, I will care for Belle at the cottage, along with the other children. I shall come to Kirkwynd in the morning, prepare her for the day and then bring her back with me. Whenever you wish I will deliver her back to you.'

That was a disappointment. All at once, the manor house loomed even larger than it was, thinking it would be only him rattling about all day long.

No, not rattling, he had work to do…accounts to keep and a business to oversee…but he was not used to being so completely alone.

'You may bring the children to the manor with you if you wish to. Bring the dog as well.'

Her expression softened. He sensed she would like nothing more than to spend time at the manor house.

'I have obligations that prevent me from living at Kirkwynd Manor.'

'Would those involve carrying out Lady Kirkwynd's every whim? I shall speak to her, persuade her to do without you for a short time.'

For an instant she blinked at him in confusion, but her expression cleared quickly, replaced with the engaging smile he was quickly becoming fond of.

'Lady Kirkwynd is away…yes, on a visit to London.'

'Searching for a wealthy husband, is she?'

Perhaps he should not have spoken so harshly about Louisa's employer, a woman he had never met, but then she laughed that sultry laugh so he was glad he had.

The sound of it hit his heart, excited his nerves from hairline to big toe.

'No, I rather think that is the last thing she is doing. I have a feeling that marriage is one thing that Lady Kirkwynd has put behind her.'

He waited a heartbeat to see if she would laugh again but she only smiled. Even that was enough to keep his heart and his nerves tingling.

'I agree, then. Belle will go with you to the cottage. What is your other requirement?'

'You must call me Louisa. I prefer it to Mrs Copeland.'

Mrs then, not Miss. Naturally a woman like Louisa would be married and could not possibly live under his roof.

He ought to be ashamed of himself, give himself a mental kick in the derrière for thinking the things he had about her, for dreaming about them without knowing for sure if she was married.

But what kind of man was she married to?

It was none of his business, but no decent husband would allow his wife to do the work Louisa had been doing last night.

'Will you need to consult with your husband about accepting my offer?'

'No, Mr Clarke, I am a widow. The decision is mine to make.'

Despite a sense of relief, he said…and meant it, 'I am truly sorry for your loss, Mrs Copeland.'

It was hard not to miss the shadow that crossed her eyes briefly before she smiled and nodded.

'I accept the position, happily.'

'Good.' He nodded because shaking her hand to ratify the agreement felt wrong. But perhaps if—'I have a request of my own, Louisa.'

'But of course, Belle is your child.'

'It's to do with me.' He shrugged, gave back her smile. 'If I am to call you Louisa, I would appreciate it if you call me Hugh.'

Once again, she laughed her sultry laugh. He felt his smile stretch to its limits.

In his heart he danced a little jig, felt carefree as if he were a boy in the throes of his first crush.

'Hugh,' she murmured with a nod.

And all at once it did not seem at all out of line to be calling each other by their given names.

Had he hired a nurse from town, the familiarity would have been awkward in the extreme.

Louisa Copeland was simply different from anyone he had ever met.

He looked forward to seeing her morning and evening… in between times if he could manage it. And somehow he would find some way to manage it.

Chapter Four

Watching the children run in circles, tossing leaves in the air to pretend it was snowing, listening to their carefree laughter, Louisa knew she would agree to care for Belle even without being paid.

What a charming little child she was. She and Emily were of an age to enjoy playing with each other and Bram appeared delighted to have someone other than his sister to have fun with.

'They get along very well together, Hugh.'

She found it pleasant using his name. In her opinion Hugh suited him, being a strong name...a dependable one.

For all that she barely knew him, she did sense he was that. There was nothing quite as attractive as a dependable man.

Some ladies' hearts quickened for dashing scoundrels. Not Louisa's. Seeing Hugh gaze in tender affection at his daughter, a child he had taken to his heart even though she was not his by blood, made her heart quiver...melt.

Hugh was not a philanderer, like so many gentlemen she had encountered in society were. He was man a woman could safely trust her heart to...had she the mind to do such a thing.

So far, she had not had a mind to give her heart.

How could she when she had been pursuing gentlemen of society and seeking a fortune, not a life's mate.

No wonder she had failed miserably. One could hardly give her heart to a cause that her heart was not in.

Hugh turned his smile from his daughter to Louisa. She blinked, caught her breath. She could not recall a man ever looking at her quite the way he was doing. There was an expression in his eyes that made her want to gaze into them for hours upon end.

Which would not do. She was not a lady of leisure with hours to be spent on daydreams. Indeed, she spent her days doing chores, caring for children…planning a joyous Christmas for them.

Yet in a sense, Hugh, as a rent-paying tenant, was her hero.

Not only had he made it possible to purchase Christmas gifts but he had given one to her.

Because of him, or the money he paid her, she had been saved from having to sacrifice her heart to a loveless marriage.

Now that she was no longer obligated to find a husband, she was free to relax and enjoy a man's company simply for the pleasure of it. How wonderful it was to not be dwelling on how to entice him into marriage.

The thought made her smile.

Hugh made her smile.

'It is delightful seeing the children having so much fun, don't you think?'

'Quite honestly, Louisa, I cannot recall ever seeing Belle this happy.'

'Is there anything I ought to know about her in order to make her feel comfortable in my care? What does she like? What does she dislike?'

He rubbed the back of his neck. Apparently, this was something he did when he was giving thought to a matter. Something about the tilt of his head, the gathering of lines between his brows struck her as endearing.

When he smiled it gave her heart the oddest tickle. Funny, a man's smile had never given her a tickle before. Chester's smile had made her feel safe…cherished, but Hugh's smile made her feel appreciated in quite a different way.

'I would say she likes being with other children. I have been raising her for more than two years and never seen her this happy.'

He shook his head, his expression something between bemusement and a frown. A lock of dark hair swiped across his forehead, making him appear dashing. 'I suppose I ought to have realised she would miss the company of other children.'

The last thing this good man needed was to feel negligent in any way.

'Hugh.' She touched his arm because she wanted to make an important point. Then she kept hold of it because his arm felt strong…manly and steadfast. 'I do not know you well, hardly at all, in fact, but it is clear to me that Belle feels safe with you. You cannot imagine what that means to a little girl.'

Louisa could imagine it, though. She would have given anything to have a father like Belle did.

'I have done what I can but…' He shrugged, one corner of his mouth curled in a compelling half-smile. 'She did not come with instructions. You see what I did to her hair?'

'Curls can be wickedly tricky. I will see to her hair from now on. May I ask you something? Do not feel bound to answer, but it does have to do with Belle.'

'Since you will become a big part of her life, I will tell you whatever you would like to know.'

'I wonder about her parents, and how you came to be her father.'

'Ah.' His glance slanted towards the children, who were playing only a few feet away, then it shifted towards a fallen tree trunk several yards away. 'Perhaps over there… I would rather that Belle not hear what I have to say. The only parent she remembers is me.'

'I could do with sitting for a moment.' Indeed she could, having been up and busy since before dawn.

When they sat down it was with a proper and respectable distance for strangers to observe.

Her mind wandered a bit, wondering what it might be like once they were no longer strangers. Would he slide closer to her, would her arm brush his sleeve? Would she inhale deeply and catch his masculine scent?

Oh! But then he did slide closer. The scent of cold air

clung to his coat, but under that... He smelled very male... so much so that she wondered if she was blushing.

'I hope you don't mind,' he said. 'It's easier to have a quiet conversation this way.'

For some reason, being so close felt appropriate rather than awkward.

At least to her, it did. Having been acquainted with him for such a short time, she had no way of knowing if he felt the same way...but then again, he was the one to have moved closer.

What she did know was that she enjoyed it, found the subtle scent of home...of Kirkwynd Manor...wafting from his coat greatly comforting.

'Belle was only an infant when her mother sought employment from me as a chambermaid. It is not regular to hire a woman with a baby, but she was quite young and a widow so of course I did.'

Here was further proof that Hugh Clarke was a decent man.

'A few months later Sarah, that was her name, caught a fever. She died of it but before she did, she asked me to make sure Belle was placed in a good home. Since I could not bear to send her to a foundling institution, I kept her with me. It did not take long to know that her good home was with me.'

'You are a rare man, Hugh. I hope you do not mind me saying so.'

Belle was an exceptionally lucky child. She would never have to see her father staring blankly at her while she reminded him she was hungry, that there had been no food since breakfast the day before.

'Belle is my heart, if you want to know the truth. I cannot imagine my life—'

'Auntie Louisa?' *Oh...my word!* Where had Bram come from so suddenly? 'We mustn't forget Mother's mistletoe.'

'We will not,' she told him. To Hugh she said, 'Their mother, Lena, is my sister-in-law. She adores mistletoe and insists that any proper home must have it.'

'It's where people kiss,' Bram stated. 'Father Christmas will not come unless people do. Since Father died, Mother kisses me and Emily.'

'We shall not go home until we find a huge bunch of it, Bram.' Hugh answered with a nod.

'I already found it.' Why was it that Bram's smile looked sweetly impish?

'Where?' Louisa stood up. 'We shall pick it at once.'

'It's on that branch, right over your head...yours and Mr Clarke's.'

Hugh stood up, too. 'I'll reach it.'

Given his height, he would have plucked it in an instant had Emily not raced forward, calling for him to stop.

'You must kiss Auntie Louisa first!'

'Oh...no...it is not necessary,' she said.

Goodness me, what must Hugh be thinking?

Perhaps that it would be lovely? Because it was precisely what she was thinking.

'It is!' Emily gasped, looking worried. 'Anyone under mistletoe must kiss!'

'Father Christmas will not come if you do not kiss her, sir,' Bram said, his tone now grave.

'I wants Father Christmas to come!' Belle cried, her bottom lip beginning to tremble.

'Will you allow me to kiss your hand, Louisa? For the sake of Father Christmas?'

'For Father Christmas, then,' she said, and presented the back of her hand.

Hugh grazed her knuckles with his lips. It felt rather like a feather tickling her skin.

'That is not a proper kiss, sir,' Emily pointed out.

'Proper enough, young lady,' Louisa said with a laugh.

'I suppose it is since the mistletoe is still hanging in the woods,' Bram admitted. 'But once it is hung up in the house a real kiss will be needed.'

Since Hugh was not likely to be in the cottage long enough to stand under the mistletoe, it would not become an issue.

'I never knew that was true about mistletoe,' Hugh said while reaching high to pluck the growth from the branch. 'Father Christmas will not come without kisses?'

Glancing down, he winked at her.

'It is family tradition more than Father Christmas's requirement,' she whispered so the children would not hear, wondering at how the warmth of his lips lingered on her skin. 'Started by my sister-in-law and her husband, who took every opportunity to kiss.'

It had been ages since she kissed anyone...or wanted to.

Looking at the man, the sprig of greenery pinched in his fingers...heavens above but she wanted to kiss someone now.

And not just any someone... She wanted to kiss Hugh on his handsome, smiling lips.

Hugh was awake and ready for the day earlier than he normally was.

This huge mansion was far too quiet for sleeping. Back in Liverpool he was used to the subtle hum of household activities going on late into the night and early in the morning. With a full staff living there, someone was always puttering about doing something.

Until last night he had not realised that quiet could be equally peaceful and oppressive. He would be glad when Christmas was over and his staff came to Kirkwynd.

Entering Belle's chamber, he found her asleep, her cheeks flushed with warmth from the covers tucked under her chin.

It would be wrong to wake her but at the same time he would enjoy having the energy of a three-year-old to liven the quietude.

He ignited the fire in the hearth and then stood beside the window. Gazing out he spotted smoke curling out of the cottage's chimney. White and wispy, it whisked away against a backdrop of dark grey clouds.

Was the mistletoe hung somewhere inside the cottage, waiting to entrap people unawares into a kiss?

He smiled, thinking about it. The business about Father

Christmas not coming if the tradition was not adhered to was charming. Especially since it had been begun by a married couple deeply in love with each other.

He wanted a marriage like theirs must have been…like he remembered his parents' being.

His dearest wish was to find a lady who would kiss him under a sprig of mistletoe without regard for his position, or the fortune that went with it.

Perhaps this evening when he fetched Belle from the cottage he would glance about for the interesting green sprig.

In his mind, he watched himself enter the charming cottage, spot pretty Louisa standing under the mistletoe with an invitation in her smile. He would go to her, she would rise to her toes, lean towards him with her lips parted just so, catching winks of firelight and then—

'Papa!' Belle tossed the blankets off the bed, scrambled down and dashed for him, hugging his legs while looking up with a grin. 'Will Auntie Louisa come for me?'

'She said she would, but the weather is threatening so she might not want to come out in it. Why do you call her Auntie?'

'Emily and Bram do…and I loves her, Papa. Take me to her…please, please, please!'

Would she love any woman so quickly, or was there something special about Louisa?

But of course there was something special. Even knowing her as short a time as he had, he felt it.

'Come downstairs and eat breakfast. We will see what happens.' He held up her robe and she shoved her arms in.

'Strawberry jam on toast!' she exclaimed on a rush towards the doorway.

'Slippers!' he called after her.

'Jam!' Her laughter chimed from the hallway.

'Jam indeed,' he muttered carrying the slippers with him. It was December. The floors were cold and her feet were small.

'Jam after slippers!' he called following her down the hallway that led to the kitchen.

Rounding the corner, he nearly dropped her slippers on the floor.

There was Louisa, lifting Belle onto a stool at the work counter in the middle of the room.

'Good morning,' she said. The welcome shone in her eyes as well as her words. 'I've brought eggs. I thought you would not wish to go to Coniston for supplies, not with threatening weather on the way.'

Along with eggs she had brought butter and milk. He glanced at the umbrella resting against the back door. It was dotted with raindrops.

'You needn't have come out in the rain, Louisa.'

She chose a skillet from one of the dozen or so that hung on hooks near a window overlooking a brown and dormant garden. It appeared she was comfortable working in the kitchen. He wondered if acting as the cook was yet one more chore Lady Kirkwynd burdened her maid with.

'But I did need to,' she answered, glancing over her shoulder with a smile. 'Employment obligation aside, I have been looking forward to seeing Belle ever since I got up this morning.'

'Me too!' Belle's expression was nothing shy of enraptured. 'I bounced out of bed. The floor was *so* cold.'

'You ran off without putting on slippers,' he said, holding her small feet in his hands to warm them for a second before placing them on her.

When he glanced back at Louisa she was smiling, but wistfully, as if she were looking at more than what was before her eyes.

'Is something wrong?' he asked.

She shook her head, her smile quickly returned. 'I was just thinking of what a lucky little girl you are, Belle.'

'Shall I get to play with Bernard today? Did Emily and Bram miss me last night?'

'They talked about you all evening.'

'They did?' Belle's eyes shone in a way he had never seen.

'Oh, indeed. This very minute they are waiting for you come back and help make garlands out of the branches and twigs you gathered yesterday.'

It occurred to him that it might be a mistake, letting Belle grow close to the other children. The lease for the house was for but one year. The last thing he wanted was for her heart to be broken when they returned to Liverpool.

Louisa set a plate of food in front of Belle and then slid one in front of him.

'Won't you eat with us?' he asked.

'I had a bite when I made breakfast for Lena and the children.' She sat down on a stool beside Belle. 'I've brought one of Emily's ribbons for your hair. I'm certain you have dozens of your own but she would like to give you one of hers.'

'Papa, may I take my yellow one for Emily?'

It was by far her favourite. Sometimes she wrapped the satin strand around her fingers while sucking her thumb.

Belle ate more quickly than usual then slipped off the tall stool. Snatching Louisa's hand, she tugged.

'Come and make my hair pretty, Auntie Louisa.'

'I will meet you upstairs after I have a word with your father.'

'Are you certain that caring for Belle is not too much for you, Louisa? Along with everything else you do, I mean?'

How early must she have risen in order to prepare breakfast for both households? This really was none of his business, her life was her own...but he did feel compelled to speak.

'It seems to me that the Baroness puts far too much responsibility on you. In my opinion she ought not to be out hunting a husband while laying so much on your shoulders. If you want to know what I think, the woman is unmindful of anyone but herself.'

He had spoken in all seriousness, but her response was to utter that sultry laugh while shaking her head.

'Do I appear so frail to you?' Well, no, she did not. 'Duty

is what duty is, my friend. You know it to be true as well as I do, being a father as you are.'

He did know it, had used that very sentiment as his own motto. Which still did not give Lady Kirkwynd leave to take advantage of this hard-working lady.

It had not been his intention that she work both positions.

'Stay with me, Louisa.'

'I beg your pardon?' Her dark brows lifted in surprise.

'What I mean is that when my year here is up, come back with me to Liverpool. I will find a permanent position for you in my household.'

'As lovely as that would be, I do have other obligations.'

'Let the Baroness hire someone else.'

'Hire someone else to care for my niece and nephew? For my disabled sister-in-law? I will tell you the truth, Hugh. If it were not for the Baroness, we would not have a roof over our heads at all.'

Apparently, she was becoming weary of him maligning her employer because this time she did not laugh but arched a brow at him. He did admire a woman who spoke her mind, but in his opinion Lady Kirkwynd did not deserve Louisa's loyalty.

He suspected now was not the time to point it out...yet again.

From the bottom of the stairway he looked up to see Belle bouncing about, impatiently waving a hairbrush in her hand.

Clearly his baby was eager to be off and going. He had a sorry feeling that he was going to miss her far more than she missed him.

He felt Louisa's gaze resting on him. No doubt she was still piqued over his negative attitude towards Lady Kirkwynd...which she seemed not to share.

Glancing sideways, he was surprised to see her smiling.

He truly did enjoy looking at her smile. She had the prettiest, the warmest of anyone he had ever met.

'Won't you join us for dinner at the cottage?'

'I would not wish to impose,' he answered as he ought

to, even though it did sound more appealing than spending the evening here alone.

'You would be doing me a favour. It would save me having to go out in the rain to bring Belle back. Besides, it will be a grand evening. We will be practising Christmas carols while we decorate wreaths for the windows and make bows for the Christmas tree.'

Christmas tree? Belle had never had a Christmas tree, only a Yule log. Not only that, he had to admit they had never spent an evening carolling.

'Thank you, Louisa. It would be my pleasure to come for dinner.'

Half an hour later he watched from the porch while Belle hugged Louisa's skirt tightly under the shelter of the umbrella, her expression shining.

Something inside him shifted, glowed. He could not hear it over the patter of rain on the earth, but he suspected they were laughing.

All of a sudden, he was very much looking forward to this evening.

Chapter Five

An utterly delicious aroma wafted from the kitchen. Judging by the scents of cinnamon, vanilla and nutmeg, it would make an inappropriate dinner.

Entering the kitchen, Louisa spotted the rump of Mildred Hooper's skirt swaying while she bent over, peering into the open oven.

'Dessert smells perfect, Mildred.'

The cook glanced over her shoulder, nodded vigorously, causing her grey-haired bun to slip an inch off centre of her head.

'It will be in about thirty seconds…all we need is a pinch more time for the pie crusts to brown. The gravy will not stick to them otherwise.'

Oh, dear…gravy over mince pie?

Mildred drew the muffins from the oven and set them on the work counter.

'My best yet, Lady Kirkwynd,' she announced with a satisfied smile.

'Far too good to smother in gravy.' Louisa inhaled a deep sniff. Oh, indeed, far too good. 'May I suggest we serve them for dessert?'

For years Mildred had overseen every detail having to do with the kitchen. Now at times it could be a difficult balance between making her feel she was still needed in that capacity and making certain appropriate food was served at each meal.

'Of course, my lady. But what shall I prepare for dinner, I wonder?'

'We will have a guest tonight, Mildred, and I have it that he enjoys a meat pie.'

'A guest? How delightful. A meat pie it shall be, then.'

Louisa heard the front door open and then a deep voice speaking.

'Thank you, Mildred. If you need help with anything, please let me know.'

She hurried out of the kitchen but stopped, looked back around the doorframe at Mildred, who was smiling at her muffins. 'Just one thing. Would you mind calling me Louisa? Since it is only family here at the cottage, it would be appropriate.'

'I shall try, Lady Kirkwynd, but you have been "my lady" for a very long time.'

'Thank you. I would consider it a great favour.'

Hurrying to greet her guest, she knew the older lady would have trouble with it.

She was not certain what would happen if Hugh discovered her true identity. Although her true identity was the one he was becoming acquainted with, not the false one she had used to present to society in her desperate attempt to get a husband.

Like so many others, her tenant appeared to have succumbed to gossip about Lady Louisa Kirkwynd. It would not do for her to lose her position if it came to light.

Father Christmas was counting upon her to supply gifts and spread good cheer. All things she adored doing!

If she was going to accomplish it, she needed to keep her employment as Belle's nurse.

It was Mildred's custom to retire to her room with a dinner tray then remain there until early morning. There was a good chance Louisa would not be exposed...not tonight at any rate.

Rushing into the parlour, she came close to tangling the toe of her slipper in her skirt hem. The sight of Hugh standing in front of the hearth, shrugging his shoulders out of his coat, quite caught her breath. Perhaps it was the glow of firelight in his hair and his smile that made him appear even more handsome than he had this morning.

My word, but he was a well-featured man.

How could a simple grin of welcome set her heart twirling?

She hurried to take his coat from him, noticing how attractive his dark hair looked with a smattering of raindrops glistening at the tips.

'It looks rather wet outside, Hugh. It is a lucky thing you are staying for dinner.'

Belle rushed for him, reached up with her small fingers flexing. Hugh scooped her up.

'I love to stay, Papa!' She patted his cheeks, her plump hands dimpled and sweet looking.

Realising that her gaze had drifted from Belle's fingers to Hugh's lips, she glanced away quickly.

Truly, though, it was not her fault his lips were so appealing. Any woman would be staring at them.

Hopefully, he would assume the blush heating her face had to do with the temperature in the room.

One thing was for certain, he would never expect Lady Kirkwynd to blush. Making others blush was what she was known for.

'And I cannot think of anything I would enjoy more, princess.' His smile was for Belle, but then he turned it upon Louisa and her nerves skittered. 'The manor is rather lonely with only me stumbling about in it.'

'Papa is nice.' Belle kissed her father's cheek then scrambled down to try and hug Bernard, who was frisking about, apparently overcome that Hugh was in the house.

Nice indeed! Lady Kirkwynd, the fortune hunter, had never been attracted to any man she had pursued. She had liked them, certainly, but her heart never became soft over them.

Funny, but she liked the frizzle Hugh caused, gave herself over to enjoying the way it made her skin flush in delightful warmth.

In a way she could not quite understand, Hugh's presence made the cottage feel complete, as if it had an anchor.

Which was an absurd idea. Hugh was a man she had only recently met, her employer. She ought not allow her heart to tumble over itself as it was doing.

Really, a bit of caution was called for.

She was the anchor of the family, the one responsible for them all.

'Please let me introduce my sister-in-law, Lena Wood. You have met her children already, Emily and Bram.'

He nodded in greeting. 'It is a pleasure, Mrs Wood.'

'The pleasure is mine, sir,' she answered from her chair.

Lena shot Louisa a sidelong glance, a knowing glance, her mouth tweaking in a teasing smile.

Louisa had never wondered where Bram's mischievous nature came from. Like mother, like son was certainly true where they were concerned.

But what was that glance about? Perhaps it had to do with the unguarded way in which Louisa had described Hugh's hair…how it tickled his neck. That had been an unfortunate choice of words and not too much should be read into it.

More than likely the children had already informed their mother of the incident in the woods involving mistletoe. That could be what Lena was secretly chuckling over.

'Won't you sit by the fire, Hugh? You must be chilled through,' Lena said.

'I'll admit to it. The temperature dropped like a stone in a well on the way over and the wind picked up. Had I spread my coat open, I'd have sailed along the path like a ship on the ocean.'

Bram perked up at those words. He dashed for the coat-rack.

'Oh, no, you don't, my boy!' Lena tried to rise from her chair and half managed. 'You will remain inside, fashioning bows.'

'But I want go sailing on the path.' He scuffed the tip of his shoe on the rug, giving his frown a dash of force.

'And after dinner we will sing carols.' Lena arched a brow at her child. 'Sailing, indeed. You may dismiss going outside in this weather from your mind.'

Sitting, Hugh glanced about the room. His gaze caught and remained on the mistletoe hanging from a wooden arch dividing the parlour from the dining room.

He did not look at Louisa. He did not need to. The twitch of his smile told her he remembered kissing her hand in the woods.

For as innocent as the moment had been, it did occupy her mind more than was prudent.

Her life was full to bursting already without this sort of distraction. She had invited Hugh to share a friendly evening with her family and nothing more.

Indeed, it was charitable to invite tenants to share Christmas cheer. Particularly when one of them was an adorable three-year-old.

And more… When the other one of them twitched his smile at her and it tickled something within her that had not been tickled in a long time.

No, she would not dwell on that. The man did not even know who she really was.

Hugh relaxed into a high-backed chair stuffed to perfection, his feet propped upon an ottoman. It was hard to decide what the best part of the evening had been.

Dinner had been superb, the meat pie the best he had ever tasted. While forming bows had been more of a trial than entertaining, learning to sing 'O Tannenbaum' had been fun. There had been more laughter than on-key notes.

If he were forced to pick the best part, he thought he would choose this moment, with happy memories settling into every corner of his mind at once. Contentment in a way he had never experienced filled this room, warmed his soul.

Outside, wind whistled under the eaves, rain pattered against windowpanes, making the cottage feel a safe harbour.

Across from where he sat, Louisa cuddled Belle in her arms.

By the look of his daughter, she was growing sleepy but fighting it. Her eyes dipped, then opened while she sucked her thumb and stroked a length of satin ribbon sewn to the sleeve of her dress.

Louisa sang softly to his child, something about Father Christmas, sleigh rides and snow.

He nearly fell asleep himself but the cook, a roundish, elderly lady entered the parlour carrying a tray of something that smelled delicious. Mince pies, unless he missed his guess.

Belle sat up, popped her thumb from her mouth.

Bram jumped up from the floor where he had been playing a game of jacks with Emily.

'Oh, yummy!' Emily rubbed her belly with her open palm.

'Here you are, my dearies.' The lady put the tray on a table, which, by chance, was set under the sprig of mistletoe now sporting a bright red bow.

The lady plucked a small mince pie from a doily decorating the tray, glanced up at the mistletoe with a wink.

Bram rushed forward. The woman bent, presented her cheek to receive his quick kiss. Grinning, he took the pie.

Returning his peck on the cheek, she took one for herself then bade them goodnight.

By turns, the family exchanged kisses then took a mince pie.

'Is this a family tradition?' he asked. If so, it was a touching one. 'Dessert in exchange for mistletoe kisses?'

'Indeed, it is.' Lena declared, taking a deep sniff of her mince pie. 'But it seems you have been left out of it.'

'I suppose I will just have to eat one without the kiss.'

'Oh, no, you mustn't.' Lena shooed his hand away from the plate. 'Christmas traditions must be upheld. They are the unity binding generations. And since you are standing under mistletoe you must give someone a kiss, pie or not.'

'Or Father Christmas will not come!' Bram reminded him through a mouthful of crumbs.

'We can't have that,' Hugh said with a sweeping glance that took them all in. Then his smile settled on Louisa…his attention lingering on her face, on her lips… 'For the sake of tradition and Father Christmas, will you allow me to kiss your cheek, Louisa?'

'It would be a shame for you to miss having one of Mildred's mince pies,' she answered playfully in the spirit of the moment.

She stepped close to him, tipped her cheek. Even before his lips touched her skin, he warmed to the scent of her. Cloves, vanilla and cinnamon…she smelled like Christmas.

Probably tasted like it too…like…like a gift? One which when opened might gladden a lonely heart.

Was he lonely? Until this moment he had not thought so. Perhaps his day-to-day life had been so busy he had not been aware of the fact. It could be that awareness of his own needs had been smothered under the responsibility he bore as Mooreland.

Now that he was away from Liverpool life was quieter. He had to wonder if, with only him and Belle living in the large home, the quietude was pointing things out to him.

Or perhaps it was spending time in this homey cottage where warmth and affection were openly displayed by the people living within that made him consider the state of his heart.

But, quite honestly, there was Louisa, her eyes sparkling while she gave him a teasing sidelong smile.

Perhaps Louisa Copeland was the reason he was suddenly examining his heart.

He grinned inside, contemplating the matter facing him in the moment. Father Christmas would not come without a mistletoe kiss.

Who was he to ruin family tradition?

He felt Louisa's cheek lift in a smile when his lips grazed her skin. Vaguely, he was aware that the children were giggling.

And a lucky thing he was aware! Had he not been, he might have skimmed his lips across Louisa's cheek. Her lips were awfully close…inviting.

Nothing would be more inappropriate than indulging in the fantasy.

While it would guarantee Father Christmas's arrival, the jolly old soul would leave a great stack of coal upon Hugh's hearth.

If he were invited to dinner in the future, it would be best for him to decline. At least until the new year when the temping green sprig would be taken down.

A man could only gaze at the beautiful face of temptation for so long before he succumbed. Although he could not imagine how to explain to Belle why they would be spending the evenings alone at the manor when at the end of the path waited warmth and friendship.

If only he had not hired Louisa, things might be different. If she were not his employee…

Then again, if she were not, he would not be seeing her first thing in the morning.

To tell the truth, he was greatly looking forward to it, which put him in a pickle and no doubt about it.

Half an hour later, he was back at home, tucking Belle into her bed, thinking about how, pickle or not, he was looking forward to seeing Louisa first thing tomorrow.

'Papa, the storm is so scary.' Belle's dark hair puddled on the pillow, she blinked up at him. 'Leave the door open, please.'

He kissed her forehead. 'I will leave my door open as well. You will be able to see light coming from my chamber and know I am watching over everything.'

She yawned, rubbed her eyes and nodded. Frightened or not, he supposed she would fall asleep before he lit the lamp in his chamber.

* * *

The children were tucked into bed, giving Louisa a few moments to help Lena strengthen her legs. She was hopeful her sister-in-law would walk again. To that end, Louisa made sure Lena exercised her limbs.

Truly, doctors who suggested this was not likely did not have the last say in the matter.

'I have been practising on my own,' Lena admitted.

Louisa touched the waist of her sister-in-law's skirt. This time she did not give support by gripping the waistband, but rather watched to see if she could manage on her own for a moment.

'You are doing splendidly! In no time at all you will take a step. Can you stand for thirty seconds?'

'Let go and we shall see. Louisa, I do intend to dance about this room one day, wait and see if I do not.'

'I was not holding onto you. You were standing on your own! For more than thirty seconds, I think.' Carefully, she lowered Lena to the chair. 'Well done, sister. Now, I'd best fasten that banging shutter or we will not get any sleep.'

It was fortunate that Hugh had taken Belle home when he had. The wind was growing worse by the moment, blowing as hard as she had ever heard it. As if defying natural law, rain blew sideways instead of down.

'I smell smoke, Lena,' she called over her shoulder.

'From the chimney, I expect.'

'No, it smells different from that…wrong.'

Barely visible through the bare, twisting branches of the woods, she spotted it. Billows of black boiled out of a second-storey window in the big house!

'The manor is on fire!'

Stepping outside, she yanked the door closed.

She ran hard but wind pressed her backwards, stole her breath. Rain slapped her face, soaked her to the skin.

No! No! No! This could not be!

Vile, acrid-smelling smoke spilled out a bedchamber window. It was too thick to know which room it came from.

Reaching the porch steps, she dashed up. They were slippery and her feet went out from under her. She banged her shin on a stone step, swallowed a yelp of pain.

Scrambling up, she ran for the front door, praying it was not locked.

To her vast relief the heavy door opened. She rushed inside.

'Belle! Hugh!'

Ominous...sinister, the crackle of unseen flames answered. She dashed up the stairs against ash drifting down.

A large figure emerged, coming at her fast.

'Get her out!' Hugh shoved Belle at him.

When he turned to rush back, she grabbed his sleeve.

'No, Hugh, it isn't worth the risk.'

'I won't be reckless.'

He dashed up the stairs and vanished into the choking black smoke as quickly as he had emerged from it.

What was rushing into a burning home if not reckless? Everything in her screamed to go after him, try and drag him out if he refused to come.

She could not...not with a screeching child in her arms.

Once outside on the porch, she took shelter in the lee of a large pillar. It was not perfect, but it did protect them from the worst of the wind.

What could have happened to cause a fire? The chimneys were clean...she had spent a great deal of money making sure they were.

In the end it did not matter how it had started...only how it ended. The one and only thing that counted at the moment was seeing Hugh emerge safely from the house.

'My papa,' Belle whimpered.

'Don't worry, baby. Keep your eyes on the doorway and count to one hundred. He will be with us before you finish.'

'I don't know how, only to ten.'

Rubbing her back to still the child's trembling, Louisa said, 'We will count together. The higher the numbers get the closer he is to being with us.'

'One, two, three,' they began. Belle lifted her head from Louisa's shoulder to stare at the doorway. 'Four, five, six.'

She did not hear flames, only the great racket of the wind and the rain but surely they were growing worse. What could have prompted Hugh to go back inside?

Nothing was worth his life!

'Seventy,' she said, which Belle repeated.

At eighty, Louisa began to pray silently.

'Ninety,' she murmured, feeling panic rise in her chest. What was she to do, leave the child alone on the porch and go in after Hugh…run for the cottage, leave her there and then come back?

'One hundred.'

'Where is my papa?'

'It is taking him a little longer than we hoped, that's all.' Stepping out of the questionable shelter of the pillar, she hugged Belle tight, for the child's comfort as well as her own.

She ran for the cottage, praying Hugh was safe…that he had not done anything foolishly heroic.

Rushing inside, she dropped Belle into Lena's lap.

Without taking time to explain, she dashed back out.

Running, she ignored the stitch in her side…the pain in her shin.

What did a bit of pain matter when her tenant…no, more than her tenant, her friend…was in danger?

What was she to do if she found him unconscious? Drag him out? How could she when he was so much bigger than she was?

Wake him somehow?

She did not know. All she did know was that she needed to run faster.

The wind died suddenly…although rain continued to fall on her head and make the path slippery.

Oh! Her foot slid sideways and she went down on one knee. The pain was intense. If only she could stay down, take the time to catch her breath. But, no, she could not possibly spare a second because good-hearted, sensible and kind Hugh needed her.

Murmuring his name along with a grunt for effort, she tried to stand. Something prevented her from rising. She was weak, yes, but not incapacitated. At least she would not be once she could rise.

The pressure on her shoulder released. She felt a large hand under her elbow, lifting her.

Hugh!

Standing, she made a move to hug him because…well, because he was there and she was relieved she would not have to drag him anywhere.

She refrained from the impulse. In fact, now that he was safe, she wanted nothing more than to shake sense into him.

'Hugh Clarke!' With her hands curled at her waist she narrowed a severe gaze on him, her heart still running wild in relief. 'What were you thinking, rushing back inside like that?'

'That I needed a place to live.'

'What nonsense! You need to be alive to be able to live in it. You are a father. Belle needs you.'

Why was the blasted man grinning? He had been vastly reckless despite his vow he would not be.

'Here I am, safe and hale,' he said, his smile grey with soot and ash. 'And I have put the fire out.'

Undeniably, that was a relief but, still, the man had no sense and she would tell him so.

'Where is your sense, Hugh? Do you enjoy rushing into danger?'

'What I do not enjoy is standing in the rain, talking about it.' He looped her arm through his and hurried her towards the cottage.

'Are you limping?'

'No.' Not enough to fuss over.

Coming to the gate, he opened it, led her under the porch roof. Rain sluiced off the eaves, hitting the stones with a noisy splat. He cleared his throat, looking intently at her for a long, curious moment. Then he touched her cheek, leaned forward as if he wished to kiss her.

And just like that, her well-focused ire evaporated.

His lips, glistening with rain, dipped close. She got lost in the heat and the enticing scent of his breath brushing her face.

Perhaps his urge to kiss her came from relief. Perhaps the kiss she would answer with came from the same place.

It hardly mattered, she did intend to have this kiss.

There was the sound of soft tapping, as if small footsteps pattered on the far side of the door.

Slowly his finger traced the curve of her chin, her cheek, and then his hand fell away.

'Thank you for coming after me, Louisa. You were very brave and I—'

The door flew open and Belle dashed out, wrapped herself around her father's trouser leg.

Apparently, she had not stepped away from Hugh soon enough. Lena sat in her chair, giving the pair of them a curious glance.

Not that there was anything to be curious about.

They had not kissed and now that the moment had passed were not likely to.

'You should not have gone back inside, Hugh,' she said hoping to distract her attention from the kiss that had nearly happened.

'I imagine Lady Kirkwynd would not see it the same way,' he answered. 'She would not appreciate her house burning.'

Of all the uncalled-for things to say! Louisa had half a mind to reveal who she was and point out that she cared more for his safety than a building.

Lena also had a mind to say something. Louisa saw the words twitching on her lips, wanting release, but they both knew she needed this job that was not a job at all but a pleasure.

The day would soon come when Belle's nurse arrived at

Kirkland and Louisa would be forced to give over care of Belle to her.

The thought made her chest ache. She enjoyed caring for Belle in a way that had nothing to do with payment for services.

'Lady Kirkwynd would go to lengths to protect her home, as any lady would,' Lena stated while helping Belle crawl back onto her lap. She snuggled the child tightly to her heart. 'But even she values human life.'

Hugh glanced about as if he wished to sit down but given the condition of his clothing did not.

'There are a pair of chairs in the kitchen, Hugh,' Lena said. 'If you would not mind bringing them.'

'I truly like that man, Louisa,' she whispered as soon as he was out of sight. 'Even if he is a bit misguided about… well, you know what I mean.'

'I loves my papa, too,' Belle said then, stroking a satin ribbon on her nightgown, promptly fell asleep.

Louisa sat down on the chair that Hugh set in front of the fireplace. Warmth chased away the chill. Indeed, she noticed steam curling from her wet clothing.

'Although I do not approve of you going back into the fire, Hugh,' Louisa admonished, keenly aware that it would have been beyond devastating to lose Kirkwynd Manor. What would they do without the big house? Memories aside, they needed the income it provided. 'I must say that you are our hero and we are beyond grateful.'

'Before you crown me, I must confess matters were not as dire as they looked. There was not as much fire as one would think with all the smoke it created.'

'How did it happen? I was sure I… Lady Kirkwynd, I mean…had the chimneys cleaned before you moved in.'

'There is no blame to be placed, unless you can blame it on the weather.'

That was a great relief. She nearly sighed aloud.

'Belle was afraid of the storm so I left the lamp burning in my bedchamber, hoping she would be comforted by the light in the hallway. While I was downstairs in the library a branch broke off that huge old tree and broke the window. The branch or the wind, I'm not sure which, knocked over the lamp and the drapes caught fire.'

'How awful!' Lena exclaimed. 'I am relieved it was not worse but, Louisa, didn't you purchase them—?' Lena nearly clapped her hand over her mouth but covered her faux pas with a smile. 'For Lady Kirkwynd?'

'I did, when she came here as a bride...she was quite taken with them.'

More than taken, it had been the first purchase she had ever made that she'd had no worry about paying for. Funny how hard times came and went and then came again. Perhaps there was hope for another turnaround of their fortunes, this time for the good.

Because they had a rent-paying tenant, she need not chase after a title to keep them safe.

In the event she did wed again it would be for love...or at least deep affection.

She held deep affection for Hugh. Perhaps...

No! What was wrong with her? She had no business thinking of marrying anyone. She had quite enough to deal with without thoughts of wedded bliss with a man she barely knew.

'You and Belle will stay the night here, of course,' Louisa said, glad to have a practical matter to occupy her mind. 'I will prepare a room for you. Belle may sleep with Emily.'

'I accept your kind offer, Louisa, but do not bother about the room. I will be comfortable on the sofa for one night.'

Louisa stood, plucked her steaming skirt away from her legs.

'My late husband was about your size.' But not figure. Being a great deal younger than Chester, Hugh was...

Never mind that.

The clothing would fit. 'I'll bring you something dry to put on.'

'We will come with you,' Lena said. 'Belle is spent and I nearly am.'

'It has been quite an evening.' Hugh stood up, came and brushed a strand of curly hair from Belle's cheek. The love he bore the child shimmered in his eyes.

'Goodnight, Lena,' he said when Belle wheeled her from the parlour.

If Louisa had a child, which was not likely, of course, but if she did, she would wish for her husband to look at it in such a loving way. Indeed, loving her child would be the same thing as loving her.

Chapter Six

Within half an hour Hugh was dry, warm and, in spite of everything that had just happened, content. He drummed his fingers on his stomach because even his belly was satisfied.

Moments ago, Louisa had limped into the parlour, bearing a cup of hot chocolate in each hand.

For an instant she resembled an angel bearing an earthly gift. But then she smiled and became the earthly gift.

Having been so recently burned by an engagement, he was surprised to find his thoughts dwelling on marriage. But there they were, quite merrily imagining the possibilities.

He should redirect his attention to something else. But how could he not wonder what life would be like shared with a woman like Louisa?

Paradise might be found in warm drinks in front of a snapping fire, with rain beating against the windows... everything snug within.

There had been a time when he had imagined contentment with the woman he had been engaged to. Had imagined but not experienced.

Now, here he sat with a woman he was not engaged to and yet he was experiencing a gut-deep sensation of well-being.

The feeling might have to do with the cosiness of the cottage. Although not the cottage itself. Unfeeling wood and bricks could not create the soul of the home.

This cottage took its heart from the woman who cared for it...and for everyone living within its walls.

If he felt this way sipping cocoa, what would he feel sharing more intimate moments with her?

With great effort he did manage to focus his attention on something else.

'I recall you telling me you were not limping, Louisa. It looked to me as if you were.'

'At the time, the important thing was to get home, which I was well capable of doing.'

He watched her silently, simply for the pleasure of sitting quietly in her presence.

'It seems to me you carry a great deal of responsibility on your shoulders.'

'Many widows do.'

'Many widows remarry.' He smiled when he said it, hoping she would not take offence to the well-meaning comment.

'Please, Hugh, show me the man who would take me, my sister-in-law and two children. I will marry him right off.'

Louisa's hair was beginning to dry. It fell over her shoulders in dark waves. Outlined in the soft fire glow he could see ringlets springing from the lustrous mass.

If she were married…to him, for instance…he would be able to touch her hair. But he would have to be acquainted with a woman for a long time before he would trust her enough to offer a proposal. A grasping woman did not only steal a man's heart and leave it bereft, she spent what she could of his funds, leaving his wallet empty.

He had not been burned by fire tonight and would not be burned by a broken heart…not again.

Hang it, he would not be touching any woman's hair for a long time. Which did not mean he wasn't tempted to lean forward, reach out his hand and do it. Greatly tempted.

'I would think a man with a child would wed as well,' she pointed out.

She was right, of course. Despite the fact that experience had taught him the wisdom of knowing a woman thoroughly before proposing, Belle ought to have a mother.

He saw the unguarded longing for one in his child's eyes whenever she looked at Louisa.

'I would have to be incredibly careful in my choice, don't you think? I would need to be certain my wife loved her and did not consider Belle an obligation to be tolerated.'

'Oh, but she is so loveable. Any woman would be pleased to call her daughter.'

Louisa would. It was clear that she already cared deeply for Belle. He had to admit there could be worse fates than being wed to a woman like her.

What if…? No, a respectable man would not consider romancing his employee, put her in a position to feel coerced into responding to his advances in order to keep her job.

'Is your leg troubling you?' he asked, needing to get his mind off marriage. 'Perhaps you ought to elevate it. I can get a cold compress if you need one.'

'Do not bother, it's much better now.'

He half believed her.

'Everything is better now, don't you think? Only an hour ago things seemed dire,' he said.

'Quite, but thanks to you they are not dire.'

She took a long, slow sip of chocolate. She could not be aware that it left a smear of chocolate on her upper lip.

'Mmm…' she murmured, licked her lip clean. 'This is delicious.'

Very well, she was aware of it. What she was not aware of was how her innocent appreciation of the treat made him feel.

He imagined he heard her name being whispered…by the mistletoe dangling several feet away. He was not normally as imaginative so it must have to do with having nearly kissed her earlier.

'You have a way with hot cocoa, Louisa.'

'It's Mildred's recipe so I cannot take the credit.'

Sipping, they remained quiet, each of them lost in thought.

Were her thoughts lost in him, as his were in her? He should not wonder, but how could he not?

'I'm anxious to take a look at the damage in the morning,' she said. 'I will be sure to take care of it right away.'

Not that he wanted her to be thinking of him. Fleeting fantasies of homey bliss were simply that…fleeting fantasies not to be trusted.

'No, Louisa, you will not. It is Lady Kirkwynd's home

and her responsibility to repair the damage. I would be unhappy if she put this upon you the way she does everything else.'

It had not been his intention to make her unhappy, merely to point out that she was being taken advantage of. However, she was unhappy, as her deep frown at him indicated.

'I get the impression that you hold a low opinion of the Baroness.' Louisa set her mug aside, tipped her head at him and arched a slender, dark brow. 'Have you met the lady? You must have in order to form such a judgement.'

'No...but women of her ilk—'

'Her ilk? My word, her infamy must be quite widespread for you to hear of it in Liverpool.'

'Social circles are smaller than one would guess. Society loves to talk.' Did she wonder how a man who was not supposed to be from 'society' would be privy to their murmurings?

He had not disclosed his title because he did not wish to be pursued by the Baroness, as he feared he might be if she knew. Now he would have to live the small lie, step about it as best he could. It would be uncomfortable to admit to the small deception now.

'Do you often believe gossip?' Her lips pressed together.

'Not the gossip, Louisa. I see how she treats you. I cannot say I care for it.'

'Might I suggest, Hugh...' She stood, picking up her empty cup and holding out her hand to take his '...that you at least meet a person before you pass a verdict on them?'

He handed her the drained cup. 'Forgive me. You are correct once again. I understand that the Baroness is your employer and you are naturally loyal to her. I shall withhold my opinion until I have met her.'

For some reason, his apology made her frown.

'Goodnight, Hugh.' She nodded towards the sofa where she had placed a pile of blankets. 'If you need more firewood it is stacked outside the kitchen on the back porch.'

She spun about, exited the parlour, back straight, hands

clenched at her sides…and with a limp she was doing her best to disguise.

Perhaps Lady Kirkwynd had some virtue that he had not heard of.

There must be some reason Louisa was so defensive of her.

Walking into the manor house, Louisa caught her breath. A fine dusting of ash covered the floor. Smoke permeated sofas, rugs, and drapes, making it seem that more had burned than only drapes.

Going upstairs, she found the odour only grew worse.

'You cannot live here, Hugh.' Louisa glanced about the master chamber, poking a section of burned drape with the toe of her boot. 'It will take a cleaning crew to get the reek of smoke out of the house.'

How on earth was she to pay for this?

She could not possibly do the work on her own, not while keeping up with everything else. She hated to admit there was something she could not accomplish, but…really, this was a bit too much.

'Surely the odour hasn't got through the whole manor. I'll find another area for Belle and me to sleep in.'

'Maybe not the whole manor, Hugh, but enough of it to make living here unpleasant. You must stay at the cottage until Lady Kirkwynd can deal with the damage.'

However she managed to do it.

It was nearly Christmas…even if she could scrub away smoke residue…replace bedding and rugs…along with dozens of other items, she could not neglect Christmas. The children were looking forward to Father Christmas's visit. Belle was especially. Happy expectation shone in her brown sugar eyes whenever she spoke of it.

No doubt, Hugh had done what he could in the past to make it merry for her, but having other children to share her excitement with would make Christmas even more special.

Indeed, more special for all of them. The idea of spending Christmas in the cottage with Hugh was exciting.

Who knew what might come of it? A deepening of their friendship, no doubt. But perhaps… Was it too much to hope he might kiss her under the mistletoe?

'Perhaps Belle and I should take a room in Coniston.' Hugh frowned, shook his head. 'I would not wish to add to your burdens.'

'If you are referring to my family, they are not a burden. What I do for them, I do because I love them.'

'That is evident, Louisa.' He smiled now, which was far nicer to look at than his frown had been. 'I have never met a person as selfless as you are.'

Wouldn't he give himself a kick in the trousers if he knew who she was? The last woman he would consider selfless was Louisa Kirkwynd.

After all, she could hardly resent him for what he had said, given that she was withholding her identity. Hugh had no way of knowing that when he criticised the Baroness he criticised her.

It would be wrong to hold her deception against him… not that it did not grate on her to be criticised unjustly. It did, but what was she to do about it now?

She could hardly admit the truth at this point.

Louisa snatched the broom she had brought with her and began to sweep up the ashes of her pretty drapes. Working gave her a moment to think of a way to convince him to stay at the cottage.

Not only because it would be nice, but because if he moved to Coniston she would feel bound to repay him some of the rent. She could not possibly do that.

Naturally, there was Belle to consider…not only the income she would lose by not watching the child, but she would miss her dreadfully. The bond between them had grown strong in a short time.

Why was that? Belle needed a mother, certainly. And Louisa longed for a child. She had lost track of the number of times she had gazed longingly at mothers cuddling their infants, turned her gaze away and wept inside. It would be wise to remember that Belle could not fill that place in her heart. She was Hugh's daughter, not hers.

She pushed the broom harder, determined not to dwell on her childless state. She had Bram and Emily which made her beyond blessed.

What on earth…? One second she was industriously sweeping, and the next the broom was no longer in her hands.

Spinning about, she was nearly nose to chest with Hugh… so close she smelled the scent of his shirt, of his skin under the shirt. He gripped the broom in one fist. A nicely formed fist, she could not help but notice.

'Why do you feel you must do everything on your own, Louisa?'

Surely it was obvious.

'I have no husband to do it for me. Neither does Lena.'

'Come, sit for a moment.' He set the broom aside. Then, of all things, he took her hand, led her to the bed and indicated that she should sit on it.

It was as comfortable as she recalled, but it had been an awfully long time since she had slept in this bed. After Chester…well, she had found it more comfortable to sleep in the Baroness's chamber.

What was interesting was that she did not feel the old ache that usually saddened her when she entered the master's quarters. Indeed, at that moment she felt comforted here. And why would she not? Chester had always made her feel comforted.

She stroked her hand on the mattress, knowing her late husband would wish her to go on with her life…to love again if the opportunity arose.

Her glance slid to Hugh then quickly away. Why would thinking of marriage turn her gaze his way? Possibly because she had come within a breath of kissing him last night. Possibly because if it had happened, she would no longer be able to see him as merely a tenant and friend?

'Let me see your leg. It is clearly still causing you pain.'

What? She was sitting on her late husband's bed and Hugh was demanding to see her leg? That was a splash of cold water tossed on her wandering thoughts.

Standing, she slapped ash off her skirt then walked out of the room. What a bold and inappropriate thing to ask.

She was halfway down the hallway before he caught up with her, took her by the elbow.

'Evidently you consider me a woman of that "ilk"! Lacking morals, as you believe Lady Kirkwynd is.'

'I'm sure you are nothing like the Baroness. I hope you do not believe I think so.'

'I might be like her.' Really, she was becoming weary of his attitude towards her...all right, not her but the persona she had created.

'I am certain you are not.'

He was correct, of course. At heart she really was nothing like the woman he believed her to be.

'You may not see my leg under any circumstance. The condition of my shin is my business, not yours. Rest assured, it will soon heal.'

'I'm sorry, Louisa. It is only that I feel responsible for what happened to you. The fire would not have happened if I had not left the lamp unattended. But I did, which caused you to race out in the storm and be injured.'

That was true. She could put the blame on him if she wished to. However, it would be wrong.

'People leave lamps unattended every day. It was the storm that caused the fire.' She shrugged out of his gentle hold on her elbow and was surprised at how she missed the warmth of his fingers. More surprised at how she imagined his fingers in her hair, on her throat... Well, she was a widow, not a maiden. It was only natural she would think of intimacy. 'It is because of your heroic effort that the house only needs to be cleaned...and new drapes to be purchased for your chamber.'

'I will buy them.'

'You needn't do that, Hugh.' Oh…please let him insist upon it!

'Despite what you say about the storm being responsible, had I not left the lamp burning, the drapes would not have caught fire. I will replace them.'

Very well, she would not say anything that might dissuade him.

'On Lady Kirkwynd's behalf, I thank you. But really, Hugh, you must stay at the cottage. Think of how much nicer Christmas will be for Belle if she gets to spend the holiday with the other children. There is plenty of room. The cottage is larger than it looks.'

'I accept.' He did? Good. 'You are correct. Belle will be overjoyed to be spending Christmas with you and your family.'

'No more than we will be with her.'

With him…

If she were to be honest with herself, she would need to admit the truth of the matter. She was looking forward to having a man in the house for Christmas.

Not just any man but Hugh. What was there about him that drew her the way it did?

Good looks, indeed, yes, but more than that. She simply enjoyed being in his company.

Perhaps it had to do with not feeling compelled to pursue him. How refreshing it was to spend time with a gentleman simply for the pleasure of his company and not for his fortune.

She knew Hugh had one because it had been necessary for him to provide proof that he could afford the rent.

Knowing he had wealth did not make her wish to pursue him as she had others.

She simply liked him, as a man.

It was going to be enjoyable to take her time, get to know him more deeply…maybe more intimately?

Having finished inspecting the smoke damage, they approached the head of the stairs. On the way down they chatted about how thrilled Belle would be when she discovered they would be spending Christmas at the cottage.

'Emily and Bram will be so—'

'I will not have you hobbling beside me, Louisa.'

All at once, Hugh scooped her up in his arms, carried her the rest of the way down.

'You may put me down now,' she said, although she rather hoped he did not.

'Not likely.' He carried her out of the house, down the front steps.

My word but he was strong.

With his slim build she had not guessed his arms would be so firm, so warm.

Oh, yes, this was a pleasure. Honestly, her attraction towards him was unlike anything she had ever felt. Having married Chester when she had been quite young and having learned to love him after their marriage, she had never experienced being starry eyed and in love.

Surely she was not now, not with Hugh. And yet something was happening.

A delightful infatuation, no doubt, even though she was past the age for it.

'I can walk on my own. it's only a bruise.'

'Perhaps, but you will not let me see it and I do not intend to watch the pain on your face with every step you take.'

'I'm not in all that much pain.'

'But you admit you are in some and so I shall not put you down.'

She laughed, which oddly caused the muscles of his arms to clench. She felt his breath catch for half a second.

'What will you do when we reach the cabin, Hugh? Carry me about while I attend my duties?'

'Would you allow it?' My goodness, he had a compelling grin…innocent and mischievous at the same time. It was rather like Bram's smile and yet vastly different.

'Naturally not. I will fight my way to the floor.'

Being carried along the path through the woods was a delightful break from the pain in her shin, there was no denying it. What an odd sensation to feel weightless, to tip back her head and watch cold blue sky and bare branches float past her vision.

She spotted mistletoe dangling from a tree branch. What if she asked him to stop…to give her the kiss she had been denied earlier?

Wouldn't that be inappropriate? But there was mistletoe hanging in the cottage where a kiss would be required were one to linger underneath it.

They arrived at the cottage quicker than she wished to. He set her down.

'Thank you, Hugh. I will admit my shin is better for not having walked all the way home.'

'You will tell me what I can do to help? The last thing I wish is to impose upon you.'

'You will not.'

Far from it. The knowledge that there was another adult in the house to help deal with whatever might arise in the wee hours was a comfort.

Yes, indeed, and not just any adult but a strong, exceedingly attractive one.

She suspected when she closed her eyes tonight, she would sleep more easily than she had in a long time.

Chapter Seven

'Papa!' Small hands yanking on his nightshirt drew Hugh from a dream of…what? The image faded before he had a chance to recall it but there had been a lingering impression of Louisa's lips. 'Wake up! Wake up!'

What time was it? Lifting himself to his elbows, he glanced out the window. Golden light was only starting to crest the fells.

'What are you doing up so early, Belle? Are the other children awake?'

'It snowed!' She slid off the bed, tugging on his arm. 'Auntie Louisa says we must eat breakfast before we go outside.'

'You will eat faster without your mittens on.' He drew them off her small fingers. 'Go and play with your friends, have something to eat. I'll join you as soon as I'm dressed.'

'Hurry! Hurry! Hurry!' she called, dashing from the room.

He did hurry but still missed breakfast.

Coming down from his upstairs bedroom, he found the children gathered by the front door. Louisa handed them their coats. Emily and Belle wiped crumbs from their lips with the backs of their hands. Bram was still chewing.

Louisa smiled at him, looking as pretty as the morning. Delight over a snowy day reflected in her eyes as much as it did in the children's.

'You are just in time to take the children outside.' She held his coat out. 'I'll be along in a moment. Lena will not want to miss the fun.'

'Mama loves snowmen!' Emily declared, drawing the front door open.

'The path will be icy! Don't slip!' he called, then held his breath while the children scrambled out all at once.

Belle was the first to go down, then Bram. Emily laughed uproariously while Bram helped Belle up.

No one was crying so he followed them out, smiling at the picture they made, laughing and tossing handfuls of snow in the air.

Standing in front of the porch, he took the scene in, awe-struck by the beauty of the fresh snow that had crept in so gently overnight.

It was as if they had been given a gift from nature.

'Look at that, Lena!'

Turning at the sound of Louisa's voice, Hugh was equally struck by her smile. He had to admit he was often struck by her smile. There was a quality to it he could not define in a single word. The closest he could get to describing her was confident, compassionate and vulnerable...all mixed with an ethereal sultriness. Although no one living here would feel a tug of the heart over those last words the way he did.

The dog rushed outside, tail wagging madly while his paws kicked up snow.

Louisa tucked a blanket about Lena's shoulders and an-other about her legs, then she dashed outside to join the children.

'Go along, Hugh.' Lena must have noticed his hesitation to leave her alone because she gave him a heartening smile. 'We will need your help if we are to have the tallest snow-man ever.'

'I'll take you down if you wish.'

'How kind of you, but really I have a better view of the fun from up here. Come next year I will be down there all on my own...you will see.'

He returned her smile but remembered he would be liv-ing in Liverpool next Christmas. Somehow the thought of his newly remodelled house did not fill him with the hap-piness it used to.

This moment, this place was where true happiness lived. He had never felt more at home anywhere than he did in this cosy cottage.

It took an hour for the extra tall snowman to be ready for the placement of pipe, nose and buttons.

He lifted Belle to put on the buttons, then Emily to set the pipe. Bram was tall enough to shove in the nose all on his own.

Louisa picked up a pair of smooth stones near the porch and placed them for eyes.

The snowman still needed a smile. Glancing at the porch, he knew who must give it to him. He picked Lena up, chair and all, and carried her to the snowman.

She pushed up from the chair on her own but he stood behind her ready to help if need be.

Laughing, Lena poked the snowman's icy face to form a grin. Unaided, she lowered herself back into the chair.

Louisa smiled but Hugh noticed she dashed what must be a tear off her cheek with the back of her hand.

Now that their creation was properly decked out, everyone cheered. Bernard barked, reminding him that Belle had asked for a dog for Christmas.

The children must be cold, but the sun was shining and when they asked for a snowball fight, he was eager to engage. Not that he meant to attack any of the little ones... but Louisa?

Mischief sparkled in her pretty eyes.

She kept glancing over her shoulder at him, grinning while she formed a mound of snowballs. Oh, yes...this was going to be the best fun he'd had in a long time.

'Are you ready for this?' she asked. As always, her laugh made his heart stutter.

'The question is, are you?'

'I will be as soon as I deliver these weapons to my partner.'

Gathering an arsenal of snowballs in her skirt she hobbled towards Lena and gave them to her.

'Two against one?'

'Well…' She shook the snow from her skirt as she came down the steps. 'Look behind you, Hugh. I think it is rather five against one.'

Turning, a grin already on his face, he saw the children, each of them holding a snowy weapon to fling at him.

'I'm outnumbered!' he cried as five balls of snow came at him at once.

'You are bigger than we are!' Bram shouted, a second before pelting him again.

Bigger, yes, and wetter as the game went on.

A snowball exploded on his chest. Mildred came out of the house, laughing along with the rest of them.

'She will be looking for clean snow,' Louisa told him.

Standing as close as she was, her scent swirled about him. What was it? Heaven on earth? Did that even have a scent?

It must have since he had the distinct impression he was speaking to a half-ethereal being. The half that was not ethereal had him sweating under his coat.

'I'll go and help her gather it.'

'Clean snow for what?' he called after her.

Glancing over her shoulder, she winked.

He took a direct hit in the face from Lena. Snow slid down his nose and he sputtered when he laughed through it.

'You will find out tonight,' Louisa declared.

Funny, he had known Louisa Copeland for such a short time but something in his soul suggested that he had always known her. More than that…suggested that he wanted to know her for ever.

Now that he had met her, he could not imagine a time when he would not see her smile or hear her laugh.

Liverpool might prove to be a dull place in the future.

Belle wrapped her arms around his leg and told him she

was cold so he would need to put aside this train of thought… of feeling…and follow it another time.

It was particularly nice having Hugh and Belle living at the cottage. Life was simply more fun sharing time with the two of them.

Why was it she felt she had known them for so much longer than she had? Perhaps hearts did not measure time in the same way day-to-day living did.

Louisa admitted to feeling more relaxed, more at ease than she normally did.

Hugh was the reason for it. Something about being in his company felt right.

But in another way risky. She had gone to great lengths to avoid going near the mistletoe, even though she wanted nothing more than to stand beneath it, open her arms to Hugh in invitation.

With everyone gathered in the parlour, she would not act on the impulse. Which was not to say that in the privacy of her own thoughts she could not imagine how lovely and exciting it would be.

'Who would like to sing Christmas carols?' she asked.

If she did not wish her perceptive sister-in law to wonder why she was blushing she had better direct her thoughts to something more proper for a family gathering.

Family? In her mind she had included Hugh and Belle among them as naturally as she took her next breath.

She sat down in her usual chair, which faced the fireplace. Belle climbed quickly onto her lap, snuggled in.

'Look, Auntie Louisa.' Belle showed her the ribbon-wrapped pinecone she had been decorating. 'It's *so* pretty. Me and Emily used the same colour for ribbon.'

'It is the prettiest I have ever seen. What shall we sing, Belle?'

'The Christmas tree song!'

Everyone, except for Mildred who had retired early, as was her custom, sang 'O Tannenbaum'.

'Now a story, Mama,' Bram said.

'"'Twas the Night Before Christmas"!' Emily clapped her hands.

Belle scrambled down from her lap and sat on the rug in front of Lena, squeezing in between Bram and Emily.

Louisa settled back in her chair, feeling her body relax while she watched Hugh finish a helping of the treat which had long ago become known as Mildred's Delight, a dessert made of custard and clean snow with a dollop of syrup stirred in. She had been preparing the delight every night since it had snowed.

Clearly, Hugh was delighted about it. She half expected to see him lick the bowl clean, which made her nearly laugh aloud.

There was no denying that Louisa was enamoured of Hugh…and why would she wish to deny it? The sensation was titillating, delectable. Once again she was keenly aware of the mistletoe hanging only feet away with a bright red bow to draw attention to its presence…just in case one was unaware.

'May I have more of this?' Hugh set his bowl and spoon aside, patted his belly.

'We would need to gather more snow.'

'Once the children are in bed would you be interested in taking a short walk? Honestly, I have been looking for an excuse to take a snowy stroll in the moonlight.'

'Of course.' With her shin much improved, she was eager to go out herself. A brisk stroll ought to take her mind off the mistletoe, which seemed to be whispering Hugh's name.

What a perfectly silly thought. Mistletoe did not whisper, it simply hung in place, causing unwary minds to imagine things.

An hour later, the household was settled into their beds, she and Hugh bundled up in warm clothing and walking out of the garden.

'This is magical,' she said, closing the gate.

While they walked through the woods, she took note of how ice encrusted each tree branch, how it seemed an otherworldly sight.

'See how the moon makes everything sparkle?' she asked.

'It is quite an icy show. Are you cold?'

He did not wait for her answer but put his arm across her shoulder. *My word.* If she had been cold, she no longer was.

'I need to ask your help with something, Louisa.'

Perhaps his lips were chilly and needed warming.

'Of course. I'll help if I can.'

'With everything that has gone on this week, I only now remembered that Belle has her heart set on Father Christmas bringing her a puppy. Do you know where I might find such a creature so close to Christmas? As long as you are sure Lady Kirkwynd will approve.'

'Since she has not spoken a bad word about Bernard, I'm sure she will have no problem with a well-behaved dog.'

'How can you know it will be behaved when it is only a pup?'

She laughed. 'You cannot. If you want to give Belle a puppy, you will need to deal with mischief for a time. But perhaps with two pups in the house they will expend their energy upon each other.'

'Do you think it is possible to find one?'

'It will take a bit of luck, but perhaps in Coniston we will. Shall we make a trip of it? I need to buy gifts and sweets for the children.'

'To return the favour I will cut us a huge yule log.'

'That would be wonderful! Last year was our first without one…without Chester. It did not feel a proper Christmas. It was all I could manage to get a small tree for Father Christmas to put gifts under.'

'I'm sorry for that, Louisa. This year I will cut us as big a tree as will fit in the parlour. I am ashamed to admit this will be Belle's first.'

'Do not berate yourself. I got my first tree after I married Chester.'

The woods were silent until an owl flew over their heads. The whisper of the cold air through its feathers was a thrilling sound, but to hear it along with seeing the bird's shadow glide across the snow was wondrous.

'Why did you never have a tree?' he asked.

'Because I never had a father like you are. Most of the time my father forgot I was there. He only became aware of me when he needed something. I will admit it was not until I married Chester that I ever felt secure in life.'

'I begin to understand why you take care of everyone with the devotion you do. What I do not understand is why you allow Lady Kirkwynd to make you work so hard.'

She really ought to tell him who she was. In the end no good would come of keeping silent about it. Indeed, it could only be a matter of time before Mildred inadvertently gave her away.

After Christmas, she would tell him. In two more days, Father Christmas would have delivered his gifts. If she lost her employment when he discovered the truth, she would still have his rent to get them by.

'Your nose is red,' he pointed out. 'You must be freezing.'

He stopped walking, wrapped both of his arms around her...hugged her tight to his chest then quickly released her as if he realised he had committed a great blunder.

'I'm not cold.'

How could she be? Gazing up at his face, seeing a flash of heat flare in his eyes...dear lord, but it might as well be summer.

'I only asked as an excuse to give you a hug. What I meant by it is to tell you that I admire you, Louisa.'

'I admire you, too.' A great deal more than admired, as odd as it seemed for the length of time she had known him.

He touched her arm, guided her with him several yards to the right, past a fallen log half-buried in snow.

Why had he moved such a short distance and then stopped? She arched a brow in a silent question.

'I only moved you over here as another excuse, this one to kiss you.'

It had been a long time…a long, lonely time since she had been kissed. Which was not to say it had not been on her mind rather often recently.

'Here and not there?'

'There is mistletoe here and not there.' He glanced up pointed his finger to a branch directly overhead. 'As I see it, we have no choice but to kiss.'

'The children are asleep in their beds…they will not know we broke the rule.'

'I'm not fond of breaking rules.' He shook his head, smiled and frowned at the same time. How did he do that? Not both expressions at once, but how did he make her heart quiver at the sight? 'What if there are elves in the woods? They might tell Father Christmas.'

'Yes, what if there are? Elves are known for being loyal to him.'

He touched her cheek, lifted her chin. She was rather fond of elves…more of mistletoe.

Also fond of the scent of his breath on her face and the warm pressure of his fingers lifting her chin.

He dipped his head, whispering, 'Duty is what duty is.'

'It's odd that now we have the same motto. Surely it means something,' she whispered.

'It means I am going to kiss you…thoroughly.'

'Because elves might be spying.'

'Elves be dashed, Louisa.'

The puff of his breath was icy white, but it was steamy, brushing her lips in the instant before he kissed her.

My word, but the man could light a fire that would melt the ice off the trees.

For all she had adored her late husband, he had never lit flames in her like Hugh was doing now.

By the time he was finished with her, she half expected to be standing in a pool of hissing water instead of snow.

'Good morning, Willard.' Louisa stroked the mule's brown nose. 'When you are finished eating we are taking a trip into Coniston.'

The mule shook his head, dislodging her hand.

'I know it is a risk. People in town will address me as Baroness,' she confessed to the beast as if he had an inkling of what she had said. 'I suggested the trip to Hugh before I gave thought to the consequences.'

Hugging her coat tightly around her, she sat down on an overturned oak barrel.

She was not nearly ready for him to discover who she was. Oh, why had she not told him the truth from the start?

'I was under a spell, you understand, and hadn't my wits about me.'

The question was, did she have them back now…and the even larger question, did she want them back?

Last night, walking in the snow with Hugh had been nothing less than enchantment.

'I might be falling in love,' she admitted to the mule. 'What do you think of that?'

Willard turned one brown eye upon her while chewing his hay. Clearly he was not as thrilled by the idea as she was.

And she was thrilled. For all that her feelings for Hugh had come upon her rather explosively, they were genuine.

'I sense that Hugh might return my affection,' she explained. 'But will he continue to when he discovers the truth?'

Willard nickered in his odd, mulish way.

'It is not as if I can simply blurt it out. He does not care for the Baroness. It would be best to take my time, don't you think? Present the news at a proper time. When he knows me a bit longer, he will understand that I am not after his fortune or his title. He has one, you know. He's never said so, but really it is an easy enough thing to discover when one is checking the financial worthiness of one's tenant.'

No, indeed, she was not after anything of his.

She was offering something instead…her heart.

Offering her heart to a man to whom she was not already wed was risky. She had never done it before and was not certain she could do it now.

Neither was it likely she could prevent herself from doing so.

As it turned out, Hugh did not go into Coniston proper. The small carriage they travelled to town in was in poor repair. Every moment of the drive from Kirkwynd to town he had feared the bench supporting them would give way.

It slid and shimmied as if it were not bolted down.

Hugh had it on his tongue to point out the Baroness's neglect of the vehicle, but he did not wish to offend Louisa again.

He could not begin to understand her loyalty to the woman, but he had determined not to speak ill of her again and would do his best not to.

When she asked him to take the carriage to the blacksmith's, wait while it was repaired, he agreed. Happily agreed. Given the choice between shopping and chatting with the blacksmith while the fellow worked, he would rather chat.

And daydream. Kissing Louisa last night had been like spending a moment in paradise. Had made him wish for a life where he would go to sleep each night with her kiss and wake in the morning still feeling the heat.

If she had any idea what he was thinking…vividly imagining…she would be scandalised. True, she had been married and was not a naive maiden but what was on his mind would…well, it even made him blush.

She was wonderful…a more decent, more selfless and honourable woman could not be found. And yet he knew he must be cautious in giving his heart this time…wary, careful.

It was what he told himself, and yet he was not certain

that his heart had not given itself away already, even without his full consent.

Just when the sun began to set, he spotted Louisa hurrying towards him, a lovely and satisfied smile on her face.

How he would adore kissing that smile. Once again feel her lips soften and grow hot under his.

She strode quickly towards him, a basket dangling in the crook of each elbow.

'What have you got there, Louisa?'

'Dinner to eat on the journey home.' She extended her elbow, indicating the basket on her right arm. 'And a gift for Belle.'

Her grin sparkled when she handed him the basket.

As soon as he took it, something shifted inside it…and whined.

'You found a puppy?' He could scarce believe it. With only days until Christmas he had feared Belle would not get what she wanted most of all.

Secondmost, he corrected himself. Belle had never said as much but given the way his daughter looked at Louisa he knew she would rather have a mother.

Which was a bit beyond Father Christmas's ability to provide…but not Hugh's.

He could propose to Louisa, give Belle the mother she craved.

While he was lost in the intriguing idea, wondering what Louisa would say if he asked her to marry him, she set the food basket next to the hem of her skirt, lifted the puppy from the basket and nuzzled the fluffy creature with her chin.

'He was the only pup left of his litter. But isn't he sweet?'

He was a pretty dog, brown with a white blaze on his nose and dotting his paws. 'He looks awfully young. Where did you find him?'

'Mr Burke, the storekeeper, sent me across the street to the dressmaker. This small fellow is only eight weeks old.' She held him close to her nose and made little kissing noises. 'I had to promise he would be well loved.'

'Unless I miss the mark, he is already.' If one day he saw such affection directed at him he would be a grateful man.

'Everyone adores puppies.'

And he adored her. How could he not? She was simply the most remarkable woman he had ever met.

There had been a time…a moment ago, was it not…when deciding upon marriage would take serious thought and long deliberation.

Watching Louisa snuggle the little dog to her throat…it hit him that he had been greatly mistaken.

'Is the carriage repaired?' she asked.

'It is. Apparently the bolts holding the seat to the frame had come loose.'

'Ah.' She handed him the basket with the pup then picked up one containing the meal they would share along the way home. 'Isn't that odd? Thank you for seeing to it.'

He helped her into the carriage, wishing he could do so repeatedly since it offered the opportunity to touch her trim waist.

After handing the pup up, he took a place beside her and turned the carriage towards home.

While they rode, they ate dinner, discussed the children, laughed at their constant antics. He wished the trip home would last all night long.

He could not deny it, he wanted not only this night but all her nights from here on.

His heart yearned for nights of long kisses and mornings greeted with laughter.

What would she think if she knew what was on his mind?

Louisa stood in front of the hearth, holding Belle on her hip and gazing at the great leaping flames of the yule log.

'Will Father Christmas get burned up?'

'Oh, no…he never does. He is magic after all.'

So was Hugh, it seemed. When the family had woken up this morning they found the tall Christmas tree in place before the parlour window, the huge yule log already crackling and warming the room.

It had been a grand surprise for them all.

Hugh would accept no praise for his efforts, claiming that he had been restless last night and had decided to make good use of his time. In Louisa's opinion he had gone above and beyond the call of duty to venture out at night and by the light of the moon cut a worthy yule log and a grand tree.

He was a man in a million…a man who deserved to know the truth about her. She had been trying to tell him…truly, all day it had been on the tip of her tongue. The problem was, it never made it past the tip of her tongue.

'Belle!' Emily tugged at Belle's skirt. 'Come down. It is time to put ribbons on the Christmas tree.'

'Oh!' Belle wriggled down. Louisa could not resist giving her a quick hug before she raced away to gather a handful of red and green bows.

Watching Belle laugh with the other children, Louisa's heart turned over. In little more than a week Belle's nurse would arrive at Kirkwynd to resume her duties.

Duties that Louisa had become fond of.

'Are you well?' She had not noticed Hugh join her at the hearth. 'You look sad.'

'Not sad, Hugh. Only a bit nostalgic…sentimental, I suppose, because everything is festive and wonderful.'

Of their own accord, the children began to sing while they secured ribbons to the tree. It was one of the sweetest sounds she had ever heard.

Glancing at Hugh she saw emotion glistening in his eyes.

'It is the season. Peace on Earth…the greatest gift ever given.' He blinked, smiled at her. 'Speaking of gifts, how is Belle's gift faring?'

'He slept in my bed all night. And Bernard has taught him to chew slippers.'

'Louisa! Hugh!' Lena called. 'I could use your help with something over here.'

'Over there under the mistletoe?' Louisa murmured to Hugh. 'Do you see anything she needs help with?'

'Family tradition, I imagine.'

He caught her hand, hurried her across the room.

'What is it you need help with?' Louisa asked.

'Not help so much as company. Aren't the children the happiest you have ever seen them? Oh, and look!' She glanced up to where the mistletoe dangled.

Hugh picked up Lena's hand, gave it a squeeze and a sweet, smiling kiss.

Then he turned to Louisa. What she saw in his eyes was simmering rather than sweet. Oh, dear, there was a clear invitation in his eyes, but she could hardly accept. Not with children in the room.

She tugged on his waistcoat, pulled him down to her level then kissed his cheek...sort of his cheek. Her lips slid a bit so that she caught the corner of his mouth, felt the stubble grown since his last shave.

'Isn't this the merriest Christmas ever?' Lena's teasing voice jolted good sense back into her.

Letting go of Hugh's waistcoat, she stepped backwards.

It was. Happy children gathered about the tree, decorating and singing. Cold wind blew outside, making the inside feel extra snug. The aroma of warm cinnamon and vanilla drifted in from the kitchen where Mildred was baking.

Father Christmas would soon to be on his way and Hugh's kiss lingered at the corner of her mouth.

At that moment life was beyond lovely.

Chapter Eight

It was late when Hugh heard steps in the hallway, then the front door open and click closed.

Going to his window, he spotted Louisa walking towards the stable. Moments after she went inside a line of light seeped from under the door.

What could be happening in the stable at this time of night...whatever time of night it was.

Dressing quickly, he went out of the house and hurried after her.

Sliding the tall stable door open, he stepped inside.

Lamplight spilled out of the last stall on the right. Walking towards it, he shivered from the chill. When he passed the mule, it bumped his shoulder, nipped his coat sleeve.

Yanking free, he walked to the rear stall, peeked over the gate. He did not see Louisa but there was a blanket spread on a pile of straw with the shape of a woman under it.

'Louisa?'

'Hugh?' She sat up, blinking. 'What are you doing out here?'

'Discovering what you are doing.'

Flashing the smile that aroused his heart, she drew the puppy from under the blanket, kissed its furry forehead.

'He smells so new... And he was crying like pups do when they leave their mothers. If Belle is to have her surprise, she must not hear him.'

What kind of woman would come outside on an icy night in order not to spoil a child's Christmas surprise?

One he was falling more in love with by the hour.

He opened the gate then sat down beside her.

'Come, Hugh, I did not light the stove and it is cold in here.' She opened the blanket, patted the straw.

'Why didn't you?'

'With how cold it was, walking over from the cottage, it seemed best to warm the puppy and then do it.'

Of course she would think of that. Louisa always put others ahead of herself.

He slipped under. The warmth she had already built under the blanket seeped around him.

'I have something to ask you, Louisa.'

'Of course.' Lamplight shimmered in her hair, giving the illusion of being dusted in black diamonds.

'Do you love Belle?'

'Why, naturally I do! She is so endearing and any woman—'

He touched her lips with one finger, shook his head. 'Any woman might care for her...but it is different with you, I think.'

'I do love her, of course.'

'May I ask you something else, of a more private nature?'

'Our friendship has grown intimate rather quickly, don't you agree? I do not mind answering personal questions.'

'Have you never had a child of your own?' She may have and lost the babe. This was a common tragedy.

She handed the puppy to him. It tried to lick his face but being too short to reach it, it bounded about like a bouncing ball in his lap.

The funny sight made Louisa smile, which in turn caused his heart to expand, his nerves to tingle.

'Chester and I were never blessed with a child, although we did want one.'

Indeed, clearly. A woman did not spend time in a cold stable to keep a puppy from crying if she was not a mother to the bone.

What would happen if she married him? Would she want a baby with him?

'The children love the Christmas tree, Hugh,' she said, so he supposed she did not wish to speak more on the subject.

'They did have a fine high time decorating it, didn't they? Can I confess something to you?'

'Oh, who does not adore a confession?' she teased. 'As long as it is not a heart-breaking one.'

'Far from it.' He leaned closer to her since confessions were best whispered. Her hair smelled like straw and puppy. 'I'm glad the curtains burned. Living in the cottage with you and your family has been wonderful. The best week I can recall having in an awfully long time.'

'It has been the best we have had in a long time too,' she whispered back. Her sweet breath brushed his ear. A delicious chill skittered up his neck. 'Although, I have found one thing to be a challenge.'

'What is it?'

'Mistletoe.'

'Hmm, here in the stable there is no mistletoe.' He touched her cheek, stroked the soft curve before turning her face towards him. It was a lucky thing he was sitting because her sigh would have brought him crashing to his knees. 'Even without it, I mean to kiss you.'

'Is no place safe?'

Not for him, not when she laughed softly that way.

'I think not, Louisa. Not for us.'

As soon as her lips pressed against his…warm, soft and loving…yes loving, he felt like he was tumbling. Because he was tumbling, bringing Louisa down with him onto the straw.

He was lost…lost in love. He took his time with the kiss, lingering because he wanted her heart to shift the way his had done.

The temptation to take this past a kiss was akin to torture. Luckily, the puppy chose that moment to nibble his hair. Good sense hit him like a bucket of water.

Louisa was far too honourable to be seduced in a stable without a wedding band on her finger.

Ah, but he did have a wedding band. A beautiful one tucked away in the desk drawer.

Here, at last, was an openhearted woman who had fallen in love with him unaware of the fact that he bore a title.

At least, he thought she had fallen in love, prayed she had. He could not imagine what he would do if Louisa did not share his feelings.

His heart sensed the truth. Louisa Copeland could be nothing other than genuine and her response to him had been guileless, fervent.

'Let's go back to the cottage,' he said. 'Now that we are no longer kissing the chill in here is noticeable.'

Reaching for the pup, she snuggled the tiny creature to her heart. 'I cannot leave him alone out here, Hugh. He would be too lonely. Neither can I take him inside. He will wake the house. But do not feel you must stay.'

'Is there wood for the stove?'

'Yes, in the stall next to Willard's.'

Within moments he had a fire going, but the stable was large so it only helped a little. Which was even more reason for him to stay with her...as if he needed an excuse.

No, rather he needed the self-control to keep his hands decently to himself.

Sitting back down, he drew the blanket over his legs, determined not to kiss her again. Where the kisses were leading would wait until after they were wed.

Wed... He wanted this, wanted her. More, he wanted this marriage right away. He could only pray that he would be granted a Christmas miracle and she would want it too.

'It is not often we have the opportunity to talk without interruption,' he said.

'It is nearly as nice as kissing, don't you agree?'

'No, I do not.'

'All right, I don't either. But it is what we shall do.'

Here was proof that Louisa was a lady of honour. Although she had shown herself to be one time and again already.

She was a woman to be trusted and he was going to propose to her tomorrow... Christmas Eve.

* * *

Sitting beside Lena in front of the warm hearth, Louisa could scarcely believe it was Christmas Eve. And what a wonderful one it promised to be.

Earlier this morning it had been necessary to spend time in the stable. Eight-week-old pups required a great deal of attention. In the end, she had enjoyed those hours greatly.

Because she had not spent them alone. Hugh had been with her. Together they had wrapped the gifts from Father Christmas. All during it he had been excited about a Christmas surprise. Although she could not imagine what would be better than when they presented Belle with her puppy.

Which was going to happen any moment. The plan was for Hugh to stop by Louisa's bedroom, tie a green bow about the pup's middle and grandly bring him down the stairway.

Lena shot her a smile of anticipation. The children sat at the foot of the Christmas tree eating fruit cake, unaware of what was about to happen.

Louisa's heart raced in anticipation of seeing Belle's joy.

'Here he comes,' Lena whispered with a nod towards the head of the stairs.

'Merry Christmas, Belle!' Hugh announced with grin that could scarcely be contained to his face.

It did not take but a heartbeat for joy to erupt…laughter from Emily and Bram, tears from Belle.

'Is he mine, Papa?'

'All yours, baby. You will need to take good care of him, feed him and hug him.'

Louisa's heart tumbled all over itself, watching Belle joyfully weeping over her new pup. She was glad that Hugh had not waited until Christmas Day to give Belle her puppy. Now they would be able to await Father Christmas's visit together.

Also, the stable was a cold place to spend the night. If she and Hugh passed another night in each other's company, she would prefer it to be in the warm parlour.

Hugh had asked if she loved Belle. Goodness, she did, deeply.

She also loved Hugh. Before last night she had thought it to be true. Tonight she had no doubt of where her heart lay.

It was past time for her to confess who she was. It was a wonder Hugh had not discovered it by now.

How could she confess her love without first admitting who she was?

'I'm going to tell him now,' she whispered to Lena.

Lena nodded, her lips pressed tightly together. 'It has to be done.'

Gathering her last ounce of fortitude, she stood, went to Hugh and plucked his sleeve.

'May I have a moment, Hugh?'

He bent to whisper in her ear. 'Under the mistletoe?'

Oh, how she would love to have one last kiss in case her confession turned him away.

'Not here…in the kitchen.'

'Alone in the kitchen?' He waggled his brows. 'I hope so because there is something I want to ask you.'

Grinning widely, he patted his shirt pocket.

She nodded, praying she was not about to crush the love light shining in his smile.

Squeezing his hand, she opened the kitchen door and led him inside.

'Ah, there you are, Lady Kirkwynd.' Mildred held out an iced cake. 'You and Mr Clarke are just in time to give it a taste.'

Hugh's fingers jerked on her hand. Slowly, he let go of her, his smile sagging.

'Lady Kirkwynd?' His breath wheezed, sounded as if it had got stuck his throat.

'Oh, dearie me… I forgot that you wish to be addressed as Louisa now.'

'It's all right, Mildred. I'm sure everyone is anxious for the cake.'

'Oh, lovely. I'll take it to them straight away.'

Hugh's stare pinned her. Seeing his pained expression, the way his mouth pressed tight, his eyes narrowed, she could scarcely breathe. The only sound in the kitchen was the bubble of boiling water in a saucepan that Mildred had left on the stove.

'Lady Kirkwynd…' He repeated her name as if it were an accusation. Why must he gape at her as if she had struck him? 'You lied to me?'

'It was not a lie as much as an omission.' The excuse did sound worthless, for all that it was true.

'An omission of the truth?'

'The truth is that I am Louisa Copeland and my husband was Baron Kirkwynd.'

'Why would you keep that omission from me, Lady Kirkwynd?'

'Because you offered me employment that I could not refuse. From the beginning you made it clear how you felt about Lady Kirkwynd. If I had told you I was her, you would have withdrawn the offer.'

'You should have had more faith in me than that.'

'Should I have?' She was feeling rather heated now…hurt and judged. 'By a man who did not feel he needed to reveal his own title, Baron Mooreland?'

His jaw dropped…his mouth fell open. She tapped her foot on the floor.

If this was not a case of the pot calling the kettle black, she did not know what was. She had not meant to bring up his identity, but he was looking at her as if she had sprouted horns…horns that she was half-tempted to poke him with.

'Why did you not reveal who you were?' She slammed her hands on her hips, tapped her fingers on her skirt.

'I knew of your reputation and had no wish to be pursued.'

'I did not pursue you. If I had, I would have donned my hunting gown.' Not that the scandalous blue garment she had stuffed at the bottom of her trunk had done her a whit of good in the past.

'I would like to believe you, Louisa…but hang it all. You knew who I was all along. Don't you see how it looks? I feel as if you planned to capture my title all along. That any affection you showed towards me was a lie.'

'My reason for withholding my title is far more valid than yours, Hugh Clarke! I needed to watch Belle in order to provide Christmas for my family...you were merely frightened of gossip.'

'What I was frightened of was handing over my heart to another woman who would step on it.'

'If that is what you think of me, we have nothing more to say to each other.' Why did tears have to be stinging her eyes? She was not one to weep. She stood strong in any situation.

Hugh strode towards the door, opened it then shot her a look that spoke of his misery, his broken and betrayed heart.

She was not guilty of title hunting! She was not guilty of not loving him either!

He believed it, though.

'Look at me, Hugh. Take a long, truthful look, tell me what you see.'

'I will gather Belle and go back to the manor house.'

'Nonsense! Just because you choose to have a broken heart, it does not mean you ought to impose one on that sweet child.'

'I did not choose it...you chose it for me.'

'Stay until the children are in bed and then come back in the morning before they wake up. There is no need for them to suffer for your needless broken heart.'

'Needless, Louisa?'

'Look at me...see me. You know the truth.'

If he did look, it was for a brief second, not nearly long enough to recognise the love she bore him.

In the space of a blink he closed the door on her.

Perhaps, for just a moment, she would indulge in a few tears.

Hugh paced the floor of his chamber, stopped, stared at his wardrobe. Only half his clothes were out of the trunk as it was. It would be no great chore to repack, close the lid and remove to Coniston, take rooms there.

It was midnight. Christmas had arrived, blown in by a gentle snowfall.

Even so, he was not merry and bright. He was miserable.

He had been duped again. Fooled by another woman not wanting him but what he could offer in position and finances.

This was far worse than when Victoria had betrayed him. Being duped by Louisa made him not want to breathe.

No, she was not his sweet Louisa, she was Baroness Kirkwynd. She did not look, sound or act any different—

Of course, she was, she had to be, and yet…

Looking at the situation fairly, it was understandable that she had not admitted to being Lady Kirkwynd. Having lived with the family, he understood she did need the money and he had made his disdain of the Baroness clear from the beginning.

If all there was to it was that she had lied about her name, he would not pack. But it was the other thing she had kept secret that he could not get past.

The worst of this all was that she had known who he was all along…known that he bore a title. It was well known that Lady Kirkwynd was a title hunter, which meant she did not want Hugh Clarke, the man. Any rich and titled fellow would have suited her purposes.

His heart felt cleaved in half. Had she kept her identity a secret, tricked him into falling in love her with the intention of seducing him into a predicament he would not be able to make right without marriage?

Sitting on the trunk lid, he stewed inside. Tried to light the fire of his anger so his sorrow would be easier to bear. He pictured her face, trying to see the hussy in her eyes, the temptress in her smile.

He stood up, paced around the trunk, cursing aloud.

Because he could not see a deceiver or a fortune hunter. Only pretty, wide and wounded eyes tearing up when he'd slammed the kitchen door.

Would a woman intent upon seduction not have seduced him in the stable…made certain he was good and stuck? For everything he had told himself at the time about behaving with honour, he would have been helpless against her had she attempted to lure him.

She had not done that. No! He had been the one to follow her out there…kissed her and wanted more.

Louisa had been the one who had given him leave to go back inside the cottage. It had been his decision to stay.

Passion might have got out of hand between them. She had been the one to say they would spend the night in conversation.

He glanced about the ash-covered chamber. It had not looked like this when he'd moved in.

Louisa…she was the one to have worked her pretty hands raw to make sure he had a comfortable place to live.

When the drapery was burning, it had been Louisa who'd tried to get him to leave the manor and run for safety. Baroness Kirkwynd had been the one to race back to make sure he had not come to harm.

Again and again Baroness Kirkwynd had borne insults to her character…and why?

For the well-being of those who depended upon her!

Oh… Louisa… He grasped his belly, feeling half-sick. She had begged him to look at her and he had drawn up his vain hood of righteousness, acted cold, wounded.

The plain truth was that Louisa was not the one who'd wounded him! That had been Victoria. All the lingering betrayal he felt for that faithless woman, he had cast on Baroness Kirkwynd.

When confronted, she had not tried to justify her secret, defend her motives.

She'd only asked him to look at her…to see her.

Well, he was looking at her now.

In doing so he saw himself, a fool of a man who had believed the lies of society gossip. A blunderhead who blamed the pain inflicted by one woman upon another.

He did see her now. Standing here in the centre of his chamber, clutching his guilty heart in his fist, he knew she was the best person he had ever met.

She had been right when she'd accused him of choosing a broken heart.

He had used his wound against her...a woman who loved his child, the very woman he had been praying to meet!

Who cared if she was the Baroness? Who even cared if the rumours about her were true?

Louisa... Lady Kirkwynd would go to great lengths to provide for those who depended upon her as any decent woman would.

What had he done? The thought that she might wash her hands of him made him ill.

She would be justified in never speaking to him again... to remember him with anger and regret.

Lifting the trunk lid, he snatched out his coat then dashed for the desk, yanked open the drawer and caught up his mother's and grandmother's wedding ring where he had angrily stashed it moments ago.

He was going to do his best to put this situation to rights... if such a thing was possible. Taking the stairs two at a time, he did not bother to button his coat.

Outside, snow fell gently, swirling across the path as if nature were dancing in celebration of this night of nights.

The first Christmas had been a miracle to mankind. Would this Christmas prove to be one for him?

He only hoped that the spirit of love Christmas inspired would help him not look such a rot-headed idiot.

He ran as fast as the snow would allow, praying he was not too late.

Louisa loved him. He did believe that. But would she forgive the ugly things he had accused her of?

He would only know when he was face to face with her. And he would be, even if he had to break into her sleeping chamber, where he would fall on his knees and lay his heart before her.

But wait! What was that? A small circle of light as if cast by a lantern bobbed among the trees, there and gone in drifting snowflakes.

The light drifted towards him, illuminating the figure clearly when she halted, set the lantern on the ground.

He stopped where he was, no more than fifteen feet from her.

Snow fell quietly in the lamplight between them, softening her image in a pristine, white veil.

But what did she have on? Some sort of blue gown that was not pristine. It left her shoulders exposed, her bosom half-exposed. The dark blue satin skirt whispered about in the breeze, as if it were bait to beckon an unwary male.

Who was she? An angel? A seductress?

He did not care because she was—

'Louisa?'

She shook her head. Dotted with snowflakes, unbound hair shimmied over her shoulders. 'Lady Kirkwynd.'

'Why are you dressed like that? Where is your coat, woman?'

'Did you not hear me say, earlier tonight, that I wear a particular gown when I am husband hunting?'

He nodded because the ice queen left him speechless.

'It must be obvious that is what I am doing. I am hunting a husband.'

'Me?' He poked his thumb at his chest. 'Even after the things I said to you?'

'Yes, Hugh. You are my prey.'

Staring at her through a drift of delicate snowflakes, he could scarcely believe she was not a dream. This seductive angel was not demanding he wallow and beg for absolution.

No! Dressed in a film of midnight satin she was the one to have come after him, offering an olive branch he did not deserve.

Why would she do that?

'Why are you wearing…that?' was the only thing he could think of to babble.

'Because I want you to see the woman you so fear.' She held her arms wide, shrugged her bare shoulders. 'Look at me, Hugh. This is who the gossip is all about… Do you see my wicked heart?'

There was a great deal exposed…but a wicked heart?

'No, Louisa. Whoever said those things about you were probably green with envy and fear. I see the most loving, caring woman I have ever met.' He spread his arms, shrugged in the way she had. 'But what do you see, Louisa? A thick-headed fool who could not see beyond a past heartache…an idiot and a blind imbecile?'

'Imbecile is rather harsh. Thick-headed fool will do.'

'I do see you, my Louisa. Can you forgive this thick-headed fool?'

She nodded once.

He ran for her. She ran for him.

Catching her in an embrace, he spun her about, feeling snowflakes whirl around them like kisses of promise.

'I love you, Louisa,' he whispered against her cheek. 'Please say you will marry me.'

'It seems you have swept me off my feet,' she murmured in the soft sultry voice that had captured him from the beginning.

He set her on the ground, noticed she was shivering and took off his coat, placed it around her shoulders.

'What do you say now that your feet are on solid ground?'

'I say I love you. Yes, Hugh, I will marry you.'

'And become Belle's mother?'

'Especially that…and, God willing, the mother of all your children.'

'When?' Please do not let her want a long engagement. He was certain he did not have the fortitude required of a long wait.

'As soon as we may obtain a special licence… By the New year and not a moment longer.'

Going down on one knee in the snow, he drew the ring from his coat pocket.

Her hand had been clutched at her throat but she extended it to him. It trembled slightly so he kissed her palm then slipped the ring on her finger.

'You honour me, Lady Kirkwynd.'

'Those are words I never expected any man to utter.'

He stood up, pressed her ringed hand to his heart. 'You will hear it every day for as long as I live.'

And then he kissed her, heard a sound, a whisper... Louisa.

Somewhere close by there was bound to be mistletoe.

Christmas morning 1892, Kirkwynd Manor

Louisa had to admit to missing Christmas at what she had come to think of as Mistletoe Cottage, but Kirkwynd Manor did not lack for the enticing green sprig. It hung in nearly every doorway of the manor, a clear reminder of the price Father Christmas demanded of one and all, according to family tradition.

It was early, the sun only just risen, but not so early that Belle, Bram, and Emily were not knee deep in gifts, with the dogs playing tug of war with discarded ribbons.

Louisa rocked in her chair, cuddling her greatest gift close to her heart.

Baby Chester, their adopted son, had been brought from the orphanage late last night. The poor mite had been abandoned on the church steps. Within hours of that he had landed in her arms and already she could not imagine life without him.

It was not as if she and Hugh had given up on having a child of their union, but they both agreed that that did not mean their hearts and arms would not be open to children in need.

Did they not love Belle as if she had been born to them? And now Chester, too?

Lena, sitting in a chair across from them, divided her attention between her and the children lost in joyful mayhem.

This year had been a gift beyond compare.

Mildred still rambled happily about the kitchen, not a bit offended that Hugh's staff had come to 'assist' her. In fact, all of Hugh's staff had settled in quite well and to a person decided they would prefer to live here rather than in Liverpool.

Lost in the pleasure of watching the children, she did not notice Hugh sit down in the chair beside her.

Leaning over, he kissed the baby's fine, downy hair.

'Happy Christmas, Chester,' he murmured. 'This time next year you will join the merriment.'

'Papa!' Belle cried. 'Come and see my dolly!'

Giving Louisa the smile that always made her feel secure and loved, he went to share Belle's new treasure with her.

Louisa watched him, the way his shoulders moved when he walked, the sound of his voice when he stooped to admire the doll…everything about him was all so dear.

'May I hold him?' Lena stood up, walked from her chair to Louisa's, reached out her arms.

She was reluctant to have his small, delightful weight taken from her arms, but it was only right to share him for a moment, so she handed him into Lena's arms.

'What a wonder our little Chester is, Louisa. I could not be happier for you and Hugh. And who knows, perhaps the two of you will be blessed with a child of your own this year.'

Louisa stood up, touching her child's cheek while he slept in his auntie's arms.

'But he is my own. Child of my heart or child of my body, I am equally blessed.'

Finished admiring the doll, Hugh returned, lifted his son from Lena's arms.

'My brother would be so proud to know he has a namesake,' she said.

'Do you need a hand back to your chair?' Hugh asked.

'No, I shall get there on my own.'

As far as Lena had come in learning to walk again, she still had some distance to go. But she had already surpassed everything that the doctors had predicted for her and Louisa could not be prouder.

'Come with me, wife.'

Hugh led her towards the sprig of mistletoe dangling in the bay window of the parlour. Snow fell prettily beyond the glass.

'A kiss under the mistletoe for love in the coming year?'

'With or without the greenery, we will have it... But, yes, let us take every opportunity to kiss that we can.'

And so they did, continuing a custom they hoped would stretch across generations.

* * * * *

THE EARL'S
UNEXPECTED GIFTS

Eva Shepherd

In memory of my kind, warm and loving mother, Freda. I miss you and think of you every day.

Dear Reader,

I loved writing *The Earl's Unexpected Gifts*. Immersing myself in a northern hemisphere Christmas with snow, sledges, short days and cozy evenings around the fireside was a real treat. I live in New Zealand and the Christmas holiday down here consists of long hot days, visits to the beach and barbecues.

My mother grew up in Carlisle, England, and never quite adjusted to Christmas in the middle of summer. For many years, she tried to create a traditional Christmas until, eventually, she reluctantly conceded that roast turkey with all the trimmings and plum pudding weren't entirely suitable when it was thirty degrees outside. After that, our Christmas lunch was more in the New Zealand tradition, with salads, pavlova, strawberries and cream. Despite this concession, every Christmas Mum would remind us that it wasn't the same and it could never be a real Christmas, not like the ones she had "at home."

Eva Shepherd

Chapter One

'*Children? Twins?* But I know nothing about children.' Rufus Deerwater, the Earl of Summerhill, stared at his lawyer, certain the man had lost all sense of reason.

Seated behind a large desk, piled high with books and files, the lawyer looked down at the papers in his hand. 'Yes, twins, my lord, aged ten. It seems you are the nearest living relative and their circumstances are now rather dire.'

'There must be someone else. Anyone else. Someone more suitable,' Rufus appealed. 'I can't become a guardian. I am wholly unsuited. And I have never heard of these cousins. They must be more than just *distant* cousins. They've been completely out of sight until now.' He shook his head. 'No, this is impossible.'

'Very well, my lord. I'll inform the executor of their parents' will that you are not in a position to help and other arrangements must be made.'

Rufus stared at the lawyer and grimaced. 'No other relatives, you say?'

'That is correct.'

'Dire circumstances?'

'Again, quite correct, my lord.'

'Orphans? Living in poverty?'

'That is what I have been reliably informed.'

Rufus drew in a deep breath, held it for a moment, then exhaled slowly. 'Well, I suppose I have no choice. I'm going to become a guardian, of twins.' He frowned at the absurdity of this situation. 'I suppose my mother can help. She's been saying for some time she wants children filling up the Deerwater estate, although she had expected them to be my children, not some waifs and strays from hitherto unknown relatives.'

'Indeed, sir,' the lawyer said, looking back at the papers in his hand. 'But very little might be expected of you or your mother, apart from providing them with a home. The children's governess still lives with them.' He paused and looked up at Rufus, as if giving him a chance to digest this news, but he was wasting his time. Whether they came with a governess or not, it would make no difference. Rufus would never get used to the absurdity of children being placed under his care.

'May I suggest that you retain the governess's services,' the lawyer continued. 'You can leave the day-to-day care of the children to her. You quite possibly will not even know that there are two children in the household.'

Rufus nodded, still frowning at his lawyer. 'Good idea. And this governess, is she happy to carry on caring for them?'

'Well, she has been working for quite some time without wages. I believe all the other servants left years ago. It was the governess who approached the executors of the family's estate, what there is left of it, and asked them to make enquiries to see if there were any relatives who might take the children on as wards. The money has all gone apparently, and it seemed the family property was to be sold, which would leave the children homeless. The governess was apparently rather desperate to see the children settled somewhere.

'It does sound as if she is rather loyal to the family. So I am sure she will be satisfied with any arrangement you make for her, as long as the children are safe.'

Rufus clasped his hands together with a satisfied clap and stood up. 'Right, it's all settled. You contact this governess and make all the arrangements. As long as she's willing to carry on doing everything necessary for the children, as you say, their presence shouldn't affect me in any way.'

The lawyer stood up and bowed as Rufus departed his office. Pleased that his duty was now done, Rufus was looking forward to the evening to come. He had wasted enough of the precious time he had left in London on the dratted business of these wards. His mother expected him back at his Yorkshire estate in a few days, where he was going to have to endure another dreary Christmas and New Year, one that would inevitably involve some serious matchmaking from his mother. He had but a few days left in London before he had to suffer that tedium, so he was determined to spend it enjoying all the pleasures that London had to offer.

His first stop after leaving the lawyer would be a visit to his club, then it would be on to a party being hosted by a friend of the Prince of Wales. Queen Victoria's son and the wild circle of aristocrats, actresses and other reprobates in which he moved certainly knew how to enjoy themselves. While Rufus never needed an excuse to indulge himself in a bit of hedonistic pleasure, if he *did* need one, the horror of becoming a guardian to two young children would certainly provide it.

Children, responsibility. He shuddered at the mere thought.

Anna Wainwright had nothing to worry about. Not any more. So why did she have a sense of foreboding as the carriage travelled up the long drive towards the Earl of Summerhill's stately home? She looked out at the extensive farmlands, coated with newly fallen snow, and tried to assuage her anxiety.

Their troubles were now over. She could relax. But worrying about the children's future and her own situation had become a habit, one she was finding impossible to shake off.

She closed her eyes briefly, then slowly breathed in and out in her practised manner for keeping calm. For many years she had successfully hidden her anxiety from the children, and she would continue to do so. Not that her worries would affect Thomas. He was leaning out of the open window, allowing the crisp, fresh air to fill the carriage, and excitedly describing all he could see. But his sister, Emily, was more like Anna, inclined to wariness. She was gripping Anna's skirt, her brow furrowed, her lips pinched.

Anna gently stroked the young girl's head. 'Isn't this just wonderful?' she said softly. 'This grand house is where we're going to live now.'

The pretty child sent her a cautious smile, and Thomas turned around to face them, his cheeky face smiling even brighter than usual.

'It's enormous and I've never seen so many windows on one building,' he said. 'Have a look, Em. It's got turrets and fountains and lakes, and statues, and more chimneys than I can count. And you should see the garden, it's enormous. It's like a palace and you're soon going to be a princess.'

'Remember, children, we will be guests. This is not actually our home,' Anna said.

While she did not want to dampen Thomas's enthusiasm, it was essential that the children know how important it was for them to be on their best behaviour at all times. The lawyer had made it clear that the Earl of Summerhill had only agreed to take the children on as his wards on condition that nothing would be expected of him, other than providing a place for them to live and financial support. He was adamant that the Earl expected the children's presence not to interfere in the way he lived his life.

The lawyer had stressed that, while many people believed children should be seen but not heard, the Earl would prefer the children to be neither seen nor heard. Something that was near impossible with a rambunctious child such as Thomas, who liked to be seen and heard by everyone, and as often as possible.

No wonder she was anxious. The children's very future depended on them not offending the Earl by their presence. If he withdrew his support, she hated to think what would become of them. There was nothing left. Even the sale of the heavily mortgaged home did not provide enough money for them to survive more than a few months.

Anna drew in another deep breath and exhaled slowly as

the carriage pulled up in front of the house, and reminded herself that the Earl would only be at his estate for the Christmas and New Year period. Hopefully, the children would behave like little angels for that short time and would do nothing to provoke the Earl's disapproval.

'Remember, children, best behaviour at all times.' Before the words were hardly out of her mouth Thomas had thrown open the door of the carriage and in one exuberant leap jumped onto the gravel path, rushed up the stone steps, and was knocking on the forbiddingly large door at the front of the house.

While the coachman lowered the steps and helped her and Emily out of the carriage, the door opened. Anna was tempted to call out to Thomas to wait for her, but she was sure a harried governess yelling at the children like a fishwife would not make a good first impression.

'Hello, my name is Thomas. My sister, Emily, my governess, Anna, and I are going to be living here,' Thomas told the impassive footman.

Taking Emily's hand, Anna rushed up the steps. 'Could you please inform the Earl that Miss Wainwright and his wards have arrived?' she said, placing her hand on Thomas's shoulder and trying to push him behind her.

The footman bowed. 'Certainly, Miss. You are expected. Please follow me.' He ushered them into the opulent entrance hall, the grandeur of which momentarily took Anna's breath away.

'Don't touch anything,' she whispered to the children as they stared wide-eyed at the porcelain vases, urns and marble statues balanced on narrow plinths, all of which seemed vulnerable to young children's clumsy hands. Under their feet, richly coloured oriental rugs graced the floors, while the solemn paintings of ancestors lining the walls seemed to glare down at them in disapproval.

The footman departed then returned a few seconds later and led them down the hallway. He opened the door to a large, sumptuous drawing room. Anna took in the floor-to-ceiling windows letting in the subdued light. They were adorned with luxurious folds of drapery, providing a sense of warmth on this cold winter's day. A fire crackled in the marble fireplace, which was surrounded by comfortable sofas.

Although the room looked welcoming, it too was unfortunately adorned with ornaments, vases and other precious objects she dreaded the children touching. A man and older woman watched them as they entered, then the man rose from his seat, just as Thomas strode forward.

'I'm Thomas Cooper and I'm pleased to make your acquaintance,' he said with a practised bow. Anna had spent some time teaching the children how to bow and curtsy when they met the Earl and his mother. Unfortunately, she had not spent enough time drumming into Thomas that under no circumstances was he to speak before he was spoken to.

'I'm pleased to meet you, Thomas,' the Earl replied, looking down at the young boy as if he were a curiosity. 'I'm Rufus Deerwater, the Earl of Summerhill, and may I present my mother, the Countess of Summerhill.'

His words were polite but the sideways glance he sent his mother did nothing to calm Anna's churning stomach.

He looked over at Anna. 'And are you going to introduce us to the ladies?'

'May I present my governess, Miss Anna Wainwright,' Thomas said. It was too late to stop him from assuming responsibility, without making the situation even worse, so Anna merely bobbed a curtsy and with a small wave of her hand signalled for Emily to do the same.

'I'm honoured to meet you, Miss Wainwright, Emily.'

She looked up into his eyes. The bemused look had left his face and that should be reassuring, but instead her stomach clenched tighter. No one had warned her that the Earl was devastatingly handsome. But, then, who would warn her of such a thing? The lawyer was unlikely to mention that the Earl's blond, tousled hair gave him a decidedly rakish quality. Neither would he have said that any appearance of foppishness was contradicted by the Earl's strong, clean-shaven jawline, which added a decidedly manly quality to his countenance.

But it would have been nice to have been warned about his striking eyes. Blue, with a greyish tinge, and a piercing quality that both drew her in and alarmed her. She lowered her gaze slightly from those eyes down to his full lips. The clenching pain in her stomach intensified. Her gaze shot back from his sculpted lips to his eyes, then quickly dropped to the floor.

Why did he have to be so good looking? This meeting was nerve-racking enough without him being so unsettlingly attractive as well.

Suddenly aware that the older woman was talking, Anna snapped out of her foolish daze. She had told the children to be on their best behaviour, and here she was, not following her own instructions and being unintentionally rude to the Countess.

'And this is my sister, Emily,' Thomas said to the Countess. 'She's a bit shy at first but once you get to know her, you'll discover that she's very clever and talented. I'm sure you'll be pleased to have us as part of your family.'

Anna cringed and drew in a quick breath. She had told Thomas and Emily how important it was that the Earl and his mother accept them, but she had not expected him to actually state it quite so blatantly.

'Indeed,' the Countess responded, raising her eyebrows. Then she smiled and the clenching in Anna's stomach eased slightly. At least the Countess was not offended by Thomas's boldness. All was not lost. Yet.

But in future she could not let her guard down. If she was to protect the children and ensure they never became a bother to anyone in the household, she most certainly could not let herself be distracted by something as trivial as the Earl's good looks.

Chapter Two

This was not what Rufus had expected. Governesses were supposed to be stern, spinsterish old biddies. His governess certainly had been. But Miss Wainwright possessed none of those qualities. She was undeniably the most beautiful woman he had ever laid eyes on, and he had seen his fair share of beauties in his time.

And he was interested. Very interested. What red-blooded man wouldn't be interested in a pretty young woman with raven-black hair and soulful brown eyes? No sane man could possibly resist that heart-shaped face and high cheekbones. And as for those lips, they had to be her most attractive feature—full, sensual, soft and just made to be kissed.

But Miss Wainwright was a temptation to which he would not be succumbing. He did not seduce women, even if they were stunningly beautiful. And he most certainly did not seduce women in his employment. Such women were vulnerable enough, without some cad taking advantage of them. He was not his father, he reminded himself as his gaze ran over Miss Wainwright's slim form. Every woman who came to his bed did so willingly of her own volition.

No, he most certainly would not be acting on his attraction to Miss Wainwright. He would stick to his type of woman, those who were merely looking for some harmless pleasure, and expected nothing more from him apart from a good time.

Rufus realised he was staring at Miss Wainwright and looked back at his mother, who was chatting to the little boy.

'Yes, we host a ball every Christmas Eve,' his mother was saying. 'We invite all the local prominent families. It's become quite a tradition and everyone looks forward to it.'

Rufus groaned inwardly. Everyone looked forward to it

except him. And as for tradition, the only one Rufus had no-ticed was his mother's tradition of trying to foist one of the unmarried young women onto him in a desperate attempt to get him married off. And each year the number of unmarried women seemed to multiply exponentially and their fierce determination to become the next Countess of Summerhill seemed to increase at an equally furious rate.

'We've never been to a ball before,' Thomas said. 'We'd love to go and Anna has taught Emily and me how to dance.' The little boy raised his hands, as if he were holding a part-ner for the waltz.

'I'm afraid balls are not for young children,' his mother said. 'Although I'm sure there will be no harm if you and your sister watch from the balcony.' She looked up at Miss Wainwright. 'Under your governess's supervision, of course.'

Miss Wainwright bobbed another curtsy. 'Yes, my lady. Thank you, my lady,' she said, and Rufus noted her charming voice. Slightly deeper than most women's voices, it contained not a hint of frippery or frivolity, something that was to be found in abundance among the women he usually mixed with.

But, then, she was a woman with responsibilities, and that could never be said of any of the women in his set.

'But we'll still be able to dance, won't we?' Thomas said.

Miss Wainwright sent Thomas a small frown, which was received with another gleeful smile. Rufus knew how the young boy felt. He too had taken pleasure in disobeying his governess when he had been Thomas's age. Although if his governess had looked anything like Miss Wainwright, he suspected he would have followed her around like a besot-ted puppy. Fortunately, he had been spared that indignity.

'Well, I have a lot still to do before tonight,' his mother said, rising from the sofa. 'I'll leave my son to show you around the house and introduce you to the servants.'

Miss Wainwright curtsied again and indicated to the chil-dren to do the same. Emily gave a small bob, while Thomas performed an extravagant bow, with much twirling of his hand, as if bidding farewell to Queen Victoria herself.

His mother watched the boy's antics with a confused frown, then sent Rufus a quick smile. What was his mother up to? He had made it clear he wanted nothing to do with these children. Was this all part of her plan to get him up the aisle, married with a brood of children? Did she really think foisting these wards onto him would soften him in that direction? Well, on that matter, she was sadly misguided.

His mother departed and he turned back to the waiting party. Although he had to admit that spending a bit more time in Miss Wainwright's company was not going to be an arduous task. 'Right,' he said. 'Let me show you your new home.'

Miss Wainwright took Emily's hand, and tried to make a grab for Thomas's, but he was too quick, and walked beside Rufus, gasping and exclaiming at everything he saw.

When they arrived at the ballroom, Thomas rushed forward before Anna could restrain him and ran down the length of the large room, skidding on the highly polished floor and coming to a stop in front of the Christmas tree.

'It's enormous,' he said, staring up at it. 'The biggest tree I've ever seen, even in a forest.'

That was perhaps a slight exaggeration, but at fifteen feet high it certainly was a large tree and dominated the ballroom. As was its purpose.

'The servants will be lighting the candles before the guests arrive tonight,' Rufus said. 'Then it will indeed look spectacular.

The two children looked up at him, all wide-eyed and appealing. 'Would you and Emily like to help?'

'Oh, yes,' Thomas said before consulting his governess. 'Wouldn't we, Em?'

The little girl looked up at her governess, who gave a quick nod, then smiled at the children.

And what a smile. Was there anything more beautiful? It softened the serious, worried line of her mouth and filled those melancholy eyes with warmth. Rufus would like to be on the receiving end of that smile. She turned to look at him, still smiling. Then it disappeared as quickly as the sun behind a cloud. He had no right to be disappointed. He did not need pretty governesses smiling at him. He did not need any encouragement to break his no-seduction rule and become his father. No, indeed he did not.

He turned back to Thomas. 'Right, let's see the rest of the house and then I'll introduce you to the servants and they can show you to your rooms.'

He led the parade out of the ballroom and into various drawing rooms, the pink one, the blue one, his mother's one, and several others that he had forgotten the names of.

He passed the library and was about to give it a cursory mention, but Miss Wainwright looked in with interest, exclaiming at the floor-to-ceiling shelves packed with leather bound books.

'My mother's an avid reader and the family has collected many books over the generations,' he said. 'Please feel free to help yourself to any books you want.'

Her brown eyes grew wide. 'Are you sure your mother won't mind?'

'My mother will be delighted to know that there is another reader in the house.'

She nodded and thanked him, still staring in at the library. It was a small thing to offer and yet she looked so grateful.

The party moved on to the music room. The moment the door opened, the barely restrained Thomas broke free once again from Miss Wainwright's grasp and rushed up to the piano.

'You have a grand piano,' he cried out, lifting up the lid. 'We only had an old upright back home and it was so out of tune. We had to sell it and I missed it so much.' The boy shuffled through the sheet music, then sat on the bench and started playing. Even Rufus could tell the boy had real talent, his fingers flying across the keyboard.

'Thomas, you must ask permission first,' Miss Wainwright admonished, reaching out to still his hands.

'It's all right,' Rufus replied. 'This piano doesn't get played nearly enough.'

Her shoulders visibly relaxed. She sent him a small, grateful smile and his heart went out to her. The lawyer had said the children had been orphaned five years ago, not long after she had joined the household, and for the last six weeks, after the death of an aged aunt, she'd effectively had guardianship of them. It all must have been such a trial for her and it was typical of him that all he had noticed was her beauty, not her worries.

He smiled at her, to try and reassure her she had nothing to concern herself with now. But rather than reassure her, her smile disappeared. Her lips once again became pinched, her posture even more rigid.

Oh, well, he had tried.

Why did he have to smile at her? Why did that enticing smile cause his eyes to crinkle at the corner in that raffish manner? And why did his smile draw her attention to his full lips? This situation was stressful enough without him adding to her worries by unsettling her with that smile. She looked away from him and concentrated on Thomas, who was now signalling for Emily to join him at the piano so they could play a duet.

Anna reached out to halt Emily's progress, then saw the little girl's confusion. She too didn't quite know how she was supposed to behave in the company of the Earl and she was only adding to Emily's discomfort. She needed to get herself under control and focus on her role as governess, nothing else. It was essential she forget all about the Earl's smile or his masculine good looks. And, in future, when walking behind him she most certainly should never look at his superb physique again. It was no matter to her how broad his shoulders were, how slim his waist or how long his legs. And it certainly was not her place to notice.

'Perhaps you should ask the Earl if he minds you playing

the piano,' she said quietly to Emily, annoyed at the choked sound in her voice.

Emily looked up at the Earl, her eyes wide and uncertain.

'I would love to hear you play, Emily,' he said gently, causing Anna's tense body to relax slightly.

Emily jumped up onto the piano bench beside Thomas, smiling for the first time since they had arrived.

Anna released a small, grateful sigh, then looked up at the Earl. She wanted to thank him for his gentleness with Emily, but the words caught in her throat and her heart gave a ridiculous little flutter in her chest.

Why did he have to be so handsome? And why was she allowing his good looks to unnerve her so much? It was essential that he provide a home for the children. It would be a disaster if she ruined their chances by failing to keep her absurd reactions to the Earl under control. It was not as if she was a young girl any more. She was a mature woman of twenty-five. One who had been in employment since the age of twenty and had virtually had sole charge of two children for the last five years. Now she just needed to act like one and not like some young chit of a girl who was easily flustered.

She stood beside the Earl while the children played, like proud parents watching their offspring perform. Anna placed her hand beneath her throat, which was suddenly constricted. Where on earth had that foolish thought come from? She pushed it away as quickly as it had emerged. What on earth was wrong with her? The anxiety of all that had happened must be taking its toll and she was now becoming somewhat delusional.

As soon as the tune ended, Anna stepped forward before they could start another one. 'I think it's time we moved on,' she said, stilling Thomas's hands on the keys. 'The Earl must have so many other things that need his attention.'

Both children pouted slightly but jumped down from the bench and Thomas closed the piano lid.

'Indeed, I have,' the Earl said. 'Unfortunately, I have to dress for tonight's ball.'

'And we're allowed to watch, aren't we?' Thomas asked, while Emily looked up at him, her eyes wide and expectant.

'Of course, you can.'

'I wish we could go,' Thomas said. 'We're really good dancers, aren't we, Em?'

Emily nodded, and looked back up at the Earl, her face a picture of appeal.

'There will be plenty of time for that when you're older,' the Earl said to them. 'And, like me, you'll quickly come to dread them. They're just a chance for matchmaking mothers to try and get their unmarried children hitched and up the aisle as quickly as possible.'

'Then Anna should go to the ball,' Thomas said, turning to look up at her. 'She's not married. Maybe your mother could find her a husband.'

'Shh!' Anna said with more force than she'd intended. 'Stop talking such nonsense.'

Surprise crossed Thomas's face and he obviously had no idea what he had said wrong.

'The ball is not for the likes of me,' she said in a softer voice.

'Oh,' Thomas said, still looking confused, not least of all, Anna suspected, because he had never seen his governess blush before.

The Earl too was looking at her with curiosity, causing the heat on her cheeks to intensify. 'I'll introduce you to the housekeeper and she can show you to your rooms,' he said, and Anna was grateful that there would be no more talk of balls, husbands or matchmaking.

He passed them over to the smiling housekeeper, who kept saying how pleased she was there would be children in the house, particularly over Christmas. Anna let them chatter on as the housekeeper led them up the stairs to their rooms and took the opportunity to try and compose herself and act more like the serious, unflappable governess she usually was.

The housekeeper opened a bedroom door and Anna was aghast at the room that had been set aside for the children.

It was enormous, bigger than the living room had been in the children's parents' home.

She entered and looked around. The walls were painted a delicate shade of dove blue, and the windows were draped with damask in the same shade. Furnished with a bed that would have filled the children's bedroom in their old home, along with armchairs, a desk, dressing table and washstand, the room seemed far too sumptuous for the children. Large bay windows overlooked the garden and, despite the dull day, soft light filled the room.

'Is this all for us?' Emily asked, looking from the housekeeper to Anna.

'No, this is Master Thomas's room,' the housekeeper replied. 'Your room is next door.' The housekeeper opened an adjoining door to an equally large and opulent room. It was furnished in the same manner, the only difference being that it was painted in soft lemon.

'And Miss Wainwright's room is across the hallway.'

All three of them stared at each other, and Anna was sure her expression was as dumbfounded as the children's. This was so much more than she had expected. Anna had assumed that she would be in the servants' quarters and that the children would have small rooms, perhaps close to the nursery. Even if the children had been taken on by the Earl under sufferance at least she would no longer have to worry about their financial security.

All she had to worry about now was herself and the absurd effect the Earl was having on her. She would have to remember at all times that the children were now part of the family and she was merely their governess. No more blushing. No more getting flustered. The Earl was her employer and at all times she would have to think and act appropriately.

Chapter Three

The ballroom looked magnificent, like a fairy-tale setting, and the children's excitement was palpable. Standing on the balcony, their hands clutching the wrought-iron banisters, they had a perfect view of all that was going on below and stared down with rapt enthusiasm.

As promised, the children had helped the servants light the candles on the Christmas tree, and it sparkled at the end of the large room, creating a festive atmosphere and filling the room with its fresh, pine scent. A large crystal chandelier suspended from the ornate ceiling sent light dancing around the room, providing an enchanting effect. Fires flickered in the many fireplaces, making the room as warm as a summer's day, which was just as well, as many of the women were wearing gowns that left their shoulders and arms bare.

It had been many years since Anna had given any thought to her own appearance but seeing the fashionable women in their lacy gowns of every shade made her painfully aware of how frumpy she had become. The dress she was presently wearing had once been a pretty shade of blue, but repeated washing had reduced it to a dull grey.

The children laughed at some private joke, and Anna admonished herself for being so frivolous. Emily and Thomas were enjoying themselves, that was all that mattered. Fortunately, she had no need to worry about them making too much noise. Their excited talking and laughter would not be heard by anyone below, drowned out by the sound of the band playing a jaunty tune and the chatter of the guests.

She turned from the children, who were now swaying to the music, and her eyes once again strayed to the Earl of Summerhill. He looked so handsome, dressed in a formal swallow-tailed evening jacket, white waistcoat, shirt and evening tie. And Anna was certainly not the only one to have noticed how well he wore his evening clothes. Every young woman present seemed to be trying to attract his attention, and many had succeeded. The Earl had not sat out a single dance, whirling one pretty young thing after another around the dance floor.

But that was as it should be, Anna reminded herself once again as he took the arm of yet another attractive woman and escorted her onto the floor. He was an eligible man, an earl no less. Of course he would be in great demand. And as for that uncomfortable gnawing sensation in her stomach, that meant nothing. Only a fool would be jealous over a man she couldn't have, and as she was no fool it couldn't possibly be jealousy. It had to be nerves, nothing more.

The band halted and the guests started to depart to the adjoining room where supper was to be served. Anna looked at the two children, who were now quiet and quite obviously fighting to keep their eyes open. The day had been a long, exciting one for them, and she was sure they were going to sleep well tonight.

She placed her hands gently on their heads. 'Come on, time for bed.'

She had expected objections, but they both looked up at her with sleepy eyes, nodded and without complaint followed her to their new rooms. Their only demand was that she leave the adjoining door between their rooms open.

'All right, but go straight to sleep, no chattering.'

They nodded again, and she was sure that tiredness, if nothing else, would make them do as she asked.

Almost before their heads were on the pillows the children fell asleep. Anna knew she too should retire for the night as it had been a long, exhausting day, but her body was too agitated after all that had happened.

The Earl had said she was welcome to help herself to any book from the library that she wanted. Now seemed like the perfect time to take him up on that offer. Hopefully, the distraction of a good book would drive out all other thoughts and help lull her off to sleep.

The tedium. Oh, Lord, the tedium. Rufus was unsure if he could stand another second of this extreme boredom. It was even worse than he had expected. He forced himself to continue smiling as the debutante beside him regaled him with tales of her coming out.

'And the Court ball was just marvellous,' she burbled. 'Queen Victoria's daughter-in-law Princess Alexandra paid me so much attention and actually told me how elegant I looked.'

Rufus continued smiling, his jaw starting to ache as he stifled another yawn. How many more of these mindless conversations would he be expected to suffer through before the night was over?

And why were all these debutantes almost exact replicas of each other, all talking, thinking and behaving in exactly the same manner? Rufus didn't know and didn't want to know.

And as for his mother's matchmaking, and the matchmaking of every mother in attendance, he was sure he would scream if the attributes of another young woman were listed for him in agonising detail. As if he cared about their marvellous watercolours, their exquisite embroidery and how well they managed the servants. These might be the qualities a man looked for in a wife, but as he was not presently looking for a wife, he cared not a fig if their singing voices were much admired or how many languages they could speak.

Eventually he would have to marry and provide the requisite heir, but he was determined to put off that catastrophe for as long as was humanly possible. His parents had married young and had suffered together for many years until his father's untimely death two years ago. At twenty-eight, Rufus calculated he had at least twenty years left in him to sow as many wild oats as he possibly could, before succumbing to his inevitable and painful duty.

Unfortunately, this plan was something his mother could never understand. She clung relentlessly to the absurd notion that all he had to do was meet the right woman and seemed to think that their annual Christmas ball was the perfect place to find such a creature.

Once again, he flicked a quick look up at the balcony. Miss Wainwright and the children were no longer present. Lucky Miss Wainwright, able to escape this tedium.

Now that supper was over, the dancing was about to begin again, but for the sake of his sanity he needed a brief respite. Like Miss Wainwright, he also had to escape.

Excusing himself from the debutante and ignoring his mother's look of disapproval, he beat a hasty retreat to the nearest door and slipped out. Free at last, he strolled off down the hallway, almost tempted to whistle as he headed towards the library. He had hidden out there in the past, and knew it was the last place his mother would think to look for him.

Entering the library, he paused. He was not the only one seeking refuge in the book-lined sanctuary. Miss Wainwright was curled up in a leather chair, her feet tucked up underneath her, obviously absorbed by the book she was holding in her lap. She raised her head. Her gaze met his. He was suddenly held captive, unable to move, unable to think.

She quickly uncurled herself and stood up, the book dropping from her hand. 'I'm so sorry…'

'I'm sorry to disturb you,' he said at the same time, and reached down to retrieve the fallen book. 'I didn't mean to intrude.'

'You're not intruding.' She shrugged one slim shoulder and shook her head. 'This is your library after all. I just wanted to read for a while before I went to bed. I hope you don't mind.'

'Not at all. And it's not really my library. I only come in here when I'm looking for somewhere to hide. It's my mother's library.' He lifted the book and looked at the spine. '*A Christmas Carol*. How appropriate for the time of year. Charles Dickens is one of my mother's favourite authors.

She's just purchased *Great Expectations* and is planning on burying herself in it after Christmas.' He handed her the book. 'Good, is it?'

She smiled at him and that strange feeling washed through him again. It was such a pleasure to see her smile. He could happily spend all night standing there like an idiot, basking in its glow.

'It's very good.' Her smile faded and that serious look returned. 'I hope your mother won't mind me borrowing it.'

'Mind? No, of course she won't. But if you don't want to spend your time in endless discussions about what you've read, I'd keep it a secret if I was you.'

She shook her head and that enchanting smile returned, causing him to smile back at her like some sort of demented clown.

'Not at all. I'd love to talk to her about this book and all the other books she's read. As much as I love caring for the children, I don't get to talk to adults very often.' She bit the edge of her top lip as if she had revealed too much.

'It must have been hard for you, being left to care for the children after their parents died.'

'No, no, not at all. I love the children,' she said in a rush.

'But they're not your children.'

'No.' She shook her head slowly, frowning. 'But sometimes I tend to forget that. And as they've known me since they were small children and I've been the person who has mostly cared for them for the last five years they tend to think of me as almost like their mother.' The furrow in her brow deepened, and she looked up at him. 'Although I do realise I'm just their governess.'

'I believe you've been more than just a governess to the children.' He signalled for her to sit, then sat down himself in the other leather chair. 'Is that why you allow them to call you Anna instead of Miss Wainwright?'

Anna. What a lovely name. He wanted to repeat that name again and again. It was such a pleasant sound.

'Yes. I made that decision after their parents died.' She

bit her lip again. 'At that stage the only relative they had was an aged aunt who had no real interest in them. We didn't know they had distant cousins. So I wanted the children to see me as family, then they would know that I would never leave them.'

Rufus nodded. 'I'll do the same then. I'll tell them they can call me Rufus. Now that we're all family.'

Her eyes grew wide and then he got his reward in the form of another small smile. 'Thank you,' she said quietly.

He waved his hand as if it was nothing, which it was. It was hardly a hardship for him to give the children a home and let them know they were family.

'So you've had a time when you have had to manage completely on your own?' he asked.

She nodded. 'The lawyer who was the executor of their parents' will managed the finances, but we didn't hear from him until he informed us there was no money left and the home would have to be sold.' She drew in a deep breath. 'That was why I asked him to make enquiries to see if there were any other family members. I was so pleased when he told us the children had distant relatives who were willing to help.'

Rufus moved in his chair, remembering his reluctance in the lawyer's office, when he had been more focused on the coming night's entertainment than he had been on the plight of those poor children.

'Least I can do,' he said, biting down his embarrassment. 'But you've had to give up so much, your own life, your own future, to care for them.'

'It's no sacrifice. As I said, I love the children. They're my whole life now.'

It was obvious she loved the children, but she must want more from her life. She was a beautiful young woman. Many men would want her to be their wife and surely that was what she wanted as well. But he could not say that. It would not be an appropriate thing to say to someone in his employment.

'What made you become a governess?' he asked instead.

She shrugged slightly. 'Sometimes you have to do what you need to in order to survive. My parents unfortunately passed away when I was nineteen. They didn't make a will, so all their property went to my cousin and I had to go out to work.' She sent him a tentative smile. 'But I was lucky. The twins' parents were very nice people and I instantly fell in love with Emily and Thomas, so I enjoyed working for them.'

'Well, perhaps now that the children are settled you can now have a life of your own.'

'I don't want to leave the children.' She stood up. Her face alarmed. 'I thank you for all you've done but please…'

He stood and waved his hand in the direction of her chair, urging her to sit down again, and smiled to indicate she should not concern herself. 'I have no intention of parting you from the children. I can see how much you love them and how much they love you. And, after all, even though I'm now their guardian, I know nothing of children. I need your help so, please, do not upset yourself.'

She slowly sat down again. 'I'm sorry. It's been a stressful time over the last few weeks, not knowing what the children's future held and how we were going to survive. I'm sorry for reacting in that manner.'

'You have nothing to apologise for. I was merely saying that now that you are free from financial worry and know that the children and their futures are safe, you can start to have a life of your own.'

She nodded slightly and looked at him as if unsure what he was talking about.

'There are often dances in the village hall,' he said. 'And other social events, such as fairs and fetes and so on, which everyone in the village attends.'

She stared at him, her dark brows drawn together. 'Um… well, yes, I suppose so. It has been a long time since I've spent much time with other adults my own age and a long time since I've attended any social events.' She looked at her skirt. Her frown deepened as she brushed down the folds.

Rufus wanted to tell her she had no need to worry about

her clothing. Even in her faded dress she looked more elegant than any of the young women who were attending tonight's ball. She would look beautiful no matter what she
was wearing. And even more beautiful wearing nothing at
all, he suspected. He coughed to drive that inappropriate
thought away and looked out the window into the darkness.

You are not your father.

He coughed to try and clear his mind of what Miss Wainwright might look like naked, moved uncomfortably on his
chair and tried to think of something else, anything else.

'So, I take it your cousin made no provision for you when
he inherited your parents' property?' he asked, moving the
conversation onto something that would drive his thoughts
away from Miss Wainwright's appearance.

She shook her head slightly, her mouth pursing. 'He found
me work with Emily and Thomas's parents. I believe he felt
in doing so he had done his duty towards me.'

Generous of the cad, Rufus internally jeered.

'And was he not prepared to help after Emily and Thomas's parents passed?'

She looked down at her hands, clasped in her lap. 'He said
they were not his responsibility.' She drew in a deep breath
and looked up at him. 'He did offer to help me find another
position, but I couldn't leave the children with just an aged
aunt. Without me I didn't know what would have become of
them, and of course they feel like family now.' She lowered
her head again. 'Although of course I'm not really family, I
know that. I'm not much more than a servant, really.'

Was she reminding him of that fact or herself? Whatever her reasons, she had been forced to endure more than
any young woman should. He would do whatever it took to
lighten her load.

'But the children see you as family and as long as you
remain in this house no one will forget that,' he said quietly. 'The children need you, and we need you to care for
the children.'

She smiled at him, that warm smile that never failed to

touch his heart. Not only was she a beautiful woman, she was also strong, clever and resourceful, and unlike any woman he had ever met. There was no denying that he was attracted to the alluring governess. Despite his constant reminders that he was not like his father, it was obvious he was falling under Miss Wainwright's spell.

So there was only one thing he could do. And he needed to do it immediately before he changed his mind.

Chapter Four

The Earl rose from his chair and looked towards the open door. 'I believe my mother will by now be listing me as a missing person, so I should return to the ball before she starts organising a search party.'

Anna began to rise from her chair but he signalled for her to remain seated. For a few moments more he paused, standing in the middle of the room looking down at her, then with a quick nod he turned abruptly and left the room.

She waited till he had gone then sighed lightly. It had been enjoyable talking to the Earl. Yes, now she came to think of it, just how long had it been since she'd had a conversation with an adult? She shook her head, unable to recall. And how long since she had spoken to a man, apart from the lawyer and various shopkeepers? That, she most certainly could not remember. No wonder her heart did that strange fluttery thing every time he looked at her. The Earl would be having no such silly reactions. Unlike her, he had an abundance of adult company in the form of those cultured young ladies who were attending the ball. It was nice of him to talk to her, but he must think her extremely dowdy and somewhat dull company.

But it was heartening to hear that her position was safe. Yes, this was all working out better than she had expected.

She snuggled up into her chair and looked down at the book in her hand but she no longer felt like reading. Finally, her agitated mind had settled down and she was sure she would be able to get a good night's sleep.

She placed the book back on the shelf. The Earl really had been so gracious to her. If he wasn't so disturbingly handsome, she might even be at ease in his company. Not that his attractive appearance should matter one iota. They were from different classes. He would not be giving her a second thought and she should be doing the same. She should just be grateful that he was a good employer, and not even notice his manly physique, those captivating blue eyes or those full lips and how they looked when they curled into an easy smile.

Suppressing a yawn, she left the library and walked down the hallway. It was definitely time she was in bed. Turning the corner towards the entrance hall, she halted.

Guests were starting to leave. Would it be ill mannered of her to walk past them? She suspected many of the guests would consider such behaviour presumptuous.

She cast a look over her shoulder. When touring the house, the servants' stairway had been pointed out to her, but the house was large and she had no idea how to get to it from the entrance hall. To find her way to her bedroom she needed to take the main stairs, but that was not possible when there were guests milling about. She ducked behind a pillar, out of sight. She would wait until they left, then quickly and quietly race up the stairs before any more appeared.

The guests left. She looked around, then darted out from behind the pillar. The ballroom door opened, releasing the sound of music and chatter. She jumped back. Drat it. She had waited too long to make her escape. The footman held back the door. An older couple and a young woman emerged, followed by the Earl.

'I do believe that was the best ball I have attended this Season,' the pretty young woman said when they reached the entrance hall and a servant helped her into her coat.

'Indeed,' the older man said, wrapping himself in a thick scarf. 'I always enjoy your balls, Deerwater. Love what you do with that tree thing.'

The Earl nodded as he handed the young woman a fur stole.

Anna should not be spying. She looked behind her to see if a discreet exit was possible. There was no way out. If she moved out from behind the column to either go up the stairs or retreat down the hallway she would be seen and it would be obvious she had been hiding.

'It wasn't the Christmas tree or the decorations that made the ball so marvellous,' the young woman said, and placed her hand on the Earl's arm. 'It was the dancing. Oh, Rufus, it's been such a perfect night. You really are a superb dancer. Although you danced with me so many times I'm sure people will be talking.' She touched her hand to her lips to cover her giggle.

'My pleasure, Lady Cecily,' he said with a small bow.

'Here's our carriage,' the older man said, taking his wife's arm and leading her out the door. 'Goodnight, Deerwater.'

'Goodnight, Lord and Lady Richely, Lady Cecily,' he said with another bow.

Lady Cecily remained standing in the doorway after her parents had departed. She whispered something to the Earl that Anna did not catch. They both looked up. Anna followed his gaze and saw the mistletoe suspended from the ceiling.

Anna's hand shot to her mouth as the Earl leant down and lightly kissed Lady Cecily's waiting lips. Her stomach clenched as Lady Cecily wrapped her arms around his shoulders and melded herself into his body. The kiss continued. This was no light goodnight peck on the cheek. Every inch of their bodies were touching and there seemed to be no indication that this kiss was to end any time soon.

Anna should not be watching. This was a private moment between a man and a woman, her employer and the woman he was presumably courting. She had to leave. And not least because of the effect that seeing a woman in the Earl's arms was having on her. Her heart was beating so hard she could feel it pounding against her chest, her cheeks were on fire and her stomach was a mass of twisted knots.

She edged herself out from behind the pillar. If she moved quickly and quietly, she might be able to get past them before they noticed her presence. After all, they were most certainly otherwise occupied.

The Earl pulled back from Lady Cecily, then looked over

her head, straight at the watching Anna. Her shame and mortification was now complete. She froze in the middle of the hallway, wanting to run but unable to move.

What must he be thinking of her? Whatever it was, it would not be good. After all the kind words he had said after his reassurance that her position in the household was safe, she had repaid him by spying on him during such an intimate moment.

She bobbed a quick curtsy and rushed past him, moving quickly towards the stairs.

The young lady spotted her and gave a tinkling laugh. 'Oh, dear. I think our behaviour has shocked the servant,' she said, intensifying Anna's mortification.

Anna increased her pace, the laughter still ringing in her ears, determined not to hear the Earl's response. If he too laughed Anna was sure she would die of embarrassment. Once she turned the corner, out of sight of the embracing couple, she ran down the hallway to her room, collapsed on her bed and buried her head in her hands. This was a disaster. After what she had done, what she had seen, how on earth was she ever going to face the Earl again?

Anna woke the next morning determined to put on a brave face. She would simply forget the entire incident. While witnessing that kiss had been embarrassing and had left her confused, it did not really matter. The Earl was hardly likely to care that a governess had seen him kissing a young woman he was courting. And how Anna herself felt about it was neither here nor there. He was her employer, what he did or did not do with any young lady was no concern of hers.

If anything, seeing him kissing his sweetheart had reminded her not to get above her station. She was not part of the family, even if the Earl had said she would be treated as such.

It was indeed a timely and unfortunately necessary reminder not to see the Earl as an attractive man but to see him as her employer, something she had been in danger of forgetting. That lack of perspective had intensified after their conversation in the library. And the strange emotions that had been whirling inside her made that plain. It wasn't just embarrassment at being caught spying that had devastated her. It had been seeing him take another woman in his arms, kiss another woman. That had cut her to the quick and left her reeling. It was ludicrous. Such feelings for the Earl were ludicrous and needed to stop.

And that was what she would do. Today, she would act in a professional manner at all times and do her best to pretend that she had not witnessed that kiss. The Earl was unlikely to allude to it. After all, her presence was merely something that had amused Lady Cecily. She was sure, or at least hoped, he had given no further thought to the fact that a mere governess had witnessed him during an intimate, private moment.

She entered the children's rooms and found a maid helping them dress. 'Your breakfast and the children's will be served in the dining room at the Countess's insistence,' the maid said. 'She thought it best if you stay with the children until they're settled in. Once you've finished breakfast, you'll be expected in Lady Deerwater's drawing room, where Christmas presents will be exchanged.'

At the sound of the word 'presents', the children started jumping up and down, only to be stilled by the maid, who had no time in her busy day for such exuberance.

Presents.

Anna had not thought of that. She had assumed the children would spend Christmas Day with her, remaining out of sight of the family, and had never for a moment considered that they would receive presents.

If she had known, she would have organised for the children to make gifts for the Earl and his mother, but it was too late now. She hadn't even had time to organise anything to give the children herself. With everything that had happened in the last few weeks, with her constant worrying and toing and froing between the executor and the lawyer, she had all but forgotten that it was Christmas. Not that there had been much money to spend on presents, even on buying materials to make gifts.

Once dressed, she inspected the children to make sure they looked their best, then led them down to the breakfast room. Trying to get them to eat their breakfast became an all but insurmountable challenge. All they could think and talk about was the prospect of presents. Once they had eaten as much as she could get them to, they all but ran along the hallway towards the drawing room, and only halted and started walking when Anna reminded them that Father Christmas did not like children who ran away and disobeyed their governess.

They entered the Countess's drawing room, which was slightly smaller and cosier than the one they had been in the previous day and was also decorated with a Christmas tree. It was not as large as the one that filled the ballroom, but still substantial enough to dominate the room, and the children had already spotted the presents at the bottom of the tree. Fortunately, her warning about Father Christmas seemed to have worked because they seated themselves on a sofa near the crackling fire, although their eyes never left the foot of the tree.

The Earl approached the tree. 'It seems Father Christmas has left a rather large gift for someone.' He lifted the label and peered at it as if having difficulty reading the writing. 'It says, Em something, and is that a Thumb, or a Thorn or a—?'

'It's Emily and Thomas,' Thomas blurted out, rushing towards the tree. 'I'm sure it's Emily and Thomas. Father Christmas has probably just got very bad handwriting.'

'Do you think so?' the Earl said with a frown. 'Perhaps you should open it and see if it's a suitable gift for two children.'

Ripped paper immediately began flying into the air as the children unwrapped their present. When it was revealed they stared at it in awe. 'It's a sled,' Thomas said, staring up at Anna then back down at the present.

'And as soon as Miss Wainwright has unwrapped her present then we'll take it outside and test it out. Shall we?'

'Oh, yes,' the children chorused, looking at Anna in anticipation.

She looked at the Earl, wrestling with confused emotions. He appeared completely relaxed, as if being seen kissing a young woman had no effect whatsoever on his behaviour towards her. That was good, wasn't it? Yes, of course it was.

It seemed her position in the household was still secure, despite being exposed as a spy. And now the Earl and his mother had given her a present. She was both delighted and surprised by their kindness. He handed her the gift and she carefully opened it. It was a copy of Charles Dickens's *Great Expectations*.

'Oh, I can't accept this,' she said, looking at the Countess. 'His Lordship said you had recently purchased it for yourself.'

The Countess waved her hand in dismissal. 'It's all purely self-interest, my dear. Rufus also informed me that you are an avid reader. The book comes with the condition that you read it to me and save my poor aging eyes from that small print. And I also expect you to provide me with some intelligent opinions on what we've read.'

'I would love to, my lady.' It was perfect. It had been such a long time since she'd had someone to discuss books with and she'd missed it terribly.

She turned to the Earl. 'I'd ask the children to thank you for your generosity as well, but I don't want to disillusion them that the sled wasn't brought by Father Christmas, so I'll thank you on their behalf.'

'It was nothing,' he said with a dismissive wave of his hand. 'Having children in the house over Christmas took us somewhat by surprise and we had no presents for them, so I had the servants bring out my childhood sled for them to use.' He smiled, a devilish smile that set off a tingling deep within her. 'And I have to admit I'm looking forward to reliving my childhood and having a go on it myself.'

'Can we take the sled out now?' Thomas interrupted, barely concealing his impatience.

'Indeed, we can,' the Earl said, picking up the sled. 'Miss Wainwright, will you join us? We'll need at least one responsible adult with us if we're to avoid getting into trouble, won't we, children?'

Emily and Thomas smiled at the Earl then looked expectantly at Anna. She nodded, which was all the encouragement they needed. They ran ahead of the Earl and headed towards the door.

Anna halted their progress at the entrance hall so she could get hats, coats and mittens on them, but it was a struggle to restrain them. The moment they were released they raced outside, followed by Anna and the Earl, who placed the two children on the sled and dragged it to a small hill behind the house. The children climbed off and raced to the top while Anna remained at the bottom and the Earl dragged up the sled.

Anna watched, still irrationally smarting from the *responsible adult* comment. Was that how he saw her? Was that how the children saw her? While they were having fun with the Earl, she was the serious one who had to make sure they were warmly dressed and did not hurt themselves. She was not the sort of woman he would laugh with in a carefree manner while he kissed her under the mistletoe, she was the sensible, serious governess.

But perhaps it was an apt description. For the last five years she had indeed been sensible and responsible and now hardly knew any other way of behaving. The moment her parents had died, she had been forced to grow up.

Her father had been a wealthy merchant and she had expected to continue living a leisurely life of reading, playing the piano and attending balls and other social events. The balls she had attended had never been as grand as the one she had witnessed last night, as they had been public rather than private affairs, but they had been fun nonetheless.

That had all ended when her parents had died suddenly in

a carriage accident and she had discovered they had made no provision for her, presumably expecting to live long enough to see her happily married. Instead of living the life of a merchant's daughter she'd had to take a job in order to survive. When the children's parents had also passed away, she'd had to effectively assume the mantle of being both their parent and their governess. There had been no room for frivolity. She knew that made her serious, and that was not something that was seen as desirable in a young woman, who was expected to be light, cheerful and full of laughter.

She sighed lightly. The debutante who had kissed the Earl could giggle and flirt, but that was not for her. Her joy was to be found in the children, not in pretty dresses, balls and flirting with eligible young men.

The Earl reached the top of the hill. Thomas jumped on board and took hold of the reins, but Emily stood beside it, looking from the sled to the slope ahead of her, then back at the sled. Anna started to move up the hill so she could reassure the little girl, but before she had taken a few steps the Earl lifted Emily up, climbed onto the sled behind Thomas and placed her between them.

With a push of his booted foot, the Earl set the sled moving down the hill. Gathering pace, it flew down the slope, Thomas's smile growing so wide it seemed to take over his entire face. After a few seconds Emily's face went from concerned to smiling. When they arrived safely at the foot of the hill, she jumped off the sled, took hold of the reins and along with Thomas they pulled it back up the hill.

'Come on, Anna, you have to join us,' Thomas called to them over his shoulder.

The Earl smiled at her. 'Well, it seems you have your orders.'

'Will it be big enough for all of us?' Anna asked.

'We'll make room,' he said, signalling with his hand for her to follow. 'Come on.'

She climbed up to the top of the hill where an impatient Emily and Thomas were waiting.

'There's room on it for all four,' the Earl said. 'If we all shuffle forward.'

Anna wasn't entirely sure, but she didn't want to just be the *responsible adult,* she wanted both the children and the Earl to see that she too was capable of having fun.

The children shuffled up to the front of the sled. Anna climbed on behind Emily and moved as far forward as she could to leave as much room as possible for the Earl. He climbed onto the sled, and Anna realised she was right. There wasn't enough room. She moved a bit closer to Emily, but it still meant the Earl was so close that his legs were wrapped around her thighs, his chest was firmly against her back, and she could feel his warm breath against her cheek.

With his body so close Anna was having trouble breathing, which was probably all for the best because each time she did breathe in she could not ignore the spiciness of his shaving soap or his warm, underlying masculine scent.

He reached out and took hold of the reins, his arms encompassing all three of them. Then pushed his boot into the ground and they were off. Like the children, Anna found it impossible not to smile as they slid down the hill, although with so many people aboard it wasn't quite such an elegant descent. They twisted and turned, the sled flinging them from side to side, until they spun to a halt at the bottom, the sled overturning with their weight, and tossing them all out into a pile of entwined legs and arms.

Still laughing, the four disentangled themselves and Anna could see the children were covered in snow. It was in their hair, down their clothes and even in their mouths. Not that they were caring one little bit and instead of brushing it off they instantly grabbed the reins and began running back up the hill.

The Earl was still laughing as he brushed some snow off her hair.

'That was such fun,' Anna said.

She turned and watched the children. The moment they got to the top of the hill they jumped on, and this time Emily was in front, holding the reins and looking completely fearless. There was no denying the Earl was a good influence on them. It was a shame that he would most probably be returning to London after Christmas. The children would miss him.

She would miss him.

Too impatient to wait for the adults, the children pushed themselves off and raced down the hill. When they reached the bottom, they deliberately leaned over to one side so once again they would be tipped out onto the snow. Then, laughing, they picked up balls of snow and began hurling them at each other.

'Let's take cover,' the Earl said, taking Anna's hand and pulling her up the hill, along with the sled. 'The children can't have all the fun,' he said. 'Now's our chance while they're distracted. Ladies first.'

He made a low bow and gestured towards the sled as if it were a stylish carriage.

Anna sat at the front and tucked in her skirts as he sat behind her. Once again, his legs wrapped around her. Once again, his chest was pressed up against her back. Once again, she was wrapped in the warmth of his body, his masculine scent, his strength. He reached out and took the reins, his arms surrounding her. Anna closed her eyes.

This felt good. Very good. Too good.

Her eyes popped open when she realised they were sliding down the hill. She had little time to think about how it felt to be held by him. Little time to contemplate how protected she felt, how warm. As if, for the first time in longer than she could remember, it was she who was being cared for, rather than doing the caring.

Neither was there enough time to consider the way her body was reacting to being in such close proximity to this sublimely attractive man. Having him so close had set off a strange throbbing deep inside her, something that was exciting and disturbing in equal measure.

Before she could fully consider what was happening to her, they were at the bottom, sliding safely to a halt, and he was standing up, holding out his hand to help her from the sled.

She placed her hand in his and he pulled her to her feet. Smiling, she looked up into his eyes and her smile faded. He was staring down at her, those blue eyes intense. Her breath caught in her throat. She should look away, but that was not what she wanted. She wanted to gaze into those entrancing eyes, to lose herself in them, to forget everything, to stop being the responsible adult.

As if her mind and body were at war, she fought to ignore the overwhelming sensation that was possessing her, fought to remind herself that he was her employer, he was courting another woman. But for once she did not want to be sensible. What she wanted was to stay staring into his eyes for the rest of her life, to lose herself in them, to once again feel his strong arms around her, to feel his muscular legs against her thighs. He pushed back a lock of hair that had been dislodged in their tumbles, then his hand gently stroked down her cheek, causing a small sigh that was almost a moan to escape from her lips.

A snowball hit the Earl full in the face, breaking the spell between them and causing him to laugh out loud. They looked around and saw Emily and Thomas laughing and clapping their hands in excitement.

'We can't let them get away with that,' the Earl said, reaching down, grabbing some snow and hurtling it in the children's direction. Squealing with mischievous pleasure, they ran off, pursued by the Earl and a barrage of snowballs.

Watching their antics, Anna did not notice the footman, who had seemed to appear from nowhere, until he coughed. 'Her Ladyship would like you to return to the house as the guests are due to arrive.'

Guests?

Anna had foolishly imagined a family Christmas dinner, with her, the Earl, his mother and the children all seated round the table, enjoying a feast. Of course it would not be like that. She would be taking dinner in the servants' hall, while the family entertained upstairs.

'Emily, Thomas, it's time we went inside.' Once again, she was back to being the responsible, sensible adult.

The laughing Earl turned to face them, saw the liveried footman, gathered up the children and led them back to her.

'Her Ladyship requests that you return to the house as the guests are due to arrive,' the footman said to the Earl.

'Yes, of course. Thank you, Charles.' The footman departed and the children grabbed the sled and turned towards the hill.

'No, children, we have to go in now,' Anna called.

In unison they groaned in protest.

'Don't worry,' the Earl said. 'There will be plenty of time for more snow fights and sled riding, and Cook has made her famous plum pudding, I'm sure you won't want to miss out on that.'

'Plum pudding,' the children said as one, then instantly ran back down the hill. The Earl took the reins of the sled, and the four headed towards the house, the children arguing good-naturedly about who had won the snowball fight and who was the best sled driver.

They approached the house, where guests were alighting from a carriage. Anna's buoyant spirits instantly deflated as she watched a young woman take the footman's hand and elegantly walk down the small steps. Dressed in a winter coat, a white fur stole around her neck and carrying a white fur muff, it was the woman Rufus had kissed last night.

Chapter Five

Rufus would have appreciated some advance warning. His mother had said there would be guests for Christmas dinner, but he had assumed it would be some of her cronies, local widows she passed her days with. But, no, his mother wasn't going to let another opportunity to indulge in some concerted matchmaking pass her by.

He bowed to Lady Cecily and to Lord and Lady Richely, then turned to the children.

'May I introduce Master Thomas and Miss Emily Cooper?'

The children once again performed a well-practised bow and curtsy, which in Thomas's case was, as usual, somewhat flamboyant.

'Oh, whose children are these?' Lady Cecily asked.

'They're mine,' Rufus replied, his answer taking him a bit by surprise, but he supposed that was now the truth.

Lady Cecily's smile wavered.

'They're his wards,' Lord Richely said. 'Children of a distant cousin or something, Lady Deerwater informed me last night.'

Lady Cecily's smile returned. 'Oh, Rufus, you have such a good heart. It's just like all those women and children you support in the village. So generous.'

Miss Wainwright looked at him questioningly, but before he had a chance to explain she had turned from him and was gathering up the children. Not that he was required to explain himself. He had been tempted to do just that last night. To chase her up the stairs and explain away that kiss she had witnessed. Thank goodness he had not done so. Thank goodness he had convinced himself he did not care what a governess had seen or what she was thinking. And now was exactly the same. He should not be considering, for one second, explaining to her why he was supporting women and children in the village. But irrationally he did not want her to think ill of him.

He continued to watch her as she ushered the children up the steps.

His eyes strayed to her hips, swaying under her skirt, and he quickly looked away.

Lady Cecily slid her arm through his, and for once he was pleased, grateful for the diversion, and he escorted her up the stairs.

'So, do you still have that mistletoe, Lord Summerhill?' she asked in a coquettish voice.

'I believe it was taken down after the ball,' Rufus replied, hoping that was the case. And hoping, that if it wasn't so, that Miss Wainwright was now well out of sight of it.

'Oh, what a pity,' Lady Cecily said with a pout. 'But perhaps we really don't need mistletoe.'

'I suspect your parents would disagree with that, Lady Cecily.'

And so would I, Rufus wanted to add. Kissing a young lady like her would mean only one thing in the eyes of her parents, a quick dash up the aisle as fast as propriety allowed. It was undoubtedly what Lady Cecily also wanted. After all, she was a young unmarried woman. It was the only thing she was expected to want. And her parents would be encouraging it, reminding her that he had a sizeable estate and income. And it was definitely what his mother wanted. She wanted him married, settled down and raising an heir and plenty of spares.

But it most certainly was not what Rufus wanted. Marriage to anyone, not just Lady Cecily, was something he wanted to postpone for as long as possible.

They entered the house and to his chagrin he noticed the mistletoe still hanging above the front door. Lady Cecily had also noticed it, paused and smiled at him.

'I stand corrected,' he said as he leaned down to give her a quick peck on the lips, and before she could wrap her hands around him again he took a step backwards. The children stared at him, wide-eyed, while Miss Wainwright kept her gaze lowered, as if something on the floor had her complete attention.

I was just being polite, he wanted to state, loud and clear, so Miss Wainwright would be under no misapprehension as to his feelings for Lady Cecily, but of course he would do no such thing. Even thinking such a thing was absurd. He did not owe Miss Wainwright an explanation.

The waiting servants helped the Richelys remove their coats and they entered the drawing room. Miss Wainwright led the children upstairs so they could all change out of their damp clothes, and Rufus excused himself to do the same.

When he returned to the drawing room he was greeted by the children's excited voices, both talking animatedly to his smiling mother, regaling her with tales of their rides down the hill and their snowball fights.

'Isn't it time the children left?' Lady Cecily said, the moment the children paused for breath. 'Shouldn't their governess take them to the nursery or something?'

Irritation briefly flitted across Rufus's mother's face before she composed herself. 'It's Christmas Day, a family occasion, and they're family. And they'll be dining with us.' She smiled at Thomas and Emily. 'If it's good enough for Queen Victoria to dine on Christmas Day with her children and grandchildren then I'm sure it's good enough for us.'

'Delightful, I'm sure,' Lady Cecily said, although her voice held no hint of the delight she was claiming.

'As will Miss Wainwright,' his mother continued.

'A servant?' Lady Cecily looked at Miss Wainwright as if it were her fault, unable to hide her shock at the impropriety.

Rufus smiled in reassurance at Miss Wainwright, who was also looking uncomfortable. 'She's the only mother the children have known for the last five years so she too is part of the family,' he said to Lady Cecily, but intending it for Miss Wainwright.

'Oh, I see.' Lady Cecily's lips moved into a strained smile, and the strain was also starting to take its toll on Rufus. If only he could be back outside, playing in the snow with Miss Wainwright, like a couple of children. She had looked so beautiful, her cheeks red from the exertion and the cold, her dark eyes sparkling and her lips smiling. Instead, he'd be stuck inside, enduring another round of sustained matchmaking.

But at least the children should liven up the Christmas dinner. He looked over at his mother, who was pointing to the tree and explaining to the children where the various Christmas decorations had come from. She was so happy with the children, and it seemed she had quite taken to the governess as well. It was unfortunate Miss Wainwright was not of their class, or his mother would see her as a very good prospect for the future Countess of Summerhill.

Rufus coughed. How could such an unwanted thought enter his head? Was he going mad? He did not want anyone to be the future Countess of Summerhill, not for a long, long time. He looked over at Miss Wainwright.

When it came to the beautiful governess, he was indeed in danger of losing his mind. Since her arrival he been fighting hard to stop himself from becoming like his father, who hadn't let a woman's status or vulnerability stop him from having his way with her, and now he was having absurd thoughts about marriage. Even if they were only thoughts and no one knew what was going on in his fevered mind, this had to stop. Now.

The footman announced that dinner was served. Lady Cecily hooked her arm through his so he could escort her through to the dining room. He looked to see what Miss Wainwright was doing and saw she was organising Emily and Thomas to link their arms and join the parade from the drawing room to the dining room. She looked up and caught

his eye. She had been smiling at the children but when she
saw him looking at her, her face once again became serious.

Any sense of friendship they had shared when they had
been playing in the snow together had gone. He was now
back to being merely her employer. Just as it should be, he
tried to console himself.

Anna took her place at the end of the line as they walked
from the drawing room to the dining room. Should she have,
for a moment, forgotten her lowly status, tagging along at
the rear, and only present for the sake of the children, would
have reminded her.

The children pranced along the hallway, enjoying playing
at being a lady and gentleman, and Anna tried to put aside
her own petty concerns. The children were enjoying themselves. That was the only thing she needed to think about.
They were now part of the family. It was everything she
could have hoped for.

They entered the dining room and the children instantly
broke ranks and ran forward to look at the beautifully decorated table. Anna knew she should reprimand them, should
tell them to exercise more restraint, but as Lady Summerhill was smiling at them indulgently, Anna held back and let
them touch the decorations. And she had to admit the stern
look of disapproval she received from Lady Cecily made her
even less inclined to rebuke the children.

And the table did look sumptuous. The large centrepiece
of holly and ivy was surrounded by candles as red as the
holly berries. The glasses, plates and silverware were lined
up with military precision and the silver and cut-glass sparkled in the candlelight. Yet another tree adorned the dining
room. An entire forest must have been felled to decorate this
large home. Small candles twinkled among the branches and
the scent of pine again filled the air.

The Earl pulled out the chair for Lady Cecily, and with
much fluttering of eyelashes she sat down. Anna stifled her
indignation. She would not be jealous of Lady Cecily. Not

for her pretty blonde looks, not for her lacy pink gown, and most certainly not because she was quite obviously the Earl's intended. If he found happiness with another woman, then that was all for the good.

All her concerns were for the children, she told herself. She could only hope that if they did marry, Lady Cecily would be as welcoming as the Earl and his mother had been. At least at the moment the children had the formidable Countess on their side. It was obvious that Lady Cecily deferred to her, but would that continue when Lady Cecily was the Countess?

The children seated themselves at the table and were now on their best behaviour, seeing it as an honour to be dining with the adults. And it was a novelty for Anna as well. She thought again of how little time she'd spent in adult company over the last five years. Although it would have been nice if her lowly status hadn't been so obvious and she was not wearing her faded dress, which, if anyone bothered to look closely enough, they would see had been mended and re-mended countless times.

The first course of foie gras was served and Emily and Thomas looked at her, their brows furrowed as if they were unsure whether it actually was food, and whether they really were expected to eat it.

'The Earl said there was to be plum pudding,' Thomas whispered to his sister, in a voice that was not quiet enough to be missed by the guests.

Lady Cecily frowned at the children, then smiled when she realised that the Earl was laughing.

'You're right, Thomas, I did promise plum pudding,' he said from the head of the table. 'And I'm a man of my word. You don't have to eat the pâté if you don't want to, but the more of the roast turkey and vegetables you eat, then the more plum pudding you'll be allowed to have. Isn't that right, Miss Wainwright?'

Anna smiled politely at him, which drew a slight scowl from Lady Cecily. 'Indeed it is,' she said.

Thomas frowned and poked at his pâté. 'I'd better save my appetite for vegetables and turkey, then.'

Emily nodded and pushed her pate to one side.

Polite conversation resumed around the table, and Anna could hear Lady Cecily questioning the Earl about this estate, and his other homes around the country. Anna tried not to be judgmental, but it did seem as if the woman was taking an inventory of all that the Earl possessed. But perhaps that was what young women were expected to do. If Anna's parents hadn't died, she too would have been expected to join the ranks of women seeking suitable husbands. Then she too might have been just like Lady Cecily, trying to work out just how rich a man was so she could make the most advantageous marriage possible. Instead, circumstances had made her grateful that she merely had a roof over her and the children's heads and they had enough to eat.

The pâté was removed and the roast turkey was served. The Earl's bribe of plum pudding proved effective and both children consumed their entire meal. They even ate their Brussels sprouts, which surprised Anna. When their plates were clear they looked up at the Earl, their faces expectant.

'Well done, Emily and Thomas,' the Earl said, cutting through the conversation at his end of the table. 'You can have as much plum pudding as you want, but unfortunately you'll have to wait until the adults have finished this course. Although you can have a second helping of sprouts if you want while you're waiting.'

'No,' both children chorused loudly.

Anna coughed and sent the children a small frown.

'No, thank you. We have had sufficient,' Emily said politely.

'Well, then, everyone, less chatter, more eating,' the Earl said. 'There are some young children desperately in need of plum pudding.'

Lady Cecily pulled her face into a tight smile and Anna said a silent prayer that he did not marry that young woman.

Only because she cared about the children's future. For no other reason.

Finally, the plum pudding arrived, proudly held aloft by a footman, the brandy burning with a blue flame.

'I think you had better serve Thomas and Emily first,' the Earl told the footman. 'And, please, children, start without us. You've done the hard work with all those vegetables, now you deserve your reward.'

Emily and Thomas's eyes grew enormous as generous servings of plum pudding were placed in front of them and they were allowed to pour on as much custard as they chose. Then, taking the Earl at his word, they tucked in immediately.

Once the meal was over Anna once again took her place at the end of the line-up as they made their way to the drawing room for coffee and fruit mince pies. Anna and the adults turned down the pies, but she was not surprised to see that Emily and Thomas managed to find some room for extra treats.

'Anyone would think those children had been half-starved,' Lady Cecily said, laughing at her joke and looking at the Earl.

He merely gave a polite smile in reply, one that did not suggest any real amusement.

'You've always been one for taking in lame ducks,' she continued, and looked with mock sympathy at Anna. 'All those other families you support. All those cottages you've let out to those unfortunate women.'

Conversation died. The Earl, his mother and Lady and Lord Richely all moved uncomfortably in their seats and drank their coffee in silence.

Who were these unfortunate women that Lady Cecily kept mentioning? Anna couldn't help but wonder. Why was the Earl supporting them? And why did it cause such embarrassment? Anna was loth to think it, but the most likely explanation was they were women the Earl had got into trouble? He wouldn't be the first man to do such a thing. Although most men in the Earl's position did not support such women but left them and their unwanted offspring to fend for themselves.

It seemed there was a lot she did not know about the Earl. Had she been lured into thinking he was a good man simply because of the way he had welcomed the children into his home?

'I'm only doing what's right,' the Earl said in a low voice, the tone making it clear it was a subject he did not want to discuss.

Lady Cecily's smile quivered, then returned brighter than before. 'Of course you are,' she said, patting his arm. 'You're a good man. Perhaps too good sometimes.'

Anna knew she shouldn't be eavesdropping, but the children did not need her, they were perfectly happy cracking nuts for the duchess, and the conversation was intriguing.

'I'm not as good as you think I am,' he replied, and looked over at Anna. Her gaze quickly dropped to her lap, embarrassed that he had caught her listening in to a conversation that did not concern her. Whether the Earl was a good man or not, it was none of her business. As long as he was good to the children, that was all that mattered.

Chapter Six

Rufus flicked a quick glance at the clock, slowly ticking away on the mantelpiece. How much longer would Christmas Day last? It already seemed longer than days were supposed to be. And it had started off so enjoyably. Riding the sled with Miss Wainwright and the children had been a romp. In fact, spending any time with Miss Wainwright and the children was always enjoyable, much more so than he had expected when he had reluctantly taken on the responsibility of being Thomas and Emily's guardian. Perhaps it was because he was nothing but a big kid himself.

Or perhaps it was because when he had put up objections in the lawyer's office, he had not known that the children would come with the lovely Anna Wainwright.

He sent her a small, sympathetic smile. She too seemed to be enduring rather than enjoying this part of the Christmas celebration. The children were still having a good time, though, he was pleased to see, as was his mother. The children had really made Christmas special for her and it was almost difficult to imagine what life had been like before they had arrived. His mother also seemed to be fond of Miss Wainwright, which was really no surprise. Who would not be fond of such a clever, loving, beautiful young woman?

It was just a shame…

His thought was interrupted by Lady Cecily, who had been talking for some time but had now raised her voice to get his attention.

'I said we should have some music.' She patted his arm. 'I've just mastered Beethoven's piano concerto number five and I'm dying to play it for you.'

Rufus suppressed a moan. He was tempted to remind her

that it was Christmas Day, a time for fun and frivolity, not for showing off her dexterity on the piano. Although, in Rufus's world view, every day should be a day for fun and frivolity.

Lady Cecily rose from her chair, followed somewhat reluctantly by the rest of the company. Even Lady and Lord Richely seemed disinclined to move from the comfort of their chairs by the fire, but they pulled themselves to their feet and joined the parade from the drawing room into the music room, where the servants were busily lighting a fire and the candles.

'You'll have to turn the pages for me,' Lady Cecily said as she seated herself at the grand piano and opened the lid.

Everyone settled themselves on the seats lined up before the piano. Then the serious piano music filled the air. Lady Cecily was reputed to be an accomplished pianist and Rufus had to pity her that such an accomplishment was wasted on him. As a child, he tried to avoid music lessons as often as he could, preferring to be outdoors as much as possible. And now his tastes ran to music-hall tunes rather than classical music. If Lady Cecily hadn't nodded each time the page needed to be turned, he would have been hopelessly lost and would have revealed himself as the philistine he knew himself to happily be.

When she came to the end everyone clapped enthusiastically, particularly her proud parents.

Lady Cecily nodded her appreciation of their applause and began riffling through the sheet music, looking for something else to show off her talents.

Thomas stood up and rushed towards the piano. 'My turn,' he said, sitting next to Lady Cecily and shuffling along so she was forced to move down the piano bench.

Lady Cecily looked at Thomas, shock etched on her face, then disapprovingly at Miss Wainwright.

'No, Thomas, Lady Cecily hasn't finished yet,' Miss Wainwright said, rising from her chair. 'Come and sit back down with your sister.'

'Let the child play,' his mother said. 'It's Christmas after all, and Christmas is about children, isn't it?'

Thomas smiled at Lady Cecily. 'We can play a duet, if you like.'

Lady Cecily looked at him as if he had suggested they roll around in the mud together. 'No, I don't think so.' She stood up, her back ramrod straight, and retreated to a chair.

'Well, Rufus, do *you* want to play a duet with me?' Thomas asked. 'Come on, Emily, you can join in too. And you too, Anna. Everyone can join in.'

Rufus had to laugh at the young boy's enthusiasm.

'You let the child call you by your given name?' Lady Cecily said, staring at Thomas with distain.

'Yes, we are family after all,' Rufus replied.

She sent him a slightly disapproving look. 'And you let the child order you around?' She looked over at Miss Wainwright, as if expecting her to admonish young Thomas.

'It seems I do,' Rufus had to admit, still laughing.

Thomas found the book of Christmas songs and began playing 'Jingle Bells' and singing along, signalling for everyone to join in. The Countess instantly started singing, and was soon joined by Miss Wainwright and Emily, followed by Lord and Lady Richely, then reluctantly by a still affronted Lady Cecily.

Their singing was enthusiastic, although even to Rufus's untrained ear hardly melodious.

'More, more,' his mother and Lady Cecily's parents chorused when the song came to an end. Thomas instantly obliged and began playing 'The Twelve Days of Christmas'.

Rufus looked over at his singing mother. The children had definitely brought laughter and joy to the household. This had to be the best Christmas they had celebrated since he had been a child himself. He could see why his mother so wanted him to marry and have children. He had always assumed it was so he could produce the required heir, but perhaps she was thinking of the happiness that could be found with the right woman. As much as he enjoyed the way he lived, he could see why people were drawn to a family life.

He looked from Anna Wainwright to Lady Cecily then back again. Until Miss Wainwright and the children had arrived, he had never given serious consideration to such things as marriage, settling down, family. But now he could see the appeal. Although one thing he did know for certain, as acceptable as Lady Cecily was as a future countess, he would not be marrying her. He did not love her. And he very much doubted if she loved him. She loved his title, his estates and most certainly loved the lifestyle that being married to an earl would bring her. But as for him? He doubted Lady Cecily knew anything about him, and probably cared even less.

He looked back at Anna Wainwright. She was still singing and had her hand lightly on Emily's shoulder, who was leaning in towards her with such love and trust. Warmth flooded through him and he smiled with something that seemed suspiciously like contentment.

'Oh, it's snowing again!' Lord Richely exclaimed when the song came to an end.

They all looked out of the window, and saw white flakes floating to the ground against the background of the now dark exterior.

'I believe we should make haste if we are to get home safely tonight,' Lord Richely said, standing. 'Come on, my dear,' he said to his wife. 'Come on, Cecily.'

He looked over at the footman standing to attention by the door. 'And you, my man, ask the coachman to bring the carriage around to the front door and the maid to bring us our coats.'

Miss Wainwright gathered up the children. 'After all this excitement and your late night last night, you two could do with an early night, so say goodnight, Emily, Thomas.'

The two children emitted small groans, but then said goodnight to the assembled company.

'Thank you, young man,' Lord Richely said, ruffling

Thomas's hair. 'Nothing like a good sing-along on Christmas Day. Capital.'

Holding the children by the hand, Miss Wainwright led them out of the room, distracting Rufus from the goodbyes and good wishes that were taking place in the music room.

He accompanied the Richelys out into the entrance hall, where the maid was waiting with their coats and the women's fur stoles.

'Please thank the Countess again for inviting us, Deerwater. It's been a simply splendid day,' Lord Richely said as the women wrapped themselves in their layers. 'Lady Summerhill is right: children really do make Christmas.'

The carriage arrived and Lord Richely escorted his wife down the stairs. Lady Cecily remained standing in the entrance hall, smiling at Rufus, then looked up at the mistletoe and raised her eyebrows in question.

Feeling uncharacteristically uncomfortable, he gave Lady Cecily another quick peck on the lips.

'Oh, I suppose that will have to do for now,' she said with a little giggle. 'After all, my parents are waiting, but I'll be expecting a bit more than that next time we meet.' With a small, coquettish wave she departed through the door and was escorted down the steps by the waiting coachman.

The carriage drove off. Rufus released a small sigh of relief, then, humming 'The Twelve Days of Christmas', he turned and saw Miss Wainwright watching him from the bottom of the stairs.

'It's tradition,' he blurted out.

She nodded. 'I've just come down to say goodnight to you and the Countess and to thank you for such a pleasant day,' she said, her voice constricted.

'I see. Well, goodnight, Miss Wainwright.' He looked up and forced himself to keep his face straight. 'And if you haven't noticed, I'm still standing under the mistletoe.' He knew he shouldn't tease, but something was making him feel reckless. Perhaps he had been infected by an impish spirit of Christmas.

She didn't move from the bottom of the stairs.

'You wouldn't want to break an age-old Christmas tradition, would you?'

She bit her bottom lip, approached him slowly, cautiously, then rose up on her toes. As her lips lightly met his, the feathery touch almost drove him mad, causing him to want more, much more. But a light kiss was all he could expect from this tradition, any more would be greedy.

Her lips lingered, close to his. So close he could feel her soft breath against his mouth. He closed his eyes, loving having her so near to him, loving her fresh feminine scent, loving the warmth of her body.

Before he had registered what he was doing, his lips were on hers again. For a second her body went rigid. He paused. Half-formed questions rushed chaotically through his mind. Should he do this, was this acceptable? Her body relaxed. The unanswered questions evaporated. He slid his hand around her small waist, pulling her hard up against him. To his mounting pleasure she moulded herself into his body, her breasts against his chest. Then her hands encased his head. She was kissing him back. And this was no tentative kiss. This was a kiss that mirrored his desire for her, his desperate need and longing.

Deepening the kiss, he parted her lips, savouring her taste as he ran his tongue along her bottom lip. A soft moan escaped from her, driving his need for her to an all but insatiable level. No longer thinking, he entered her mouth, plunging, probing, wanting to possess her.

All restraint now gone, his passion for her unleashed, he kissed her harder, with more desperation, and she responded. Her body moved seductively against his, her breasts rubbing against his chest, her back arching, her buttocks moving sensuously. How could he possibly stop now, how could he resist this temptation? How could he not do what he fervently desired, to rip off her clothing, to take her, here and now, and make her his own?

No woman had ever affected him the way she did. This

was what he had wanted to do since the first moment he had seen her, had been dreaming of doing. Now she was in his arms the reality was even better than the fantasy. She was an intoxicating woman and he was drunk with his need for her.

He nuzzled the side of her neck. 'Anna, you're so beautiful,' he murmured. 'I want you so much. I must have you.'

She tilted her head back as he once again kissed the soft flesh of her neck. Her breath was coming in fast, short gasps, the mounds of her breasts rising and falling, inciting him further. If only he could rip off her protective clothing right now and expose her breasts to his gaze, his touch, his lips.

He looked down the hallway, no one was around. He looked back down at the woman in his arms. Her lips were parted, her eyes hooded. Her arousal was as obvious as his own. He could take her right now, right here, and she would put up no objections.

Just like his father would have done.

Those words crashed into Rufus's fevered mind. He jumped back as if hit by lightning. What was he doing? He did not need to search hard to find the answer to that question. He was seducing a vulnerable woman, just as his father had done countless times before him. He had despised his father for his behaviour, had hated the way the man had thought only of his own pleasure and nothing of the women whose lives he was ruining.

She looked up at him, her eyes questioning, but he had no answers for her, as he hardly knew himself what he was doing, what he was thinking. She stared at him for a moment longer, then abruptly turned and all but ran up the stairs.

'I am so sorry, Miss Wainwright,' he called to her retreating back, unsure if she had heard him.

Chapter Seven

'Do you think we can have plum pudding for breakfast?' Thomas asked Anna, while Emily stood beside him, nodding encouragement.

Anna suppressed a smile. His innocent question, asked the moment she entered the children's rooms first thing in the morning, took her out of herself. All night she had agonised over what had happened between her and the Earl. But now that the children were awake her focus had to be on them, not on herself, not on why the Earl had kissed her with such passion, and not on why she had reacted with such abandon.

'I don't think plum pudding is suitable for breakfast,' Anna said, adopting her most serious tone. 'But if you behave yourself, you might be able to have some later on in the day.'

'We always behave ourselves,' Thomas said, looking affronted.

'Well, show how much you can behave by getting washed and dressed as quickly as possible.'

'And then will Rufus take us out on the sled again?' Emily asked.

At the mention of his name Anna's stomach lurched and her heart seemed to miss a beat. She covered up her disconcerting reaction by smiling even more brightly at the children. 'I don't know, but don't pester the Earl. If he wants to take you out on the sled he will offer, but he's a very busy man.'

Emily's smile faded.

'But that doesn't mean we can't take the sled out,' Anna said, trying to cheer up the young girl.

'But it will be more fun with Rufus,' Thomas said. 'I'm so pleased we came here.'

The gripping sensation in Anna's stomach intensified.

'So am I,' she said, not sure if that was entirely accurate. 'Now, quickly, off you go, get washed and dressed.'

Anna returned to her room, pulled her skirt and blouse out of the wardrobe and began washing from the jug and bowl of warm water the maid had left for her. She had told the children they had to be on their best behaviour, and that was an order she was going to have to follow herself.

Nothing could endanger the children's future. After just two days they were settled in this house. The Countess and the Earl had welcomed them into their home and were treating the children as if they were family. She would do nothing to jeopardise that.

Nothing else. She had no idea what damage kissing the Earl might have done. She had no idea what he now thought of her. Had no idea why he had kissed her. If he had been any other man, she would have demanded answers to these questions, but this was about more than just her and the Earl. It was about the children's futures.

But she did so want to know what he felt, why he had kissed her that way. Did she mean something to him? The way he had looked at her, the kindness he had shown her, suggested he did. But did he treat all women like that? Or, worse, did he kiss any compliant woman the way he had kissed her last night? Was he the sort of man who seduced all and any woman he could?

All those *unfortunate women* who lived in the village.

Lady Cecily's words, which had whirled through her head all night, returned to her mind. She put down her washcloth and stared straight ahead. Was that what was about to happen to her? Was she about to be seduced by the Earl? Then when she fell pregnant he would graciously provide her with a home and she could join all the other women in the village who were raising the Earl's unwanted children.

Anna was determined that would not be her fate. There was no denying she was attracted to him, hopelessly, helplessly attracted. But she needed to keep that attraction firmly under control. She did not want to become one of the women in the village who people were embarrassed to talk about. It was therefore essential not to let him kiss her again, and to spurn his advances should he try.

And hopefully that would be the end of it. From what she had seen of him, it was unlikely that he would be a vindictive man and hold her rejection of him against her, or against the children.

She resumed washing, pulled her hair up into a bun and dressed in her faded skirt and blouse. Brushing down her skirt, she breathed slowly and deeply. Her best course of action was to pretend that the kiss had been nothing more than the two of them following tradition and kissing under the mistletoe. It had meant nothing. Not to her and not to the Earl.

When Anna entered the breakfast room with the children, Rufus said good morning, and tried as hard as he could to behave as if nothing untoward had happened last night. If he pretended that it had merely been a friendly peck under the mistletoe that meant nothing, maybe, just maybe, Miss Wainwright would forgive him for his impropriety, and ultimately they could forget that it had ever happened. Although he knew it would be a long time before he could forget the enticing touch and taste of her lips, or the feel of her soft, warm body pressed against his.

He coughed and shook out his napkin.

'So, children, are we ready for some more riding on the sled today?' he said.

The children both cheered and looked at Miss Wainwright.

'Say thank you to the Earl,' she said, then turned to his mother. 'My lady, would you like me to begin reading *Great Expectations* to you today?'

It seemed Miss Wainwright was trying to avoid spending time with him. He had to admit that was a very sensible course of action, even if it had caused a ridiculous sense of deflation inside him.

'Oh, Anna, that would be perfect,' his mother responded. 'But it will have to wait until this evening. Today I will be distributing the Christmas presents to the servants, then visiting the village to distribute food parcels and more presents.'

She turned to Emily and Thomas. 'Would you like it if Anna read to all of us once you have finished playing on the sled?'

'Yes, I love it when Anna reads to us,' little Emily said.

'And we can have plum pudding at the same time?' Thomas added.

The Countess laughed. 'Well, I don't know about that. But I'll ask Cook if there is any pudding left and perhaps we can have it with our luncheon.'

'Yes,' Thomas said, clapping his hands together and receiving an admonishing frown from Miss Wainwright.

Breakfast continued, with the children chatting happily and his mother being the one to respond. Miss Wainwright hardly ate a thing and kept her head lowered most of the time. Rufus doubted if he could feel more wretched. Yesterday, when they had played in the snow, she had given every appearance of enjoying herself and today she looked so uncomfortable. And it was all his fault. He wanted to tell her how sorry he was, tell her it would never happen again, that he didn't know what had come over him.

But looking at her he knew exactly what had come over him. The effect she had on him was unlike anything he had experienced before. It wasn't just that she was beautiful, lots of women were beautiful. It wasn't just that she was clever, lots of women were clever. It was also her gentle nature, her compassion, her caring for the children, and something intangible that he could not name. Something that made her special. Something that had captivated him, that had caused him to act in such a reckless manner.

She looked up at him and he realised he was staring. He quickly looked down at the eggs and bacon on his plate, drew in a deep breath and looked up again, trying to pretend that nothing had happened. But it had not been missed by his mother, who was looking at him, her head inclined, her eyebrows raised.

He just hoped his behaviour was not bringing back memories of how his father had behaved around the servants. He had already upset one woman at the table, he did not need to upset his mother as well.

With breakfast over, the children rushed out towards the front door, where the servants had anticipated their needs and had hats, gloves, coats and scarves ready and waiting.

Before Miss Wainwright and Rufus had even made it down the hallway, the children were dressed and hovering at the door. Once they were in their own outdoor clothing, Rufus picked up the sled and the children rushed down the steps, ran up the hill, and began entertaining themselves with a snow fight.

He walked along in silence with Miss Wainwright, wishing they had the diversion of the children, who would have broken this uneasy silence.

Rufus had to say something, now, or he might not get another opportunity. 'Miss Wainwright,' he started, unsure how he was to continue.

'Yes?' she said quietly.

'Miss Wainwright,' he repeated, starting to feel like an ass. 'I must apologise for my behaviour last night.'

She shook her head, but he had no way of knowing if that was a dismissal of his apology or whether she was merely uncomfortable talking about it. But he needed to let her know just how sorry he was.

'My behaviour was completely unacceptable. I had no right to kiss a woman in your position. It was something I have never done before and, I promise you, I will never do it again.'

She turned and looked up at him, her expression questioning. 'But what about…?'

Thomas and Emily came running down the slope, fast,

both emitting a loud 'Whee!' When they arrived in front of Rufus and Miss Wainwright, Thomas grabbed the reins out of his guardian's hands.

'Come on, we're wasting time. Let's get sledding.'

'I think you and Emily can do it on your own now,' Rufus said. 'Miss Wainwright and I will watch you.'

The children seemed to require no more encouragement and immediately rushed up the hill.

'What were you saying, Miss Wainwright?'

She looked down at the ground, her hands held demurely in front of her. 'I'm sorry, it's not my place to question you.'

'Under the circumstances I believe you have every right to ask me anything you want, and you deserve an explanation.' Although Rufus was not sure if he would be able to explain his behaviour because he wasn't entirely sure himself what had come over him.

She drew in a deep breath. 'Yesterday, Lady Cecily alluded to women and children in the village that you care for.' She bit her lip and looked up at him. 'Who are those women and children?'

Rufus exhaled loudly. 'Those women are a constant reminder to me why I should not kiss servants or any other vulnerable woman.'

'Oh, I see.' She looked back down at the ground.

'My father was a scoundrel,' he said, something that was if anything an understatement. 'He was notorious for seducing women.' Rufus was unsure whether this was a suitable conversation to be having with a young woman, but she had asked, and she did deserve to know the truth. 'And attractive servants and tenants' daughters were certainly not an exception.' He drew in another deep breath.

'Unfortunately, the inevitable outcome of this was that some fell pregnant. These are the women who live in cottages owned by the estate, where they are able to raise their children without having to face the terrible consequences that befall unmarried mothers.'

'I see,' she said quietly again, nodding slowly. 'It was

your father?' She bit her top lip, drawing Rufus's reluctant attention. He looked away. He should not be staring at her lips, should not be even thinking about her enticing red lips. Surely talking about his father should remind him of why this was necessary. And she had thought he was responsible for those unfortunate women... She thought he *was* just like his father.

'But at least he took some responsibility,' she said. 'Most men in his position just sack the unfortunate servant and turn their back on her, leaving her to fend for herself.'

'I'd like to be able to say my father did take some responsibility for his actions, but he didn't. It was my mother who made provision for them.'

'Your mother?' She looked up at him, her eyes wide with surprise. 'But wasn't she angry, hurt...?' She looked back down at the ground. 'Humiliated?'

Rufus shrugged. 'She probably was all those things the first time it happened, but I think she almost became immune to his behaviour. My parents' marriage was an arranged one that was advantageous to both families. They tended to live separate lives and once she had given birth to the heir, they had little to do with each other. So I don't believe it affected her as much as it might have, and she has always cared for others.'

Miss Wainwright nodded. 'Yes, she has been nothing but kind to me and the children, more than kind, she has treated me almost like a member of the family.' Her hand shot to her mouth. 'But I am aware of my position within the household.'

Rufus nodded. 'I know,' he said quietly, wishing it wasn't so. 'And that is why I am so sorry. I should not have kissed you and why it will never happen again.'

'Thank you,' she said quietly.

Rufus swallowed his disappointment. What had he expected? That she would insist that he kiss her again? That she would tell him to seduce her and to hell with the consequences? He had no right to be disappointed. This was the best possible outcome. They had discussed what had happened like sensible adults who knew how to control their feelings. They would now be able to put the entire incident in the past and carry on as if it had never happened. That was exactly what he had hoped for. Wasn't it?

The children came whizzing down the hill again. Rufus forced himself to smile. Their enjoyment should not be ruined by his own despondency.

'Come on, Anna, Rufus, don't just stand there talking,' Thomas said, grabbing the sled and pulling it back up the hill. 'You should play too and have some fun.'

Rufus looked at Miss Wainwright. 'Once again, it looks like we have our orders.'

She sighed and nodded but joined him as they walked up the hill. Once at the top, the four of them climbed onto the sled.

If he really was determined to actually put their kiss behind them and pretend it had never happened, climbing onto a sled behind Miss Wainwright was perhaps not the best thing to do. Being so close to her, wrapping his legs around hers, was most certainly not conducive to putting her out of his mind. Although he had to admit Thomas was right, this was much more enjoyable than standing around talking.

Once they were all settled on the sled, he pushed off with his foot and they whizzed down the slope, this time with more finesse than they had yesterday. As soon as they reached the bottom, Thomas and Emily jumped off and dragged the sled back up the hill, insisting that Rufus and Miss Wainwright keep up.

With each slide down the hill Rufus found himself relaxing more, laughing more, and the awkwardness between himself and Miss Wainwright seemed to slip away. She too seemed to be enjoying herself. He could only hope that she now trusted him and knew that he would never try to kiss her again. And that he could trust himself to be true to his promise.

Arriving at the bottom of the hill once again, Rufus looked up to see a footman arriving.

'Luncheon is being served. Her Ladyship has requested you return to the house.'

'You know what that means, don't you?' Rufus said to the two children.

'Plum pudding!' the children cried out together, and ran towards the house.

Laughing, he picked up the sled reins, and he and Miss Wainwright walked back.

'It's a joy to see them laughing again,' Miss Wainwright said, looking in the direction of the children, who were now rushing up the steps to the house, pulling off hats and scarves as they went. 'I can hardly remember a time when they were so happy.'

'It must have been hard for you, looking after the children when their parents died.'

She nodded. 'It was hard, and at times very frightening. Then when I discovered there was virtually no money left, I was so scared that they'd end up in the workhouse.'

He was tempted to reach out and take her hand, but he forced his hands to remain at his sides. 'That was the fate my mother was trying to avoid when she offered the women and children cottages in the village,' he said. 'She wouldn't want any child to suffer that fate and particularly children who were related.'

'And you did the same. You graciously agreed to take Thomas and Emily because they were related, even if it was only distantly.'

Rufus cringed slightly, remembering how reluctant he had been in the lawyer's office. But that had been a reluctance to spend time with children, not a reluctance to help family members in difficult circumstances. He had expected to find spending time with children to be tedious, but the last two days had been among the happiest he had experienced. Being with Miss Wainwright and the children made his other life seem empty, frivolous, a way of mindlessly filling in time.

As for the women who entertained him, well, had he even thought about another woman since he had met Miss Wain-

wright? He had no interest in carousing with actresses and
dissatisfied married women who craved the excitement their
husbands couldn't provide.

'I believe the children have given me and my mother much
more than we have given them. This has been the most enjoyable Christmas we've had at Deerwater that I can remember.'

They reached the steps and he escorted her up.

'But you have a ball every Christmas Eve. That must
be fun.'

Rufus rolled his eyes, then nodded his thanks to the footman as he opened the door. 'If you think it's fun to have
your mother foist an endless stream of debutantes in your
direction until you feel like you're going to suffocate under
a mountain of tulle and satin, and drown in a sea of inane
small talk then, yes, I suppose it is fun.'

They entered the entrance hall and he tried not to notice
that she stood well away from the mistletoe as the servants
helped them out of their coats.

'Don't get me wrong,' he said as they walked down the
hallway towards the dining room. 'My mother means well.
She thinks being married with a brood of children will make
me happy.'

'So what does make you happy?'

He paused before the door to the dining room, and the
footman waited patiently while he considered her question.
Once he would have believed, if not said to a young woman
such as Miss Wainwright, that all the pleasures that London had to offer made him happy. That being in the arms
of a beautiful, willing woman, one who expected nothing
more from him than a good time, would make him happy.
But now he was no longer sure if that was true.

'It seems when it comes to happiness, nothing can compare to sliding down a hill, falling off an overloaded sled
and getting a mouthful of snow.'

She laughed, an enchanting, joyful laugh and he was so
pleased that it was in response to something he'd said.

They entered the dining room, where Emily, Thomas and

his mother were already seated, the left-over plum pudding sitting in the middle of the table.

'You may serve yourself some luncheon, if you choose,' his mother said, indicating the dishes set up on the sideboard. 'But the children and I have decided to be rebels and have our plum pudding first.'

Miss Wainwright laughed again. 'That sounds like an excellent idea.'

Once they were seated, the footman served them all generous amounts of plum pudding and custard. Rufus had been dreading this Christmas, had expected to be desperate to get away from his country estate. Instead, here he was, happily eating plum pudding, and wishing Christmas would never end.

Chapter Eight

As soon as there was no more plum pudding left, the children asked to be excused and rushed outside, eager to continue playing.

Anna could see why they were so eager, for her too it had been a long time since she had last enjoyed herself so much. Playing in the snow with the Earl and the children had made her feel like a carefree, young woman without a worry in the world. Not so long ago she would not have thought such a thing was possible.

'Well, shall we join them?' the Earl asked. Anna nodded her head, almost as excited as the children had been.

'While you are off larking about, I have some serious work to do,' the Countess said, rising from the table. 'But don't let me stop you,' she said waving her hand towards the door. 'Go, go.'

The Earl escorted Anna back outside, and the moment the door closed behind them they seemed to turn back into children, and ran through the snow, up the hill to join Emily and Thomas.

While they were riding down the hill, they all waved to the Countess, who was departing with several footmen in tow, carrying an assortment of covered baskets.

The afternoon past in a whirl of laughter as they spent their time riding the sled, throwing snowballs at each other and making a snowman family. When the footman arrived and signalled it was time for dinner, Anna could hardly believe the entire afternoon had passed so quickly.

After dinner, as promised, they all settled in front of the crackling fire and Anna began reading *Great Expectations*. Thomas and Emily snuggled up beside her on the sofa and the Countess and the Earl sat in large leather chairs, also listening in rapt attention. Anna knew it was wrong of her to think such things, but it really was as if they were a family group enjoying a winter's evening together in complete harmony.

And it *was* wrong. The children, fortunately, were now part of this family, but her position would always be that of an outsider. Her role had always been to ensure the children settled in with their new family, and she had fulfilled her role. The children *were* settled.

No doubt she would soon be expected to adopt a role more suited to her status. She would not be spending as much time with the family, and rather than acting like a mother to the children she would become their governess once again. But when that happened, she would just have to accept it, just as she had accepted so much else in her life.

She looked up from her reading and glanced over at the Earl. Her position in the household also meant she would have to accept he could never be anything other than her employer, and she would have to bury her feelings deep within her and never, ever let them come to the surface again. They had agreed to put the kiss behind them, and she would try as hard as she possibly could to do exactly that.

But it was not going to be easy. Every time she looked at him, she remembered. Remembered what it was like to be held in his arms, to feel the touch of his lips on hers. And every time the memory came crashing back, her body weakened, yearned to feel it again, until the thought of it was almost like a torture.

But it was a torture she was going to have to endure. There was the option of giving in her notice and leaving. But she would never do that. She loved the children too much to ever leave them, not while they still needed her.

Part of her hoped the Earl would return to London, but another part of her hoped he would never leave. The children would miss him, that was one reason. But she would miss him as well. Being in his company was such a pleasure. He made her laugh, and it was a long time since she had truly laughed with such carefree joy.

Pleasure and torture, what a dilemma.

Emily and Thomas's eyes started to close and Anna could see they were forcing themselves to stay awake.

She paused in her reading and looked at the Countess. 'I believe the children need to go to bed now,' she said quietly.

'Yes, of course. We can continue reading tomorrow,' the Countess said. 'It's been so pleasant having you read to us, Anna. It really is wonderful having you as part of the household.' She looked at her son. 'Isn't it, Rufus?'

'Indeed, it is,' he said. 'And please allow me to help you with the children.'

She looked down and could see that Emily had fallen asleep and would need to be carried. While Anna took Thomas's hand, the Earl scooped Emily up into his arms and followed her out of the room.

Anna had to fight the thought that they were loving parents taking their children up to bed after spending an enjoyable day together as a family. She had no family. Even the children, whom she loved with every fibre of her being, were now part of the Deerwater family. She was the outsider but, oh, for now it was a lovely fantasy.

They entered the bedrooms and Anna indicated which bed to place Emily on.

'Right, I'll leave you to put the children to bed,' he said when he returned to Thomas's room. Thomas was sleepily trying to remove his clothing, so Anna assisted him.

'Thank you for your help, my lord,' Anna said over her shoulder.

'Think nothing of it.' He remained standing in the room a few seconds more. 'Right, I'll be off, then.'

'Goodnight, my lord,' Anna said, as he remained standing in the room.

'Goodnight, Anna, I mean, Miss Wainwright.' He nodded and left.

Anna savoured the moment. It might not be real, but she allowed herself to indulge in the fantasy for a moment longer.

Rufus paused outside the door then reluctantly walked off down the hallway. That was perhaps how a father felt when he helped to put his children to bed. He looked back at the room, sighed, then turned the corner and headed down the stairs.

Yes, he could certainly see why his mother wanted him married. Caring for children could give you such a sense of purpose and contentment that he had never thought possible before. Yes, that must be what his mother wanted for him, a good marriage and a family. One that provided that warm feeling, as if you were exactly where you belonged.

He looked back up the stairs. But didn't that depend on being married to the *right* woman? Marriage was not always like that. His mother's marriage had been an unhappy one. Most of the marriages he knew were equally miserable. He just had to think of all those unhappily married women who were so eager to spend time in his bed. But with a woman like Anna Wainwright he was sure marriage could be happy. It was just a shame he didn't know anyone in his class who was like Anna.

He continued walking down the stairs, surprised at where his thoughts had taken him. Meeting her had changed him so much in such an unexpected manner.

A few days ago, the thought of caring for children had filled him with trepidation. And as for marriage, well, every time he thought of that it was with horror. Now it was something he could see as a definite possibility. Although it could never be to any woman who wasn't just like Anna Wainwright.

Rufus stopped in his tracks, halfway down the stairs. It couldn't be to anyone who wasn't just like Anna Wainwright. Who wasn't Anna Wainwright. He looked back towards the children's rooms. She was the only woman he would ever consider marrying, and she was out of the question.

Slowly, he continued walking. How could he have got himself into this untenable situation? He wanted Anna more desperately than he had ever wanted any woman, more desperately than he thought it possible to want a woman, and he couldn't have her.

It was a situation that could not continue. He could not live with a woman who he wanted with his heart and soul, knowing that he could never have her. He could not see her every day and know that he could never hold her again, kiss her again. He was going to have to put this right and do something about this unbearable situation as soon as possible.

Chapter Nine

Anna awoke the next day full of determination. It was time to put all fantasies behind her and live in the real world. She would get her emotions under control. It was something she was certain she could do. Hadn't she already proven to herself just how resilient and resourceful she could be? When her parents had died and she had been forced to leave the family home and take up employment, she had buried her emotions and learned to cope. When the children's parents and then their great-aunt had also passed away, she had just carried on. She hadn't wallowed in self-pity or fallen apart because things had got tough.

And she would do that again. She would bury her emotions. Forget that she had any feelings for the Earl. Put aside any memories of how it felt to be kissed by him, push away all irrational fantasies and concentrate on caring for Emily and Thomas.

The children were already up and chatting in their beds when Anna went through to their rooms. Emily asked whether they'd be able to go sledding again today and Thomas asked if they'd be able to have plum pudding for breakfast. She answered yes to Emily's question and no to Thomas's.

'Remember, you ate all the plum pudding yesterday,' she reminded him.

Thomas frowned briefly, but then jumped out of bed, anxious to get the day's entertainment started as quickly as possible.

'We'll have to get Rufus to come sledding with us again,' he said as he pulled on his clothes.

'You've proved you're old enough and strong enough to

pull the sled up the hill yourself,' Anna said, going through to Emily's room to help her get dressed. 'I'm sure the Earl has lots of important things he needs to do today other than playing with children.'

'Like kissing Lady Cecily,' Emily said with a frown, causing Thomas to make vomiting noises.

'Did you see them under the mistletoe on Christmas Day?' Thomas called out. 'Yuck.'

'Don't talk like that. You need to be polite to Lady Cecily.' Despite what had happened between her and the Earl, there was still a possibility that the Earl might one day marry Lady Cecily and become the children's guardian. That was what men of his position did, they married suitable young women of the same class. Anna fought to ignore the pain gripping her heart as she ran a brush through Emily's long hair.

Once the children were ready, she led them downstairs to the dining room, where they helped themselves to hearty breakfasts, still chatting animatedly. Anna picked at her food, reminding herself not to wonder what the Earl was up to, why he had not joined them for breakfast and whether he had returned to London. Her heart clenched. It was inevitable that he would eventually return to London. Then she might never see him again.

She told herself not to let her thoughts stray in the direction of what the Earl may or may not be up to, even though it seemed that was the only pathway they were prepared to follow.

After breakfast was over, the children ran to the entrance hall so the servants could help them into their warmest clothes, then waited expectantly for Anna to arrive.

She passed the Countess's drawing room and could hear voices. It seemed the Earl had not left for London, but was sequestered away with his mother, deep in discussion. Anna's heart sank, hoping the discussion was not about her. She shook herself and continued walking. Of course it would not be about her. She was merely the governess. They probably never gave her a second thought, as long as she was doing her job properly.

Maybe they were discussing his future with Lady Cecily. Her heart sank further. It was not her place to speculate about such things, she reminded herself, standing up straighter and continuing to walk along the hallway.

The door opened and the Earl emerged. 'Miss Wainwright, may I have a word with you, please, in the library?' he called out to her.

She stopped in her tracks, her stomach clenching tighter. To steady herself she drew in a few deep breaths and then turned to face him.

'Of course,' she said quietly, with a slight dip of her head. 'Children, once the maid has helped you into your clothes, you can take out the sled and I'll join you soon.'

He continued to stare at her as she retraced her steps down the hallway. He held open the door to the library then followed her in.

'I have something I need to tell you,' he said as he gestured towards a chair. Once she had seated herself, he sat down opposite her in the same chairs they had occupied when they had talked together so companionably on Christmas Eve.

After all that had happened, she suspected this conversation was not going to be quite as companionable. She closed her eyes briefly and said a silent prayer.

Please, even if you are going to marry Lady Cecily, please, please keep me on for the sake of the children. I promise to secure my feelings for you under lock and key, and you'll never, ever know how much that kiss affected me.

He coughed lightly, as if preparing himself to tell her bad news, and she gripped the edges of the chair to brace herself.

If Lady Cecily expects me to act more like a servant than a member of the family, I'll happily do that as well. Just, please, let me stay with the children.

'Anna... Miss Wainwright,' he said, then coughed again.

'After everything that has happened between us, I feel there needs to be some changes in the household.'

Anna's grip on the chair intensified. 'I see.'

'As you know, my father had a reputation for seducing servants. Well, for seducing any pretty young woman, and that caused a great deal of pain to the young women, and to my mother.'

Anna nodded her head and looked down.

'I vowed I would never be like my father.'

She nodded her head again.

'And yet I almost broke that vow with you. For that I am eternally sorry.'

Anna bit the edge of her top lip to stop herself from blurting out that she was not sorry. While kissing him had been a mistake, she was not sorry for it. How could she be sorry for something that had been so wonderful? But she also knew it was something that could never happen again.

'I'm very sorry, Anna,' he said again, quietly.

She looked up at him. If they were to continue living together and if she was to continue working in this house, it was essential that he think it meant nothing and she had put it all behind her. 'You do not need to apologise. It was just a bit of fun under the mistletoe. It meant nothing really. You were not being like your father.' She gave a little laugh as if to dismiss the entire incident.

'We both know that that isn't the truth,' he said, staring at her in a disconcerting manner.

'No.' Anna lowered her eyes. 'But, please, don't let it affect my position in the house,' she said in a quiet voice. 'I love the children and they love me. No one knows what happened and I promise they never will.'

He quickly rose from his chair, crossed the room, knelt in front of her and took both her hands in his. 'Oh, Anna, no. I would never separate you from the children. And certainly not because I had kissed you, that would be unforgivable.'

'Thank you,' she murmured, trying to remain calm, despite the fact that the man she knew herself to be falling in love with was kneeling in front of her, an imploring look on his face.

'But we cannot continue as we are,' he said, standing up and walking over to the bookshelves.

Anna looked up at him, her mind awhirl.

'That is why I propose to change things but don't worry, I hope this will be something that you will approve of.'

She waited, her anxiety mounting with every word he spoke.

'I have spoken to my mother and she agrees that the best course forward is for me to make some essential changes to your situation.

Anna froze, unable to breathe, hardly able to think.

'The lawyer informed me that for quite some time you worked without wages.'

Anna nodded her head, then shook it, unsure what this change in the conversation meant.

'As you made such a sacrifice for two members of our family we have decided to provide you with a large financial settlement and your own home on the estate.'

Anna stared up at him, unsure what this meant. 'You don't need to. I was happy to—'

He held up his hand. 'This isn't just for you, Anna, Miss Wainwright. It will provide you with financial independence. The ability to make your own decisions, to no longer be dependent on your job here at Deerwater for your financial security.'

Anna stared at him in disbelief, scrambling to get the words whirling round in her head into some order. 'You are so kind,' she finally said. 'This is more generous than I could have thought possible.'

He looked down and shook his head. 'I'm not being kind or generous.' He looked up at her. 'I'm doing this for completely selfish reasons.'

Anna shook her head. She could think of nothing selfish about this extreme generosity.

He crossed the room once again, and again knelt down

in front of her. 'I've done it so you will be free to make your own choices about your future. About us.'

'Oh,' Anna said, trying to take in the implications of his words.

'Anna, I have fallen in love with you and I wish to court you,' he said, his voice low and serious. 'You will be under no obligation. I give you my word, I will never come between you and the children and you are now a completely independent woman.'

He drew in a deep breath, looked down at her hands held in his, then looked up at her, his eyes imploring. 'I never thought such a thing was possible, but it's true. I have fallen in love with you. You are the most beautiful woman I have ever met. You have a beautiful heart, a beautiful spirit.' He looked back down at their hands. 'I have never met a woman like you. I have never been affected by a woman in the way you affect me. It's as if I lost my mind the moment I saw you.' He looked back up at her. 'Whatever you decide, I will respect your decision. But, Anna, will you allow me to court you?'

Warmth flooding her body, a smile threatened to consume Anna, but she fought hard to keep her face straight. 'What? Is that all you want to do? Court me?' She failed in her attempt to be serious, and a small giggle of delight escaped. 'Aren't you at least going to try and seduce me?'

He stared at her in surprise, then joined her in laughing and pulled her to her feet. 'Well, if you insist, I'll give it my best shot.'

With that he took her in his arms and kissed her, and there wasn't a piece of mistletoe anywhere in sight.

Epilogue

Six months later

Rose petals fluttered around them while bells chimed out a joyful tune. The last six months had been the happiest of Anna's life, and as she stood on the steps of the local church on the arm of her new husband, she knew her future would be just as happy.

She looked down at Thomas, dressed in his formal suit, still puffed up with self-importance after playing the role of pageboy, and Emily, twirling round, her pretty attendant's dress spinning out around her. Like her, the children could not have been happier.

Being courted by Rufus had been like a dream and she knew he was going to be a perfect husband and a perfect father to Emily and Thomas.

'You look beautiful,' the Dowager Countess said, kissing Anna on the cheek. 'Just as the Countess of Summerill should look.'

Despite the differences in their stations, the Dowager Countess had put up no objection to Rufus courting her. She had told Anna that the one good thing to come out of her own unhappy marriage was Rufus, and what she wanted more than anything was for her son to be happy. When Rufus had told her he had fallen in love with the governess, the older woman admitted she was taken aback, memories of her own husband's behaviour flooding in. But then she had realised this was different. This was love, and she had given them her blessing.

The fact that the Dowager adored the children had also

During their courtship, Rufus had been true to his word, treating Anna as his equal and always letting her know that she was free to make her own choices.

Not that there was ever really another choice. From the moment he had kissed her under the mistletoe she had been lost. She had fallen hopelessly, heedlessly in love with him and knew that, no matter what had happened, there would never be any other man for her than Rufus Deerwater, the Earl of Summerhill.

'Kiss her, my lord,' one of the local lads called out, followed by much ribbing and laughter from his friends.

'Well, what do you think?' Rufus said, giving her that wonderful smile that was one of the many things she loved about him.

'I think that young man's suggestion is a very good idea,' Anna said, laughing.

His lips met hers. They were still smiling when they kissed, and Anna was sure her life would now be full of smiles, laughter and love.

* * * * *

*If you enjoyed these stories, you won't want
to miss these other Historical collections*